Praise for
LOSING YOU

"Lose yourself in this smart nail-biter of a tale about a mother's desperate search for her missing teenage daughter." —*People* magazine

"A seamless first-person account...This engrossing read captures the importance of the often overlooked and underappreciated minutiae of everyday life while commanding a deeply personal reaction in readers." —*Publishers Weekly* (starred review)

"What gives *Losing You* its chief distinction...is its unusually emotive color and its flinty protagonist.... Nina is the parent we'd all like to be under duress, and I find I've become nearly as protective of her as she is of her daughter." —*Salon.com*

"The pace and tension accelerate as the identity of Charlie's abductor remains deliciously uncertain. This is a quick, enjoyable read." —*Library Journal*

"[French] renders psychological chillers that manage to generate great suspense... This latest offering is sure to keep readers furiously flipping pages through the night." —*Booklist*

"The novel's greatest strength is its cool-eyed portrait of an English village." —*Washington Post*

Also by Nicci French

LOSING YOU

Nicci French

St. Martin's Paperbacks

First published in Great Britain by Michael Joseph, an imprint of The Penguin Group

This is a work of fiction. All of the characters, organizations, and events portrayed in this novel are either products of the author's imagination or are used fictitiously.

LOSING YOU

For information address St. Martin's Press, 175 Fifth Avenue, New York, NY 10010.

Library of Congress Catalog Card Number: 2007051828

ISBN: 0-312-94316-4
EAN: 978-0-312-94316-5

Printed in the United States of America

St. Martin's Press hardcover edition / April 2008
St. Martin's Paperbacks edition / March 2009

St. Martin's Paperbacks are published by St. Martin's Press, 175 Fifth Avenue, New York, NY 10010.

10 9 8 7 6 5 4 3 2 1

To Jamie, Sophia, Maya and Cassie

Sometimes I still felt that I had fetched up on the edge of the world. The wintry light slanting on to the flat, colourless landscape; the moan of the wind, the shriek of sea-birds and the melancholy boom of the foghorn far out at sea all sent a shiver through me. But I stamped my feet on the ground to warm them and told myself that in a few hours I would be far away.

Rick dropped the spanner and straightened up from the open bonnet of the car. My car. He rubbed his grazed knuckle. His unshaven face was raw from the cold north-easterly that whipped over us, carrying the first drops of rain, and his pale blue eyes were watering. His curls were damp and lay flat on his head so that I could see the shape of his skull. He blew on his whitened fingers and tried to flash me his boyish smile, but I could see it was an effort.

"Rick," I said, "it's kind of you, but you don't need to do this. It was just a rattle in the engine and I thought something had come loose. I would never have called you otherwise. I can take it to the garage after we get back from holiday."

His wife, Karen, came out of the front door with three mugs of coffee on a tray, three Digestive biscuits laid out neatly beside them. She was a tall woman, almost as tall as Rick, big-boned but thin. Sometimes she looked striking, nearly beautiful, and then I could understand why the pair of them had got together, but too often she seemed gaunt and unfinished, as if she hadn't paid proper attention to herself. Her hair was brown, already peppered with grey, and pulled back in a hasty bun. Her skin was bracketed with worry lines, her nails were bitten down to the ends of her fingers. She rarely wore makeup or jewellery, except for the wedding band on her finger. Her clothes didn't quite fit together. Today it was a strawberry-pink quilted jacket and a thin black skirt that was trailing on the ground. I worried she would trip over it. She had the bossy abruptness of someone who was fundamentally shy, and once, late at night, when she was a bit tipsy, she'd confided to me that life rushed at her out of a fog, constantly taking her by surprise. Maybe that was why she often seemed to talk in non-sequiturs, and her manner often swung between sprightly sarcasm and barely suppressed anger.

"White no sugar, right? How's it going, then? All sorted?"

Rick grimaced at her in exasperation, then down at the ground on which lay the battery from my car and a couple of other parts that I couldn't identify.

A little gleam appeared in her eyes. "You said when you came back that it would only take a couple of minutes."

"I know," said Rick, wryly.

"That was before ten." She glanced ostentatiously

at the watch on her wrist. "You've been out here for nearly three-quarters of an hour."

"I know that too."

"Nina's got a plane to catch." She cast me an amused smile that said, *Men*. I looked away guiltily.

"I know."

"It's all right," I said. "I've done most of the packing for me and Jackson, and Charlie promised she'd be ready by the time I was back."

Rick's head disappeared beneath the bonnet again. There was the sound of several sharp taps and a mumbled curse. It might have seemed funny but he was so obviously not finding it funny that I bit my lip to forestall even the tiniest hint of a smile. I pulled off my gloves to pick up my coffee mug and wrapped my fingers round it, grateful for the warmth, the curl of steam that licked at my cold face.

"Christmas in the sunshine instead of this endless cold, grey drizzle," said Karen, and pulled her jacket more closely round her, shivering exaggeratedly. "What time does your plane go?"

"Not until just before six. I'm picking Christian up on the way to Heathrow."

I said it casually, but felt a small prickle of nervous happiness in my chest: Christian and I had been friends for nearly eighteen years, lovers for just a few months, and now, for two weeks, the four of us would all be together in the Florida Keys. We would be the family unit I'd thought had been smashed to pieces: going on trips, making plans, collecting shared stories that we could tell and retell later, even eating breakfast together. Except Charlie never ate breakfast: she acted as though toast was immoral. I hoped she would behave herself.

"I think Christmas should be cancelled," Karen was saying. "Eamonn has a kind of ideological objection to it anyway, and is always trying to make us celebrate the winter solstice instead, stand around a bonfire at midnight like witches. Rick tries to make us play board games and Charades and Wink Murder, even though you can't play Wink Murder with just three people, and I . . ." She raised her eyebrows at me. "I'm the one who drinks too much and burns the turkey."

Rick came round to the driver's door, leaned in and turned the key in the ignition. "Right," he said determinedly. There was a hasty splutter, then silence.

"You *hope* you're picking up Christian," said Karen, who seemed almost pleased.

Rick pulled a face that was a caricature of confusion, anxiety and distress. This was what he did in life. He helped people, he fixed things; he was unflappably, charmingly capable. People turned to him, just as I had this morning.

"At least you've solved the rattle," said Karen, gaily, and gave a small, explosive snort.

"What?" said Rick, with a glance at her that she pretended not to see.

"The car won't rattle if you can't switch it on."

His face went a scary shade of crimson. He looked at his watch and I cast a surreptitious glance to it as well.

"Shall we just call the garage?" I suggested. "Or the AA? I'm a member."

"Well," began Rick. "It might just be—"

"Don't be ridiculous," said Karen. "You've got nothing on today, have you? Just working on your boat. Though God knows why you want to work on your boat on a day like this, and it's the first day of your holiday. You can't just take Nina's car apart and leave it like that. She's got to get to the—"

"I *know*. How old is this car, anyway?" Rick stared at the rusty little Rover as if it was one of his more hopeless pupils.

"About ten years," I said. "It was already quite old when I got it."

Rick gave a grunt as if the car's age was to blame for the situation.

"Can't you work backwards?" said Karen. "At least you could get it back to the way it was when Nina drove it here."

"What do you think I'm doing?" Rick asked, with effortful calm.

"Don't worry, Nina," Karen said reassuringly.

"I'm not worried," I said, and it was true. I knew that in a few hours, even if I had to get a taxi all the way to Heathrow, we'd be in the air, far from the pinched, icy days of English winter. I imagined sitting beside Christian and gazing out of the window as London became an intricate grid of orange and white lights. I raised my head and looked past Rick and Karen's house to what lay beyond.

For thirty-eight years, I had lived in a city where I could go a whole day without seeing the horizon. Here, on Sandling Island, it was all horizon: the level land, the mudflats, the miles of marshes, the saltings,

the grey, wrinkled sea. Now it was mid-morning
and from where I stood—facing west towards the
mainland—I could see only the glistening mudflats
with their narrow, oozing ditches of water where
waders were walking with high-stepping delicate
legs and giving mournful cries, as if they'd lost
something. It was low tide. Little boats tethered to
their unnecessary buoys tipped at a steep angle to
show their blistered, slimy hulls; their halliards
chinked and chimed in the wind. From my own house,
a bit further round to the south-east, I could make out
the sea. Sometimes, when I woke in the morning and
opened my eyes on its grey, shifting expanse, I still
wondered for a moment where I was, how on earth
I'd landed up there.

It was Rory who had wanted to come, who for
years of our marriage had dreamed of leaving London, of giving up his job as a solicitor and running a
restaurant instead. At first, it had just been a day-
dream, an if-only that I didn't really share, but bit
by bit it had taken on the harder edge of an obses-
sion, until at last he'd found premises on Sandling
Island and dragged his reluctant family with him to
begin a new life. It was only sixty miles from London but, rimmed as it was by the tidal estuary and
facing out to open sea, it had the feel of a different
world, gripped by weather and seasons; full of wild
spaces, loneliness, the strange call of sea-birds
and sighing winds. It was even cut off from the mainland every so often, when the highest of high tides
covered the causeway. From my bedroom, I could

hear the waters lapping at the shingle shore, the foghorns booming out at sea. Sometimes at night, when the island was wrapped in the darkness of the sky and of the rising, falling waters, I could scarcely bear the sense of solitude that engulfed me.

Yet I was the one who had fallen half in love with Sandling Island while Rory had been driven mad by it. Somewhere in the dream of the austere restaurant decorated with lobster-pots, nets and etchings of fishing-smacks it had gone wrong. There was an argument with a supplier about the ovens, cash stubbornly failed to flow and the restaurant had never even opened. As he found himself trapped by the fantasy he'd held for so long, he no longer knew what he was for or even who he was. Eventually the only way out was to run away.

"Sorry." I turned my attention back to Karen, who was saying something.

"It's your birthday, isn't it?"

"That's right."

"And not just any birthday."

"Yes," I said reluctantly. "Forty. It's one of the ones you're not supposed to be happy about. How did you know?"

She gave a shrug.

"Everyone knows everything about everyone round here. Happy birthday, anyway."

"Thanks."

"Do you really mind about it?"

"I'm not sure. A friend of mine once told me—"

"I minded," she said. "I looked at myself in the

mirror, and I thought, That's you now. No escape. That's who you are. Nothing turns out the way you expect, does it?"

"I think I'm getting there," said Rick. "Give me my coffee, will you?"

He had a streak of black grease on his jaw that rather suited him, and a rip in his jacket. I watched as he took a large gulp of cooling coffee, then posted half a Digestive after it. I had a list in my mind that I kept adding to: pack swimming stuff, goggles and suncream; remember the Christmas presents, including the snorkel and flippers I'd bought for Christian, who was a marine biologist yet lived many miles from the coast; some dollars; books for the plane; packs of cards. Leave out the dog food and instructions for Renata; the Christmas money for the postman, the milkman, the bin men . . . My toes were getting chilly now; my face felt stiff in the cold wind.

"I've been wanting to ask," Rick moved closer to me and spoke in a low tone, "how's Charlie doing now, Nina? Are things better?"

"I think so," I said cautiously. "You can't really tell. At least, I can't with Charlie. She's quite private, you know."

"She's a teenager," said Rick. "Teenagers are meant to be private. Especially with their parents. Look at Eamonn, for Christ's sake."

"What's this?" asked Karen, moving in closer, a flicker of interest in her eyes.

"Charlie's had a rough time at school," I said. I didn't want to talk about this because it was Charlie's story, not mine. I didn't want to discuss it lightly, give it a trite meaning. I imagined Charlie's pale, truculent face, its look of withdrawal behind the turbulent fall of her reddish hair. "Rick found out about it. He talked to the girls who were bullying her, and to their parents. And to me. He was very helpful. As much as anyone can be."

"Girls can be cruel," said Karen, with a sweeping sympathy.

"She was at a sleepover at one of their houses last night," I said. "Tam's. Maybe that's a breakthrough. I haven't seen her yet. It would be a good way to end the term."

"She'll be fine, you know," said Rick, putting down his mug, reluctantly picking up the spanner once more. "Being bullied is horrible. Sometimes I think we forget how horrible it can be, how undermining. Especially if we're teachers, because we come to take it for granted, don't you think? But Charlie's a resilient young woman. Very bright, with a mind of her own and wide horizons. I always enjoy having her in my class. You should be proud of her."

I smiled gratefully at him.

"She's got all those piercings, hasn't she?"

"For God's sake, Karen, what on earth has that got to do with anything?" Rick tweaked a knob with his spanner.

"I just thought that maybe she got picked on because she seems different."

"Different? Have you seen Amelia Ronson recently? She's had her right eye half sewn together, and talking of different, look at our own son . . . Oh, speak of the devil."

A baroque figure had appeared on the doorstep, wrapped in a bottle-green trench coat that almost reached the ground, bare grubby feet poking out beneath it. Eamonn had a face so pale it almost looked like a mask, although a mask that was pierced several times with rings: on his eyebrow, through his nose and ears. His eyes were Rick's eyes, but sad. His mane of tangled matt-black hair had green streaks in it. His fingernails were painted black and he had a swirling tattoo on his right forearm. He always appeared unwashed, hung-over, drugged-up and ferociously glum, though when he smiled, he looked sweet and lost, younger than his seventeen years. I knew from Rick that he was a problem-child, an all-out Goth on a small island that regarded him with suspicion or hilarity; a loner; a bright lad who felt he didn't belong. I also knew that he and his parents, Karen particularly, could hardly manage to get through a minute together without arguing. But I'd always got on with him. He liked talking to me about funny little number problems he'd come across in books—after all, I am an ex-accountant who is now masquerading as a maths teacher—and about God (or the lack of any God). And he liked being around me in case Charlie walked through the door. Mothers notice these things.

Karen looked at her watch. "Do you know what time it is?" she said.

"No," said Eamonn.

"It's gone half past ten," she said.

"Low tide's in ten minutes," Eamonn said, as if it was the most logical response. He wrinkled his face in distaste. "We're surrounded by putrid-smelling mud."

"I thought you might have got up and gone out."

"How do you know I didn't?"

"That'll be the day," said Rick, from somewhere inside my engine.

"Hello, Eamonn," I said brightly, trying to forestall another argument.

"Happy birthday." He gave an abrupt half-bow; his trench coat opened slightly and I could see he was naked beneath it.

"Everyone really does know." I laughed. Flip-flops, I thought. Remember flip-flops and the camera-charger.

"Charlie told me," he said.

"Have you seen her recently?" I began, but then my mobile sang in my pocket, an irritating jangle that Jackson must have programmed without me realizing, and I turned away from the car. He was already in mid-sentence by the time I brought the phone to my ear, and it took me a few seconds to separate out the stream of sounds into recognizable words. It was as if I had tuned in to a radio programme that was already half-way through.

". . . and if I'd known, fuck it, that you'd turn out to be the kind of mother who'd take my children away from me at Christmas and not only take them away but fly off with a man who hardly knows them to the other side of . . ."

"Rory, Rory, hold on . . ." I walked a few steps down the driveway.

"Just because I went off the rails a bit, does that

mean I've forfeited the right to see them and they're growing up so quickly my little children only of course they're not so little any more and now there's this Christian and soon they'll stop thinking of me as their father that's what you want isn't it only you always used to say—"

"What's up?" I hated the way my voice took on a calming, gentle tone, as if I was murmuring nonsense to a scared horse, all the while wanting to slide a bridle over its head. I knew what his face was like when he was ranting, screwed up in wretched anger, an unnerving replica of Charlie when she was upset. I knew there were tears in his eyes and that he'd been drinking. "You've known for weeks we were going away. You said it was fine. We discussed it."

"At least you could have let me see them before they go," he said.

"What do you mean?"

"Just for a bit, to say happy Christmas."

"That's not possible," I said. I heard a crunching on the gravel behind me and turned to find Karen making exaggerated semaphores with her arms and mouthing incomprehensible words at me. Behind her, my car's engine coughed and hacked and rasped, then stuttered into life. I held up a finger, signifying I'd only be a few seconds. I felt like a terrible hypocrite. I was having a suppressed row with Rory while making a pathetic attempt to suggest to the eagerly eavesdropping Karen that I was in a perfectly civilized discussion. "We're leaving in an hour or so for the airport."

"I'm speaking theoretically. I'm speaking about principle. You know that word? Principle? The principle of a father seeing his daughter."

"You've got a son as well," I said. I had always hated the way he was besotted with Charlie and often seemed barely to notice Jackson, who adored him.

"Of a father seeing his children. That's what I'm speaking about." His voice broke up.

"You're on your mobile. You're not driving, are you?" Drunk-driving was what I meant but didn't say.

"I got your solicitor's letter."

I was wary now. I'd asked my solicitor, Sally, who was also a close friend, to write a letter to his solicitor. It had been the first step on an unpleasant road. The letter warned him that if his behaviour with Jackson and Charlie didn't become more rational I would be forced to seek a restraining order. I'd done it after their last visit, when he'd got drunk and knocked Jackson over. The children hadn't told me about it until I'd insisted on knowing how the bruise on Jackson's shoulder had come about.

"You just want to take them away."

"I don't," I said hopelessly.

"It's Christmas and I won't see them."

"I've got to go. I'll ring you from home."

"Don't cut me off."

"I'm not. I'm saying I'll call you in a few minutes. Have a strong coffee or something and I'll call you."

"What does that mean, 'have a strong coffee?'"

"'Bye, Rory."

I clicked the phone off. I blinked and hoped it might look as if it was just the wind in my face.

"Oh dear," said Karen. "Upset?"

"He's fine." I felt my pity flare into protectiveness before Karen's blatant curiosity. "I mean, no."

"Christmas can be difficult for the absent father, can't it?"

"I guess."

"And, after all, Rory was always rather . . ." She was searching for the exact word. "Volatile," she said at last, with heavy-handed tact. "Like Charlie," she added. "Not like you and Jackson. You're always so polite and methodical."

I turned with relief to my now nicely chugging car. "That's fantastic, Rick. Thanks so much."

"Don't mention it."

"Now go and work on your boat," I said. I stood on tiptoe and gave him a kiss on both cold, stubbly, grease-stained cheeks.

"Not just yet," said Karen. "I need him for something else."

I sensed that I should escape before a really serious row broke out.

"I'm going to collect Jackson and finish the packing. 'Bye, Karen." I kissed her too, missing her cheek and landing on her nose. "Thanks for the coffee. Take care, Eamonn."

I got into the car, pulled the door shut and wound down the window.

"Happy Christmas," I called, as I reversed down

the drive. I waved, then swung into the narrow lane. "And new year."

I put it into first gear and drew away, free. The car rattled happily as I went.

As soon as I had turned inland and was out of sight, I pulled over, tugged my mobile out of my back pocket and phoned Christian. The engine was still running, and the heating system blew warm air on to my hands while my feet remained cold. Outside, gusts of wind rattled in the bare branches of the trees and blew twigs and tin cans along the road. He didn't answer his landline, so I tried his mobile but only got his voicemail.

"It's just me," I said into it. "And I don't really know why I'm calling."

I had first met Christian when I was in the third year of my degree in maths. He was a graduate in marine biology. I was going out with Rory by then and I used to spend every weekend in London with him. We were planning our future together, and university already felt like part of my past. I liked Christian and his circle of friends. But because he was of the world I was preparing to leave, I didn't remember him very well. I've tried, but he's a blur, a half-remembered face. We had a drink together a few times. I think I once went to his house and had a meal with lots of other people there. He says we danced together more than once; he swears he once put his arm round me when we were in a pub by the river. A few weeks ago, he showed me a photograph of himself as a student, his thin face, the tumble of dark hair, the cigarette in the corner of his mouth. I studied it and felt desire stir in me for the youth he was then, but at the time I had felt nothing like that. He was a figure I passed on the road and, though we promised to keep in touch, we hadn't really. He sent me a postcard from a conference he was at in Mexico several years ago, and it took me a few seconds to work out who "Christian," signed with an inky flourish under a couple of lines I could hardly decipher, actually was. Two years ago I heard from a mutual acquaintance that the relationship he'd been in had broken up and I thought then of getting in touch, but I never did. I sent him a change-of-address card when we moved to Sandling Island, but assumed it would never reach him. I wasn't even sure where he lived any more.

Six months ago, he called me up out of the blue to say he was going to be in East Anglia for a conference, and maybe we could meet. I almost made an excuse. Rory had left in a maelstrom of tears, unpaid bills, smashed dreams, and I felt lonely, bewildered, reclusive and sad. By that time, I had already had a forlorn, short-lived fling, and I knew it wasn't the answer to anything. Certainly not to loneliness, certainly not to sadness. All I really wanted was to spend time with the children, and when I wasn't doing that, to work on the house and the small, nettle-filled garden. I was trying to create a tiny haven for us, filled with the smell of fresh paint and baking, and I didn't really want to make an effort for a man I used to know but who was now a half-remembered stranger.

In the end, I arranged to meet him because I couldn't think of a reason not to quickly enough. I told him as much at the end of that first meeting, because even by then—two and a half hours in—I wanted to be honest with him. I felt I could trust him. He didn't seem to be trying to impress me or pretend in any way to be someone he wasn't. Had he always been like that, I wondered—and why hadn't I noticed?

He was still slim, still boyish-looking, but his unruly hair was shorter and streaked with grey, and there were crow's feet round his eyes and brackets round his mouth. I tried to fit this fortyish face with the smooth, eager one from the past, and I could feel him doing the same with me. Our ghosts were with us. We walked along the sea wall, with the tide going out and the lovely light of a May early evening gradually thickening into dusk, and we talked or sometimes were silent. He told me the names of the birds that glided on the currents, although as an islander I was the one who should have known. But that became part of the flirtatious joke. He came back and had a glass of wine at my house; he played a computer game with Jackson (and lost), and when he met Charlie, who burst into the room with mud on her shoes and a dangerous glint in her eyes, he was gravely friendly without being sycophantic or matey. He rang me almost as soon as he had left the house. He told me he was crossing the causeway and the water was nearly over the road, and would I invite him for dinner the next day? He would bring the pudding and the wine, and what did the children like to eat?

I set off once more, turning inland, to drive through the centre of the town, past the shops and the church, the garage, the old people's home, the garden centre; past the building that had been going to be Rory's seafood restaurant and now had a "To Let" sign swinging in the wind above its blank windows. I already felt slightly detached from it all, as if I were five miles high and safely away. Mixed with the detachment was a twinge of guilt. I'd dropped Jackson off with his best friend, Ryan, just after breakfast and promised to collect him very soon. "Soon" is an elastic concept but I'd heard Ryan's mother, Bonnie, talk about Christmas shopping and the day was advancing. I got to Ryan's house in just a few minutes—practically everywhere on Sandling Island was a few minutes' drive from everywhere else—and knocked on the door. I was carried inside on a wave of apologies.

"I'm so sorry," I said to Bonnie. "You were going out. I've sabotaged your day."

"It's no problem," Bonnie said, with a smile.

That made it even worse. Even though we'd been on the island for less than two years I still felt I was finding my feet, but Bonnie had been one of the people I had decided would be my friend. She was in the same position as me—bringing up a young son alone—and she was doing it with uncomplaining cheerfulness. She had short hair and a pale face with red cheeks and she was quite large and I felt that it wouldn't take very much makeup to turn her into a circus clown.

"But you said something about Christmas shopping?"

"That's right. I have a rule, or maybe it's more of a challenge: all Christmas shopping has to be done in one day. And this is the day."

"Or, in fact, half a day, in this case," I said anxiously.

"Three-quarters of a day. It's not eleven yet. Which is plenty. Ryan and I are heading into town and we'll be back in about six hours, laden like pack-horses."

"So I'd better say happy Christmas," I said, "and a happy new year and everything."

"That's right," said Bonnie. "You're flying off. That's the way to turn forty. I'm so sorry I can't get to—" She stopped.

"Get to what?" I said.

"I mean, that we won't get to see you over the holiday. But let's meet up properly in the new year."

I said I'd like that. Then I went to retrieve Jackson from where I'd left him, in front of a computer game with Ryan, who grunted but barely looked up as we gave Bonnie a Christmas-and-new-year hug and went out. When we were back in the car, Jackson retrieved another miniature computer game from his pocket and started to play. I glanced across at his serious face, the tip of a pink tongue sticking out in ferocious concentration and his lick of black hair tickling his screwed-up brow, and didn't attempt conversation. I was going over my mental list again: passports, tickets and credit cards. If I got to the airport with those, two children and one nearly new boyfriend, nothing else mattered.

I took the scenic route home. Instead of snaking through the back-streets, I drove down the main street, imaginatively named The Street, wound to the left to reach the beach and turned right past the deserted caravan site, the closed-up beach huts, and the boat-maker's yard, which was now full of boats pulled up for the winter.

Our house was in a motley line of dwellings just across the road from the boathouses and -yards and mooring jetties. They were all old enough to date from a time when people evidently didn't see much point in a sea view as against the disadvantages of an icy wind and occasional floods. The grand Georgian houses, the manor houses and rectories were safely tucked away inland. The cottages that lined The Saltings were odd, ill-sorted and squeezed in at strange angles as if each had had to be fitted into a space slightly too small for it. Ours was probably the oddest of all. It was made of clapboard and looked more than anything like a square wooden boat that had been dragged on to land, turned upside-down and been unconvincingly disguised with a grey-slate roof. It had been hard to sell because it had a tiny garden at the back and almost none at the front, it was damp and the rooms were poky, but Rory and I had fallen in love with it immediately. From our bedroom window we could see mud and sea and beyond that nothing except sky.

As Jackson and I approached the door, we heard

a desperate scratching, whimpering and groaning
from inside.

"Stop that, Sludge," I shouted, as I fiddled with
the key in the lock. The door opened and a black ap-
parition flew at us.

The time between our arrival on the island and
Rory leaving was mainly a disaster of bills and half-
finished building work, then more bills. Almost
Rory's sole contribution to the household in that terrible period was to give in to the drip-drip-drip en-
treaties of Charlie and Jackson over many years for
a dog. In a blur of events that happened almost simultaneously, he obtained a Labrador that looked like
an oversized mole, christened her Sludge, left her
with me and left me. When Rory walked out, I
couldn't believe it. I literally couldn't compute in
my brain that he could be somewhere else from me;
well, after the last few weeks together, I could imagine that. But even so, I didn't see how he could be
away from the children.

However, it quickly became all too clear that
Sludge would never leave us. In fact, she seemed to
suffer acute separation trauma if we left the house to
go to the shops. As we came in and she went through
her emotional welcome home, Jackson asked for the
hundredth time why we couldn't take her with us on
holiday and I said because she's a dog, and he said
that we should get her a pet passport and I said that
pet passports took a lot of time and money, and I
didn't even know if they had them for the States, to
which he said, unanswerably: so?

Charlie and I had had an animated discussion on the phone the previous evening. I had said that I wasn't sure it was such a good idea for her to be out the night before we went away. She had hardened her voice in a way I knew well, and asked why. I said there was a lot to do and she said she could do it when she got back. It never became an argument because really I felt relieved, and she knew it, that her enemies were, perhaps, becoming her friends. So when she said that she would come back early and feed Sludge, put the washing out, tidy her room and do her packing, I didn't say anything sarcastic, I didn't pull a face down the phone at her, I didn't laugh. I did mention that she had a paper round to do as well, but she had said she would do that on her way home and then she would get everything else done. There was plenty of time. And she was right. There *was* plenty of time.

I hadn't fed Sludge this morning because Jackson or Charlie liked to do that: she's so pathetically grateful. And Sludge had done what Sludge always did when she hadn't been fed: she found something else to eat or, failing that, something to chew. In this case it was a box of porridge oats. Oats and fragments of box were scattered through the living room. I took a deep breath. This was the first day of the holidays: nothing could make me angry on the first day of the holidays. At least she hadn't eaten the mail, which had been pushed through the door in my absence—a larger pile than usual, and mostly birthday cards as far as I could see.

I put them to one side to open later. I picked up the fragments of box, then took out the vacuum cleaner and in a few minutes the room was as it had been. Jackson fed Sludge, not that she needed much feeding, full as she was of oats and cardboard.

Nor was I angry when I went into the kitchen and found the clothes still in the washing-machine. If Charlie hadn't fed Sludge, it was hardly likely that she would have hung out the washing. Of course, it meant that the clothes we needed for our holiday would now have to be put into the dryer but that wasn't a significant problem. I bundled them in and turned the dial to forty minutes. That should do it.

And, of course, it was almost a logical necessity, just about as certain as that two and two make four, that if Charlie hadn't fed Sludge and hadn't hung out the washing, she wouldn't have tidied her bedroom or packed. I went upstairs and gave her room the most cursory glance. I knew that the bed hadn't been slept in but it looked as if it had been, then jumped on. Clothes lay on the carpet where they had been dropped. There were a belt, an empty violin case, a fake tigerskin rug, pencils, a broken ruler, scissors, a pair of flip-flops, CDs with no cases, CD cases with no CDs, a string bag, a couple of teen magazines, a book splayed open, the top half of a pair of pyjamas, a large stuffed green lizard, a couple of small piles of dirty clothes, a broken hairdryer, scattered items of makeup, disparate shoes and three bath towels. Charlie seemed to prefer using a clean towel after each bath or shower, though not to the extent of putting the dirty ones in the washing-basket.

Her laptop computer sat on her desk with a tartan pencil case, several notebooks, a pink-capped deodorant, a bottle of Clearasil, a shoebox, a furry cow, various assorted piles of schoolwork and much, much more.

I felt a sense of violation even peering into her room through the gap of the open door. Since she had had this new bedroom she had been firmly private about it. I didn't clean it. Well, neither did she, but we had an agreement about that. I would leave her to do as she pleased in her room, order it as she wished, so long as she tidied up in the rest of the house. She hadn't exactly kept her end of the bargain, but I had kept mine. I felt a pang about it, of course. In the past, she had always been open, almost terrifyingly so, with me about all her fears, troubles and problems, until sometimes I felt heavy with the weight of her confessions. That had changed, as it had to, as she changed and grew. It wasn't that I believed she had important secrets to keep from me. I knew that she needed a door she could lock and a space she could call her own. Sometimes I felt excluded but I couldn't separate that feeling from all of my emotions at watching my only daughter become a woman; someone separate from me with her own life.

So I didn't do any clearing up. I didn't do any of her packing. I looked at my watch. It wasn't on my wrist. Where was it? On the side of the bath? On the floor next to my bed? In a pocket somewhere? By the sink? But at that moment a sheep emerged from Charlie's ridiculous sheep clock and bleated the hour. Eleven o'clock. No rush. So I left the room—except that I took her flip-flops off the floor to pack because she would probably forget them and I'd end up having to buy new ones.

I carried them to my bedroom and tossed them into my suitcase, which was now almost full. Walking down the stairs I almost collided with what looked like a peculiar half-boy, half-robot coming up. It was Jackson, looking through the camcorder Rory had bought for us a year ago and which I'd never even got out of the box. I'd planned to take it to Florida and had already packed it, but Jackson can sniff out electronic equipment just as Charlie can sniff out chocolate.

"What are you doing?" I asked.

"Filming," he said. "It's brilliant."

"That was meant for the holiday," I said. "There's no point in filming our house. We know what it looks like."

"It doesn't matter," Jackson said.

"Yes, it does. I charged it up specially."

"I'll charge it up again," he said, proceeding on his way, leaving me on the stairs with my mouth open. Holiday films are boring enough without being preceded by a ten-minute wobbly journey round your own house. But I knew that once Jackson had attached himself to something technological, it required major surgery to detach him from it. Besides, I had other things on my mind. Eleven. Charlie deserved a lie-in at the end of what had been a difficult, tiring term at school but she had a paper round to do, she had packing, she had a holiday to prepare for. I picked up the phone from the low table at the bottom of the stairs and dialled her mobile. I was immediately connected to her voicemail but that didn't tell me much. As I'd found to my cost over the previous year, there were several dead zones on Sandling Island where mobile phones lost their signal. Charlie might have switched off her phone or left it in a drawer in her room or she might have been on her paper round already. I made a mental note to call her a few minutes later.

I stood in the living room, briefly at a loss. I had about eight things to do and there seemed no compelling reason to choose one to do first.

It was my birthday, my fortieth birthday. I remembered the unopened mail and decided that, before anything else, I would have a cup of coffee and look at the cards and intriguing little parcels that lay on the kitchen table. I put the kettle on, ground some coffee beans, pulled out the white porcelain cup and saucer that Rory had given me this time last year. I remembered opening it as he watched me, sitting at this very table. One year ago, as I turned thirty-nine, I was still married, and we had been starting our new adventure together. Looking back with the merciless clarity of hindsight, I could see the ominous signs. Perhaps if I had recognized them at the time, I could have saved us. I could recall the day clearly. Rory had given me the lovely cup, and a shirt that was several sizes too big, and later in the day we had gone for a long walk round the island in the rain.

Now I was forty and single, with the wreck of my

marriage smoking behind me. But because of Christian, I felt younger than I had for a long time, more attractive, energetic and hopeful. Falling in love does that.

The kettle boiled and I poured the water over the coffee grounds, then opened the first card, from my old school-friend Cora. I hadn't seen her for years but we remembered each other's birthday, clinging to our friendship by our fingernails.

There were about a dozen cards, and three presents: a pair of earrings, a book of cartoons about getting older, and a CD by a sultry young female singer I'd never heard of. I nearly didn't bother with the large brown envelope at the bottom of the pile, addressed in neat capital letters, because I assumed it contained a brochure. As I ran my finger under the gummed flap, I saw a glossy sheet inside, and I drew it out carefully. It was an A4 photograph of Jackson and Charlie, with "Happy Fortieth Birthday" written in Charlie's flamboyant scrawl along the white border at the top and their signatures underneath.

I smiled at the faces smiling at me: there was Jackson, rather solemn and self-conscious, his neat dark hair with its widow's peak, his tentative smile, his dark brown eyes gazing directly into the camera. Charlie stood beside him, her copper hair in a glorious tangle, her wide red mouth flashing a smile that dimpled one cheek, her blue-green eyes in her pale freckled face.

"Jackson!" I called up the stairs. "This is lovely!"

"What?" came his voice.

"The photo. It arrived in the post."

"That was Charlie's idea. She said it was more exciting to get things by post."

"It's really good," I said, looking at the image once more, the two pairs of bright eyes. "Who took it?"

He put his head round the kitchen door. "What?"

"Who took it for you?"

"Oh, I dunno. Some friend of Charlie's when you weren't here on the weekend."

"On Sunday?"

"Yeah. I can't remember her name, though."

"Thanks. I'll always treasure it."

He wandered off once more, as if he hadn't heard.

Later I would frame it but for the time being I pinned it to the fridge door with a magnet. But what to do now? What to do first among all the things that needed doing? I mentally tossed an imaginary eight-sided coin. First, I put the bag with the snorkel, the flippers, our bathing suits and towels into the back of the car, to get it out of the way. I put the dollars I'd ordered from the bank last week into my wallet. I wrote a note for the milkman, cancelling the milk for the next two weeks, rolled it up and put it into the neck of an empty bottle, which I placed outside the front door. I washed the dishes in the sink, dried and cleared them away, and swept the kitchen floor thoroughly—I wanted Renata to arrive at a tidy house. I stripped the sheets off our beds and threw them into the kitchen to deal with. At eleven thirteen by the clock on the oven, I rang Charlie again, and once more got a message.

I decided I would wash my hair before she got

home and took over the bathroom: she's the only
person I know who can single-handedly empty a water tank with one shower. I was half-way through
rinsing off the conditioner when I heard a knock at
the door. I groaned, assuming it must be the man who
called round every Saturday morning, selling fish
from the back of a van. This was particularly irritating because a fresher and cheaper selection was
available at a fishmonger's three minutes' walk along
the waterfront. But occasionally I took pity on him,
which gave him just enough encouragement to keep
coming.

The knock sounded again, louder this time. Charlie, I thought. She's lost her keys again. I stepped out
of the shower, pulled on the ratty grey dressing-gown
that Rory hadn't taken with him when he left, and
ran down the stairs, rubbing my hair as I went. I
opened the door starting to say something like "The
prodigal daughter returns," but stopped, because it
wasn't Charlie and it wasn't the fish man.

Someone was singing loudly. Several people were
singing loudly. I could see at least a dozen faces at the
door. I felt a flash of horror of the kind you experience when you know you're about to have an accident
and there's nothing you can do to prevent it. When
you have elbowed the vase off the shelf and it hasn't
yet hit the floor. When you have put the brake on too
late and feel your car skidding unstoppably into the
one in front. I realized that I was the victim of a surprise birthday party.

At the front was Joel, head and shoulders taller
than anyone else and dressed in his working clothes

of jeans and a heavy green jacket. He was smiling at
me apologetically. At least he wasn't singing. He'd
promised never to come to the house again, yet there
he was and there—right behind him, not grinning
and not singing—was his wife Alix. And, as if that
wasn't bad enough, there was the vicar. He was certainly singing. He was leading it, as if he was in
church, trying to rouse a sluggish congregation. Behind me, Sludge was moaning in panic. She was never
much of a guard dog.

"Happy birthday to you-ou-ou-ou!" they finished.

"Surprise," said Joel.

For one moment, I thought I would slam the door
in their faces and lock it. But I couldn't. These were
my neighbours, my fellow islanders, my friends. I
made an effort to change my expression of dazed
shock into a smile.

"Charlie arranged it," piped up Ashleigh, who was
standing beside the vicar, dressed in a trailing black
velvet coat over a small, flouncy green skirt. Her face
was glossy and fresh: full red lips, arched brows and
smooth, peachy skin. Tendrils of dark hair snaked
artfully down her neck. Ashleigh is Charlie's best
friend. Sometimes I worried about what they might
get up to together.

"Oh, did she?" I said. "Is that why she's not here?"

"She said eleven, but we thought that was a bit
early."

"Eleven fifteen seems a bit early for a party to
me," I said weakly. Maybe this was the way they did
things in the countryside.

"Not when it's your birthday!"

"Not when it's Christmas!"

"Anyway, I think we can be certain it really is a surprise," said Alix, drily, as I tugged the belt of Rory's oversized dressing-gown tighter and tried to look nonchalant.

"Let us in, then, Nina. We're getting cold out here."

I looked at the man who was brandishing a bottle of sparkling wine. Had I met him before? He was familiar, but I couldn't place him, or the woman his arm was wrapped round.

"I'm packing," I said.

The man—was he called Derek or Eric?—pulled the cork from the bottle and a spume of smoke and froth oozed over its neck. I stood back as the group advanced over the threshold like a small army. Someone thrust a bunch of flowers into my hands.

"I'm leaving in a couple of hours," I tried to say.

As I was about to shut the door on us all, I saw more people coming round the corner, carrying bottles and parcels: Carrie from the primary school and her husband; Ashleigh's mother; the nice woman who's a solicitor, Joanna or Josephine or something. Behind her Rick and Karen and, trailing them, Eamonn, who wasn't even wearing a jacket, just a T-shirt.

I turned to face my visitors. "Make yourselves at home," I said, although most of them already had. Alix was shaking crisps into one of my serving dishes and the vicar had dug out some glasses for the champagne. "Can you answer the door for me? I'm going to get some clothes on."

"Take a drink up with you," someone called.

"I can't," I said. "It's not even midday and, anyway, I'm driving later."

"Just one. It's your birthday! I'm certainly going to."

"I'll make you some coffee," said Joel.

"Thanks," I said.

"Go and change. I know where everything is. Sorry to be dressed like this. I've got some work to do afterwards."

"It doesn't matter," I said, meaning that it didn't matter how he was dressed, it didn't matter whether he had work to do. He didn't need to tell me about his life.

I escaped up the stairs and put my head round Jackson's door. He was sitting on his bed, in an immaculately tidy room, filming his feet, as far as I could see.

"There's a horde of people downstairs," I said, in a hiss.

Jackson aimed the camcorder at my face.

"Charlie said something about it. She told me not to tell you."

"Yes, I can see that."

"Shouldn't you put some clothes on, though?"

"Good idea. But where's Charlie? Has she prepared something else?"

"Dunno."

I heard the sound of more knocking on the front door and Sludge barking. The swell of voices and laughter from downstairs grew louder.

"Please stop filming me," I said.

He put the camcorder down on his bed.

"She'll be here soon," he said. "You know what she's like. She only did it because she thought you'd be pleased."

I went to my room and rang Charlie's number again.

"Where are you?" I said, leaving a message. "Charlie, this is getting ridiculous. Come home now. There are dozens of people drinking downstairs, thanks to you, and we're leaving for Florida soon. You haven't even packed and—oh, never mind, just come home."

Making no concession to the impromptu celebrations going on without me, I pulled on the jeans and top I planned to travel in and brushed my hair in front of the mirror, then tied it, still damp, in a loose bun. I put on the earrings Christian had sent me days before as an early present. I knelt in front of my suitcase and rifled through its contents: light skirts, bright shirts, shorts, sandals. Had I packed enough books, I wondered. I could always get more at the airport. I wished we were there now, just the four of us, loitering together in the timeless, placeless limbo before departure, buying things we didn't need. On an impulse, I called Christian again on his mobile. This time he was there.

"Hi," I said softly. "Me again. That's all I'm ringing to say, really. And I'm looking forward to seeing you."

"Me you too," he said. His voice sounded as if he was smiling. "Are you all packed?"

"Not as such."

"Where are you? You sound like you're calling from the pub."

"I'll tell you about it later."

"Don't be late."

"I won't. Unless I can't find Charlie."

"What does that mean?"

"Never mind. We'll be there."

I stood for a moment at the window. The tide was advancing now, creeping up the mudflats. Far out at sea, boats floated free at their buoys. It was misty, a fine gauze hanging over everything, but I could still see from where I stood the shapes of the old hulks and, beyond them, the stocky concrete pillboxes. They had been built as a defence against invasion during the war. Soldiers would have hidden inside and poked their rifles out of the narrow slits to prevent the Germans coming ashore on Sandling Island. So much effort, so much concrete, but the Germans never came and here they were, still waiting, cracked, immovable, half toppled on the cliffs and sands.

On the way downstairs, I had to push through a group of young people. I didn't recognize any of them and they didn't seem to recognize me.

"Hello," I said. "I'm Nina." Blank faces. "Charlie's mother."

"*Is* Charlie in her room?" The youth who spoke was tall and skinny, with a shock of black hair and eyes that were green in the subdued light of the stairwell. Everything about him seemed a bit undone: the laces on his heavy boots were trailing, his shirt was half unbuttoned, his sleeves frayed.

"No," I said. "Only Jackson. Where *is* Charlie anyway? You haven't seen her?"

He shrugged. "I said I'd meet her here. Typical Charlie, to be late at her own party."

"My party, theoretically. If you do hear from her . . ."

But they were gone and I proceeded downstairs to where the party had become an independent noisy organism. I stood and looked at it, feeling like an imposter in my own home. Nearly two years ago I had moved from London. I had left behind an old world and this was the new. But I hadn't really made it my own, not the way Jackson and Charlie had. This was where their friends were, this was where they felt comfortable. I hadn't settled in that way. There were people whose names I knew, people I nodded at in the street, people I drank coffee with. And there was one person I had slept with. But even so, as I gazed at these islanders I wondered if they were laying claim to me, if they were asking me for something I couldn't give them.

They were crammed into the tiny kitchen, and the living room beyond. I knew enough about them to recognize the different strands that connected them. I saw Karen speaking animatedly to Alix, gesturing largely with one hand, pausing only to drain her wine glass, then refill it from the bottle she was holding. They worked together: Karen was the receptionist at Alix's GP surgery in the town. Rick was in conversation with Bill. Probably about boats. Rick was a senior science teacher at Charlie's school, a few miles from the one I taught at, but his passions were sailing, kayaking and windsurfing, anything out on the

water. He taught them during the summer. And Bill
worked at a boatyard. His face was like carved dark
wood from years of toil in the sun and wind.

There was a cluster of people round the fridge, and
Eamonn was sitting on the rocking-chair by the window. He was wearing a black T-shirt with widely
flared sleeves, black fingerless gloves and wide black
trousers that came down over high black boots. His
hair was tied back in a beautiful green and black
ponytail. He looked ready for a night out in some
sleazy London club and didn't seem to notice that he
was sitting in a kitchen surrounded by middle-aged
men and women, talking about Christmas presents
and traffic congestion. I felt a kind of admiration for
him. Sludge was wedged beneath him, whining piti-
fully. I bent down and scooped up the pile of dirty
sheets on which Eamonn was resting his boots.

"You don't know where Charlie is, do you?"

I noticed the flush that made him look so young
and awkward. "Isn't she here?" he asked.

"She's disappeared on me. Unless there's some
extra surprise she's arranged, the icing on the cake."
I turned and searched among the crowd. "Ashleigh!
Ashleigh, you have to tell me now. Has Charlie got
some secret plan she's going to spring on me? Is that
why she's not here?"

Ashleigh shrugged and raised her perfect eyebrows. "She didn't say anything to me, Nina. Honestly. She just said come to your birthday party at
eleven, and don't smoke."

"So you haven't heard anything from her?"

"Hang on." She pulled out a pink phone the size

of a matchbox and jabbed at it with casual expertise. "No," she said, after a few seconds. "Sorry."

"Happy birthday, gorgeous Nina," said a portly man, ambushing me from the side and giving me and the laundry a bear-hug. "Bet you didn't expect to see me here, did you?"

"No," I said truthfully. "I didn't. Did Charlie—"

"Yup. Lovely girl, your daughter. Growing up, isn't she?" He winked.

"Will you excuse me for a minute?"

I wriggled free and crossed the room to the washing-machine, pushed in the sheets and selected quick-wash. That way I'd still have time to hang them out before we left. A cork shot past my face as I stood up, and there was another knock at the door. I squeezed my way through the crowd to get to it. A woman with untidy dark hair and a flushed red face was standing on the step. I had been so destabilized by the shock of the party that for a few seconds I didn't speak, even though I knew her and had been expecting her. "Nina, what's going on? It was today I was meant to arrive, wasn't it?"

Renata was my cousin, or a sort of cousin. I'd known her all my life without really knowing her, and now she was here to look after Sludge while we went to Florida. Or that was the excuse. She had just been left by her husband, having tried and failed for ten years to have children, and she had spent the last two months crying, unable to get out of bed. I'd thought maybe our house on Sandling Island, so far from her own where she'd been humiliated and abandoned, might do her some good. She had clearly put on her country clothes: green wellingtons, sensible trousers, a waxed jacket that looked brand new with a scarf tucked tidily into it. But nothing was quite right on her: it was as if she was acting a part whose lines she hadn't properly learned. She had lost a lot of weight, so that her clothes hung off her. Her face was a bit puffy; there were wrinkles that hadn't been there a few months ago. Her smile was too bright and brave. I'd always found her rather brisk and bossy, but now I softened. I hugged her, kissed her icy red cheeks. "How lovely to see you. Come in out of the cold. It's the right day. Sorry. It's all a bit mad, an aberration, but we'll be gone soon and so will all of them."

"I'll get my luggage, shall I?"

"Do you mind if I leave you to it? I'll put the door on the latch."

I edged back into the house. Someone pushed a glass of wine into my hand and I put it down on the nearest shelf. I sat on the stairs, half watching Karen jabbing the vicar repeatedly in the chest, making a point I couldn't hear through the din. I had first met him the day after we arrived on the island. He had sat in my kitchen and drunk coffee, said I should call him Tom and told me about the best local shops and beaches. Right at the end he had wondered in an almost guilty murmur whether he might see us occasionally at St. Peter's. Everything in me wanted to say yes. I had already spotted and loved his church, a small medieval building, worn soft and smooth by the north wind and centuries of devotion. I could imagine being there and singing hymns alongside the islanders, except that, almost with regret, I lacked the belief. He had said with a smile that that didn't stop most people. I had promised myself that I would go to his church at Christmas, but things had turned out differently and I would instead be on a beach in Florida.

If we ever got there. I called Charlie's mobile again. This was getting ridiculous. Surely she wouldn't still be at the sleepover if she'd arranged all of this? I made out Alix in the living room, talking to a woman called Sarah, and reluctantly made my way over to her. "Sorry to butt in," I said.

"Yes?" She still talked to me in that voice of brittle, exquisite politeness. Perhaps she always would now.

"I don't know where Charlie is. Was she still at your house when you left?"

She frowned. "I don't think so—but that's what these teenage sleepovers are like. You don't know who's there and you don't know when they depart, unless you happen to bump into them in the bathroom. You just hope they're not drinking vodka and that they clear up the mess when it's all over."

"So you didn't see her leave?"

"I'm afraid not. Have you lost her?" She made Charlie sound like a bunch of keys.

"Is Tam still at your house?"

Tam was Alix and Joel's daughter: petite, blonde, fragile, demure, beloved of all teachers, and Charlie's most persistent persecutor in and out of school.

"I'm not sure." Alix gave her chilly smile again. "But you know how it is with teenagers, they—"

"Can you give me her mobile number, please? Charlie's not answering hers. I'm getting a bit anxious. We're meant to be leaving for a holiday in a couple of hours."

I punched in the number as she said it and listened to the ringing sound. The voicemail picked it up and I left a message, asking Tam to ring me back at once and leaving both my numbers.

Behind me, I heard Karen say, "Well, there's something to be said for toy-boys."

Renata came down the stairs. She had taken off her jacket and scarf, brushed her hair and put on some lipstick that was too bright for her. She looked a bit like a ghost, but she was making an effort. "Tell me who everyone is, then," she said. "You seem to have made a lot of friends here already."

"I don't know who half of them are. Charlie invited them as a surprise. Anyway," I looked round the room, "that's Joanna—or Josephine. She's a solicitor. She lives in a lovely house further to the north of the island. That's Carrie. She taught Jackson last year and he liked her. That's Karen."

"The woman who's a bit the worse for wear?"

"Yes. I think she'd already had quite a bit by the time she arrived. She's the medical secretary, and she's married to a teacher at Charlie's school, Rick, but I can't see him at the moment. No—there. Tall, rather good-looking, curly dark hair. Her son, Eamonn, is the one who's walked straight out of a scary movie. I think he's all right, though. That's Bill—you might bump into him because he works at a boatyard across the road. I'll introduce you to him in a

bit if you want. And that girl who's smoking and
thinks I can't see is Ashleigh, Charlie's best friend."

"Who's that? He was trying to catch your eye. He
looks nice."

"That's Joel. He's a tree-surgeon—that's why
he's wearing those things."

I half turned away to hide a blush. My description of Joel had been incomplete. When I first met
him, he had been separated from Alix for much of
the year, by her choice and not his, and not long
ago I had been left by Rory. We knew each other because of our daughters. He was the opposite of Rory
in almost every way: capable, steady, practical. We'd
drunk wine together, told each other stories of our
life and relationships, practised our versions of what
had happened to us, swapped confidences, become
maudlin, sad and weepy together. We had tried to
comfort each other. And we'd slept together a few
times, although it had never been about desire. For
me it had felt too much like two drowning swimmers
clutching at each other, dragging each other down. I
suppose I had wanted to know that I was still capable of attracting a man, but very quickly I felt guilty
for allowing Joel to fall in love with me and to need
me more than I needed him. I'd quickly broken it off
and then a few weeks later Alix had taken Joel back.
I thought it had all been kept secret but it had become apparent that Joel had told his wife everything. She communicated this only through icy stares
and dry comments. I didn't like to think of what had
been said about us in the conversations between
them, as they tried to repair their relationship. It

wouldn't have mattered if it hadn't been for Alix's un-friendly looks and Joel's more covert friendly ones.

The phone rang in my pocket.

"Excuse me," I said to Renata. "Hello. Nina here."

"This is Tam." Her voice was wary. "You said I should ring you."

"Yes, thanks. I wanted to know if Charlie was still there."

"Charlie? No. She left ages ago."

Something tightened in my chest. "What time did she go?"

I heard Tam talking to someone else: "Jenna, what time did Charlie go? Do you reckon? Yeah, we think about nine thirty. Maybe before that. She had to do the paper round and then get things ready for your—um, you're having it now, right? Your party?"

"Yes," I said.

"She was going to bake a cake or something. Or buy it."

"So she left about nine-thirty and you haven't heard from her?"

"Right."

"How did she seem?"

"Fine," said Tam, breezily.

"So there was nothing . . ." But I stopped. I didn't know what I wanted to ask. "Thanks, Tam," I said, and rang off.

"Not there?" asked Renata.

I shook my head distractedly, noticing out of the corner of my eye that Sludge had come out from un-der the rocking-chair and was now chomping her way through a bag of salted cashew nuts, her tail rotating wildly. "I don't understand it. I mean, I know Charlie's not the most reliable of girls, but we're supposed to be going on holiday."

I made my way out into the back garden and, standing in the lee of the wall to shelter from the vicious wind, dialled again. "Christian?"

"Hi again."

"Sorry. Listen. I don't know where Charlie is. I'm sure it's fine, but I thought I ought to warn you that we might be running late."

"You don't know where she is?"

"I know it's nothing to worry about," I said, to damp down the immediate concern in his voice. "She's probably had a flat tyre on her paper round or something. Or is rescuing some stray cat or . . . well, you know Charlie. She's very impulsive. But she hasn't packed and everything's getting a bit behind schedule."

"It's odd, though."

"I'll call you as soon as she turns up."

Back in the house, the party showed no sign of coming to a close. Karen was half-way up the stairs now, swaying gently and trying to open another bottle of wine. Beneath her, Renata was being introduced to Sludge by Jackson, who still had the camcorder slung round his neck. Only Rick, coming down the stairs with his thick coat on, was mercifully making his way to the door.

"Escaping to your beloved boat at last?" I said to him. "I don't blame you."

"The light starts to fail so early," he said. "This was a terrible idea of Charlie's, wasn't it?"

"Terrible. And she's not even here."

"If I see her, I'll give her an earful."

"Just tell her to come home. I'm going to chuck everyone out now."

"That was a quick party!"

"I've got things to do, Rick. Pack. Find my daughter. Catch a plane."

"Right. Well, then, I'll say—"

He never got the chance to finish. There was a yowl, and then a flying mass made up of black dog, a human figure or two and a terrible smashing of glass. Pieces fell and shattered on the hard floor. Sludge shot past me and up the stairs, a flash of whining black, and on the floor in front of us lay Karen and Renata, surrounded by a sudden silence.

"Wow," said Jackson, and started to pull the camcorder into position, until I slapped down his arm.

"Well," said Renata, getting up slowly, pulling her jacket into place, glancing from side to side as if she had wandered by mistake into a staged farce. "Well."

Karen, however, did not move, not at first. She had fallen from half-way up the staircase, and now lay at its foot, a smashed bottle beside her, and her arm twisted unnaturally at her side. I squatted down to her and smelt the sweet stench of alcohol on her breath. At least she was breathing. She opened an eye and stared glassily at me.

"Fuck," said Rick. "Fuck fuck fuck. Now what?"

"If she has to get drunk," said Eamonn, loudly, slouching over to where his mother lay, "she should have more fun."

"Shut up," said Rick.

All I could think, as I gazed at Karen's spreadeagled body and blotchy face, was that I had to get hold of Charlie and none of this was going to get in my way.

"Joel!" I shouted, springing up. "Can you find Alix? There's been an accident. Are you all right, Karen?"

"I don't think anything's—"

"Good. Sorry about all of this. Right, everyone, I think you'd all better go now. The party's over."

Alix hurried into the room. Professional, concerned, she was a different person from the baleful presence she'd been earlier. She bent over Karen, who was now her patient. "Let's see," she said. Karen was blearily opening her eyes and trying to shift into an upright position. She gave a shout of pain, and then there was another knock at the open door, which swung in on Ben from down the road, his bearded face beaming from behind a great bunch of flowers.

"Sorry I'm late but I . . . Have I missed something?"

Alix looked up at me as if I were nominally in charge. "She's broken her arm," she said, "and there's a nasty gash on her shoulder that needs attention before she loses more blood. I think we'd better call an ambulance."

"Shit," said Rick. "Are you sure it's broken? It might just be—"

"It's broken. Look."

"Ow! That's agony! The dog jumped on me."

"You jumped on the dog," said Jackson, indignantly. "You fell like a tree."

"Call the ambulance, Rick," I said. "I've got to find Charlie. Renata, can you get rid of everyone?"

"But—"

"I've only just arrived," said Ben. "I thought this was going to go on for ages. Can I at least have a drink?"

"No. Sorry, but no."

I ran up the stairs, away from the heat and the noise, the mess and the confusion. I saw the clock radio by my bed. Eleven thirty-six. For just a few seconds I stood by the window, staring out at the sea that was drawing closer all the time, at the grey sky that rocked gently against the grey water, the grey light falling in wide faint shafts. I could see how the wind was riffling the waves into the tightly corrugated patterns of squalls and how the sea-birds, a long way out, gathered in spiralling patterns around a lone fishing-boat, half shrouded in the faint mist.

I lifted the phone. "Christian? It's me again . . . Yes . . . No, no, she hasn't. Listen, I'm very sorry about this but you'll have to make your own way to Heathrow. I'll join you there . . . Yes, once Charlie's come home. Sorry, sorry. 'Bye."

I took a deep breath and walked downstairs. Alix was talking on the phone in an authoritative tone. She had taken control now. For just a tiny fraction of a second I resented this, then told myself not to be so bloody stupid. Karen was lying on the floor covered with one of our blankets. Her face was white. Her eyes were open but she looked sleepy. The shoulder of her blouse was dark with blood.

Alix put down the phone and addressed Rick decisively: "You have to drive Karen to the hospital," she said. "I'll come with you. Joel can follow behind us."

"The tree," said Joel. "I've got to see to the tree."

"But the ambulance . . ." said Rick. He seemed dazed, as if he was finding it hard to take in the seriousness of what had occurred. In a way that was almost comic, he seemed to want to pretend that this was a normal Saturday, that he could carry on with the weekend he had planned.

"It'll take too long," said Alix, in a tone that permitted no disagreement. "I'm concerned about shock and loss of blood. We must go at once." Now she turned to me. "Sorry to spoil your party."

That was pure Alix. In the middle of a crisis, she still had the presence of mind to aim a jab at me. Clearly her feelings about me and her husband were still raw.

"Is there anything I can do?" I said.

Alix asked if they could take the blanket with them. Since it was wrapped round Karen and possibly preventing her falling into severe shock, I wasn't about to refuse. It was a grim conclusion to what had already been an awkward social occasion. Karen was half led, half carried out to her car by her husband and Joel. She was laid on the back seat, then Rick and Alix drove away.

Joel gave me a constrained hug. "Sorry," he said.

"Don't be ridiculous."

He looked round to see if anybody was within earshot. "Alix is still a bit funny about all this," he said. "I mean about us."

"That's all in the past," I said, wishing he would leave.

"You're going away for Christmas," he said.

I opened my mouth to tell him that this wasn't the time or the place for a chat about holidays, then shrugged. "If I can track down Charlie," I said.

"You're going with your new, er . . . you know . . ."

"Joel," I said. "You're meant to be following Alix."

"I know the way," he said. "So." He paused, as if we were still at the party having a desultory conversation, rather than in the middle of an emergency. "So, have a really good holiday. And happy Christmas and I hope you have a really good new year."

He leaned across and gave me a peck on the cheek.

"You've got to go, Joel. And I've got so much to do."

He still hovered as if he was trying to think of a pretext to stay.

"So if I don't see you—" he began.

"Go," I said, in as soothing a tone as I could manage and almost pushed him into the car.

I watched him drive away but I wasn't really seeing anything. I was thinking. This was ridiculous. I had to do something straight away. Did you dial 999 for something like this? Was it enough of an emergency? When I got back into the house I opened a cupboard and fumbled for the phone book. I looked in the *Yellow Pages*. There was nothing between "Point of Sale Advertising" and "Political Organisations." Finally I found a whole page of police numbers. There were numbers for recruitment, a drugs-crackdown hotline, abnormal loads. There was a gay and lesbian helpline, victim support, Crimestoppers, ChildLine, domestic violence. You could even report a crime online. I ran my thumbnail down the page and found the number for the service desk for Sandling Island.

Unbelievably, the party in my house was still going on, like an organism that refused to die whatever was done to it. I retreated with the phone into the utility room that led off the kitchen, and shut the door behind me. A female voice answered and I realized I hadn't considered precisely what I was going to say.

"This may sound stupid," I said. "I think my daughter may be missing."

The woman stopped me right there and took my name and address, then Charlie's full name and age. She didn't sound impressed by my answers.

"How long has your daughter been missing?"

"It's difficult to put it like that. She was staying with a friend last night, but she was due back a couple of hours ago and . . ."

"A couple of hours? And she's fifteen years old? I'd really give it a bit longer than that."

"Hang on," I said. "I know it doesn't sound like much time but something's gone wrong. We're due to go away on holiday. We're supposed to be leaving before one and it's twenty to twelve now. She knows about that, she's excited about it. She had to get back—she had to pack her things. It's not just that. She organized a surprise party for me this morning but she didn't turn up at it. Why would that be? Something's happened."

"She's probably been held up."

"Of course she's been held up," I said. "The question is, what has held her up? What if it's something serious?"

We were locked in a battle of wills. I didn't know who this woman was. Was she a policewoman? Was she a receptionist? I could tell she wanted me to go away and wait for the problem to sort itself out. But I wasn't going to go away. I stayed on the line, argued and insisted, and finally she asked me to wait. She had her hand over the receiver and I heard her muffled voice asking somebody something. When she came back on the line, she told me that an officer would drop round to see what was happening.

"Soon," I said. "If anything has happened to Charlie it's urgent. Time is very important."

I only ended the conversation when the woman had agreed that the officer would be with me in a few minutes. Now I had to wait for the police to arrive. What did I do in the meantime? I couldn't just stand there. I had to finish my packing. I could throw out the last of my so-called guests. No. All that could wait. Charlie was all that mattered. Was there anything productive I could do before the police came?

I opened the door. A teenager I didn't recognize was opening my fridge. She looked round at me unconcernedly.

"The newsagent on The Street," I said. "Do you know what it's called?"

She paused, a carton of orange juice in her hand. "Walton's," she said, and poured juice into a glass.

I found the name in the phone book and rang it. "Hello," I said, when a woman answered. "Mrs. Walton?"

"No," said the woman.

"But this is Walton's?"

"That's right."

"My name is Nina Landry. I'm Charlotte's mother. Did she do her paper round this morning?"

"I think so."

"Didn't you see her?"

"Gerry," the woman shouted, "who did the papers this morning?"

I heard a voice say something I couldn't make out.

"Yes," said the woman. "She did them."

"What time did she get there?"

"That was before I arrive. Probably between nine and nine thirty. That's when she usually comes."

"Thanks."

I rang off. Was this good or bad news? She had been around, but that was hours ago. Suddenly it became clear. My soon-to-be-ex-husband. I dialled his number. A woman answered.

"Hello, is Rory there?"

"Who's this?"

"I'm sorry, who are you?"

"You first."

"I'm Nina." There was a pause. Further explanation was called for. "His ex-partner."

"Yes, Nina. I know all about you. I'm Tina."

Tina. At his flat. Answering his phone. Knowing all about me. I hadn't heard anything about a Tina. Where had she come from? When? I grimaced into

the phone, happier to know that Rory had found someone else as well and also feeling strange that both of
us had moved on so quickly. How could so many
years of marriage just disappear?

"Is Rory there?"

"He's out."

Tina seemed to want to talk but I rang off immediately and dialled Rory's mobile.

"Hi, Nina," he said.

"Rory, is there something I should know?"

"I think there's rather a lot you should know. Is
there anything particular you had in mind?"

I steadied myself. For a long time, all conversations with Rory had been like teetering on the edge
of a steep hill. One careless step and we would tumble into an increasingly bitter argument.

"You were talking about seeing Charlie earlier."

"I was talking about seeing the children, about
missing the children."

"That's what I meant."

"Are you ringing to apologize?" he asked.

"What about?" I said, regretting the words as soon
as I had spoken them.

"I don't think we should go into that. All I want to
say is that I know we've got our differences, but I really hoped you'd keep the children out of it."

"Rory, if you knew the lengths I'd gone to to do
just that."

There was a silence on the line: he'd hung up. I
redialled.

"Feeling better?" he said.

"Is Charlie with you?"

"Would it be a problem if she was?"

"Don't mess about. We're meant to be leaving for the airport in a few minutes. If you've picked her up, then—"

"Then what?"

Deep breath. Slow deep breath.

"Just drop her back. We're in a desperate rush."

"But I haven't picked her up."

"She's really not there?"

"Are you saying I'm lying?"

"I don't understand this," I said. "I've already called the police and an officer is on his way. So if—"

"What the hell are you accusing me of?" Rory said, his voice turning angry. "I'm her father. What's going on? Where is she?"

"I don't know. I hope it's nothing—well, it's bound to turn out to be nothing. Probably she'll just turn up."

"But you've called the police?"

"It was just in case."

"Just in case what?"

"I thought it was sensible."

"Right. I'll be over. I'm coming now."

"No, Rory. Please—"

It was too late. He had hung up again.

With no compunction, embarrassment or shame, I went round the house emptying it of people. I shooed some teenagers off the stairs, I told the vicar how nice it was to see him but that I was about to leave. (Didn't he have a church to go to? A sermon to write?) I hustled Derek or Eric along the garden path. I woke Eamonn up from the sofa. But I found time to ask them all about Charlie. If they saw her, tell her to ring me. It was urgent.

Jackson and a friend were wandering around, the camcorder still recording. I pulled the friend away, reunited him with his mother and wished them a happy Christmas as I steered them out firmly into the street. I saw on my mobile phone that it was eleven minutes to twelve. In half an hour or so we were meant to be heading for the A12, on the way to meet Christian, on the way to the holiday we'd been planning for so long.

At the gate, I turned and held Jackson tightly by his shoulders.

"Listen now," I said. "Charlie's missing. At least, she's not here. And though I'm sure it will be fine, it's a bit odd. Do you have any idea whatsoever of where she might be?"

He shook his head mutely.

"She said nothing to you?"

"No."

"If she doesn't turn up soon," I continued, "we're not going to get that plane."

"We'll be able to get another one later, though, won't we? Mum?" His eyes filled with tears and he wrenched himself away from me and kicked at a stone.

"The important thing is to find Charlie," I said.

"Yeah," he mumbled. Then, "She'll be all right, won't she?"

"Yes," I said.

In the house, Renata was clearing glasses off surfaces and stacking them in the dishwasher, not briskly but with a lethargic sadness that made me want to scream. The party had barely started before I'd ended it, and yet there was an extraordinary mess everywhere—bowls of crisps, saucers with cigarettes stubbed out in them, mud on the carpets and tiles, a smear of blood leading from the bottom of the stairs into the hall, a smashed bottle by the front door.

"Right, Nina," she said, picking up a bowl and staring at it hopelessly. "You can leave all of this to me. I'll put all those flowers in water for a start." Tears were rolling down her cheeks, and I saw that she was hobbling a bit, presumably from her collision with Sludge and Karen.

"No," I said. "I'm sorry, and I know this isn't what you came for, but here's what I want you to do, Renata. Can you take Jackson and Sludge and walk through the town? Ask if anyone's seen Charlie."

She looked doubtful. "Who? Anyone?"

"Jackson will point people out, won't you, my darling?"

"Oh," said Renata. "Yes, of course. I'll just get my jacket on . . ."

"Have you got a mobile?"

"Yes."

"Call me if there's any news."

"Are you staying here?"

"The police are coming."

"Oh." Her face became grave. She glanced sideways at Jackson and pulled her features into unconvincing cheeriness. "Right, then," she said heartily. "Let's be off. Lead on, Macduff."

"What?"

At any other time, I would have laughed at the sight of Sludge racing down the road with her demented crab-like gait, red tongue lolling and ears turned inside out, pulling Renata after her in a stiff-legged, braking run. Jackson jogged behind them, looking like a troll in his oversized skiing jacket.

I went back into the house. Where were the police? They'd said just a few minutes. The timer-clock on the oven told me it was eleven fifty-three. I picked up a small bunch of flowers and put my face into the satin cool of their petals, thinking furiously. She'd left the sleepover at between nine and nine thirty and I knew she'd gone straight to the newsagent . . .

The bell rang and I ran to the door.

"Nina Landry?"

The man who stood there was quite short and stout, and he wore a uniform that was slightly too tight for him. He had short brown hair and jug ears. His face was weathered and inappropriately cheerful. "PC Mahoney," he said.

"Come in," I said. "Mind the broken glass."

We walked through the living room, which looked a bit like a crime scene, and into the chaos of the kitchen. He probably expected me to offer him tea but I didn't have time for that. I pulled out a chair for him, sat down myself at the littered table and looked at him. He pushed away a bowl of crisps, pulled out a notebook and a pen, licked his finger and flipped over several pages. He wrote the date at the top, then glanced at his watch and wrote the time as well: 11:54, I read upside-down.

"Let me take a few details."

"I've already done that. When I called."

"Your daughter's full name and age?"

"I already gave it," I said. "To the woman at the police station."

"Please," he said.

"Charlotte Landry Oates. Landry after me and Oates after her father," I added, forestalling his next question.

"Is Mr. Oates here?"

"He doesn't live with us," I said, and watched the expression on his face become shrewd as I said it. "He left at the start of the year." I didn't wait for his next question. "Charlie's fifteen. She was born on the third of February."

"So she's nearly sixteen."

"Yes, but—"

"And when did she go missing? The duty officer said it was just an hour or so ago."

"I don't know exactly. She was at a sleepover, and then she did her paper round. I was out, doing errands, and I expected her to be here when I got back, which was later than I'd thought because on the spur of the moment I rang up a friend to look at my car and then—oh, that doesn't matter. The point is, she wasn't here when I got back."

"And that would have been when?"

I remembered Karen telling Eamonn, as he shuffled out of the door of their house in his bare feet and trench coat, that it was gone half past ten. And when I'd gone into Charlie's room her sheep clock had sounded the hour.

"It must have been about eleven. She wasn't there and that was odd because we're going on holiday. *Were* going on holiday. I don't think we'll make it now. We needed to leave at one or one thirty at the latest, and she was going to come home and pack. Plus she arranged this party for me. I wouldn't have worried otherwise, but this makes no sense. She was so excited. We've been planning this for ages."

"Where are you going for your holiday?"

"Florida," I said impatiently.

"Nice. Just the three of you?"

"Four. My boyfriend is coming as well."

"New boyfriend?"

"Quite, why does that—"

"Does your daughter get on with him?"

"Yes. I mean, there've been . . . but yes, basically."

"Mmm. Does Charlotte have a mobile phone?"

"I've been ringing it. No answer. I've rung the friend she was with last night. I've rung the newsagent to check she did the paper round. I've spoken to her best friend. Nobody knows where she's got to."

I wanted him to tell me it was nothing to worry about, and when he did I felt frustrated because I knew he was wrong. "I know Charlie," I said insistently. "I *know* this isn't in character. Something's wrong. We have to find her."

"Ms. Landry," he said kindly, "I understand what teenagers are like. I've got one myself."

"You don't know what *Charlie*'s like."

"Teenagers," he continued, as if I hadn't spoken, "go missing all the time. You wouldn't believe how often they're reported missing and then they turn up, a few hours later, the next day. I'm sure your daughter will come home soon. Have you had an argument recently?"

"No."

That wasn't strictly true, of course. I rarely lose my temper, but Charlie quarrels with everyone, whether they participate or not. She has a strictly confrontational attitude towards the world. When I picture her, she has her hands on her hips or her arms folded provocatively. She challenges people, she glowers, she squabbles, she storms out of rooms and slams doors. But she's like Rory, or like Rory used to be: quick to anger and quick to apologize or forgive, generous and contrite to a fault, never bearing grudges. She argued with me yesterday, and she argued with me the day before that and probably the day before that as well, about the fact that she'd lost her physics coursework on her computer and hadn't backed it up, about whether she and Ashleigh could go to London for a concert on a school day, about why she had to go to her father's when there was a big party on Sandling Island that evening, about eating an entire pack of ice-cream but leaving the empty tub in the freezer as an irritating decoy, about borrowing my shoes without asking and breaking the heel . . . But those were small tiffs, the daily stuff of Charlie's life.

"No," I repeated. "We hadn't argued."

"Boyfriend trouble?" he asked.

"No," I said. "Charlie doesn't have a boyfriend."

"As far as you know," said PC Mahoney, smiling humorously at me.

"She would have told me," I said. "She tells me things." For she did. Charlie gave me her anger and impatience, but she also offered me her confidences, often in a touchingly candid way. She'd told me about the boys who'd asked her out; she'd confessed about getting horribly drunk on Bacardi Breezers at Ashleigh's house, so that she'd thrown up on the neat green lawn; she'd asked my advice about spots and period pains, talked about how she felt stifled by her father's over-protectiveness. "Look, this is all irrelevant."

"How about at school? Was she happy? Any trouble with her peer group?"

"Nothing that would have made her run away from home."

"There was trouble, then?"

"She was bullied for a bit," I said shortly. "She was the new girl and didn't fit in. You know how vicious girls can be in a group. But that's all stopped now."

"Mmmm." He stood up suddenly, tucking his notebook back into his pocket. "Let's pay a visit to Charlotte's bedroom."

"What for?"

"Up the stairs, is it?"

He was already on his way, and I followed him.

"I've already looked. There's nothing to see."

"This one?"

"Yes."

PC Mahoney stood stolidly in the doorway, gazing in at the catastrophe of Charlie's room. The air in here smelt thickly fragrant: Charlie loved creams, lotions and bath oils. After she had taken one of her epic showers or lain for hours in a sudsy bath, she would drip her way into her room and rub cream into her body, spray perfume over it and into her coppery hair.

"Not very tidy, is it?" he remarked mildly.

He stooped down, picked up a Chinese wrap that lay at his feet, like a bright, wounded bird, and placed it carefully on the unmade bed. He frowned at the havoc around him. He stepped further into the room, his substantial frame making the space seem smaller and darker. There were lace knickers on the floor, two bras, fishnet tights, a puddle of trousers, as if Charlie had only just stepped out of them. There was a box of chocolates a boy had given her recently, most of which had gone. A notebook with her slapdash writing in it. A poster of a rock star I didn't recognize was coming away from the wall, a photograph of a younger me and Rory, holding hands, smiled from the corner. A collection of postcards Blu-tacked above her bed showed pictures of a giant stone foot from the British Museum, a white beach, a blue Matisse collage. A mosquito net was suspended from the ceiling above Charlie's pillow and PC Mahoney had to bend his head to avoid getting caught in the white gauze. His thick black boots moved softly across the carpet and I could almost hear Charlie's voice hissing in my ear, "Get him out!" There was an empty beer can next to the overflowing waste-paper basket and he touched it with his foot as if it was evidence.

"Is anything missing?"

I gazed around in despair. I opened the wardrobe

and peered inside. Charlie's clothes are a mixture of exotic and grungy: black jeans, a flounced purple skirt, an old leather jacket, an embroidered gypsy blouse, a tiny red dress, stompy boots, slouchy train-ers, camisoles and strappy tops, grey and black hood-ies, T-shirts with incomprehensible slogans stretched across the breast. Most things lay scattered around the floor. I closed the door. "I don't think so," I said cautiously.

"Nothing she would have taken with her if she was thinking of staying somewhere else?"

"I don't know."

I glanced round again, searching for absences in the frenetic jumble, spaces.

"Her mobile, for instance."

"She had that with her last night, so of course it's not here." I looked at the desk. Her computer was turned off. I picked up a shoebox. Inside, there was a pair of long, jangly earrings, a bath bomb, a snarled-up bead necklace, a strip of four passport photo-graphs of her and Ashleigh squashed into the booth, making silly faces for the camera, a folded square of lined paper, which, when I opened it, read, "Remem-ber dinner money," an inky rubber, a stick of glue, a bottle of hardened clear nail varnish, two pen lids and several hair-bands. I put the box down and stared at the surface in concentration. Clearasil, deodorant, CDs, her pencil case. Suddenly I saw it. Saw what wasn't there.

"Her washbag," I said. "It's blue with lighter blue patterns on it, I think. I can't see it." I picked up the towels and threw them to one side. "It's not here. Or her makeup bag. It's pink. Maybe it's in one of her bags. That's odd."

I started picking up all the garments on the floor and putting them in a pile to make sure nothing was hidden beneath. I held the pyjama bottoms and frowned at them, suddenly breathless.

"What?" asked PC Mahoney.

"She wears these with a nightshirt. Where's the nightshirt?"

"There's a simple explanation, Ms. Landry."

"What?"

"These are all items she would have taken to a sleepover."

"She didn't."

"She didn't take them, you mean? You're sure?"

"Absolutely sure. She wasn't going to stay over. She just went round there for a party. Tam suggested she stay over. She called me to say she wasn't coming home but she'd be back the following morning. I know she didn't have her things because we talked about it. I even offered to bring them round to her, but she laughed and said she'd clean her teeth with her finger and have a shower and change her clothes when she got back. I don't know if she had her purse with her. Just her phone."

"There you are, then."

I sat on the bed and rubbed my eyes. "I don't understand," I said. "When did she take them? I mean, they were here last night, so when did she take them? Why? We were going on holiday."

"Ms. Landry, I know it must be very distressing but we see things like this all the time."

"Like what? What are you saying?"

"For some reason Charlotte has gone to stay somewhere else for a while. I'm sure she'll be back soon."

"No."

"She's taken her makeup bag, her night things, her wash-bag, her mobile and maybe her purse."

"She was happy. It's not right, it can't be. There's some other explanation. Not this. She wouldn't."

"Your daughter is fifteen years old, two months off sixteen. I'm sure I don't have to tell you what a difficult age that can be. It sounds as if she's got a lot on her plate at the moment. Her father has left, you have a new boyfriend, she's had problems at school."

I closed my eyes and tried to think rationally. The evidence was there, incontrovertible. At some point, Charlie had come home, taken her things and gone again. I couldn't argue with that, yet at the same time I remembered that yesterday, before she'd gone out, she had seemed—had *been*, I was sure—carefree and affectionate with me. We had talked eagerly about Florida. We'd even discussed what clothes she would pack. She'd said she'd have to wax her bikini line. She had even been nice about Christian, kissing my cheek and saying that she supposed he was all right, really. "She would have told me if something was wrong. I know she would."

"Teenagers have secrets, Ms. Landry. My wife often says that—"

"So what's going to happen now?"

"As soon as you hear from her, get in touch with us."

"No, I mean what are *you* going to do?"

"We'll put her on our lists, keep an eye out—you can come down to the police station later and make a statement."

"That's it? That's all?"

"She's probably quite all right, just needs a bit of time to think things through."

I looked at his pleasant, unconcerned face. "I'm afraid I don't agree with you. If she's run away, that's because something happened to make her do so. You may well be correct—she could simply walk in through the door at any moment. But presumably it's the job of the police to think about the bad scenarios as well as the good ones. That's why I called you in the first place. We can't just wait and see. We have to find her now."

"I understand your concern, but your daughter is nearly sixteen."

"She's fifteen. She's a child," I said. "Please help me find my daughter."

The phone rang loudly and I started up off the bed.

"That's probably her right now," said PC Mahoney.

I ran down the stairs two at a time and picked up the receiver, my heart thudding with hope. "Yes?"

"Nina, it's Rick."

"Oh."

"I wanted to apologize for the rumpus we caused earlier."

"It doesn't matter," I said. "I hope Karen's all right."

"Has Charlie turned up?"

"No," I said. "She hasn't."

"I'm so sorry. And your holiday . . . I wish there was something I could do, Nina, but I'm stuck at the hospital. Have you thought of calling the police?"

"They're here now. And they think—" I broke off.

"What?"

"They think she's run away," I continued reluctantly. "It doesn't make sense, Rick. I don't think Charlie would do that. She seemed absolutely fine yesterday."

"I'm sorry I can't be much help," he said. "I'm in the middle of things here. All I'd say, as a teacher—as Charlie's teacher—is that teenagers often don't behave in the ways you'd expect."

"That's what I'd say, in your position. That's what the police officer says, too. He doesn't think there's anything to worry about."

"I'm sure there isn't."

"Thanks, Rick. I've got to go now. She might ring and I've got to keep the line clear." I remembered where he was calling from. "I'm sorry, Rick. How is Karen?"

"The doctor's seeing her now."

"I'm so sorry."

"That's all right," he said. "I'd better go. Let me know when Charlie gets back. She will, you know."

I put the phone down and turned to PC Mahoney as he came down the stairs.

"Not her?"

"No. You're going?"

"I'm sure she'll come walking in through that door right as rain . . ."

"And if she doesn't?" I said dully.

"I'll send a patrol car round the island now, to look out for her. Perhaps you could give me a recent photograph of her."

"Yes. Yes, of course. Look, here."

I pulled the photograph they had sent me for my birthday off the fridge—Charlie and Jackson, smiling at me, their eyes bright in their young and lovely faces. "This was taken a few days ago," I said.

"Thank you." He studied it for a few seconds. "Pretty girl."

"Yes."

"Well, as I said . . ."

I opened the door for him. I could hear the sea and the wind in the masts of the boats in the yard. A few drops of rain splattered against my burning face. I closed the door after him and leaned against it, dizzy with the unreality of what was happening. My daughter—my beloved, tempestuous, impulsive, honourable Charlie—had run away from home. From me. I took deep, steady breaths through the heaviness in my chest, then went into the kitchen and splashed water on my face. "Right," I said.

I dialled Christian's mobile.

"I'm on the M25. Where are you?" he said.

"Charlie's run away."

"What? Charlie has? But why?"

"I can't talk now. We're not coming." There was silence on the line. I thought we'd been cut off. "Hello? Are you there?"

"Yes, I'm here. What's happening?"

"What do you think's happening? Go without us. I'll be in touch. I'm so sorry."

"Nina, listen. I'm sure it'll be all right, but I'll come back and help you look. It's going to be all right."

"You're breaking up," I said, and ended the call.

I hadn't eaten anything all day and suddenly felt terribly hungry. I was trembling violently and even thought I might faint. I went to the kitchen, found some breakfast cereal in a cupboard and ate it as it was, in handfuls, without milk. I filled the electric kettle with water. I rinsed out the cafetière. I had to dismantle it and hold the pieces under the running tap to rid it of the last of the coffee grounds, cleaning them away with my fingers in the fiercely cold water. I took a pack of coffee beans from the fridge, ground them and tipped some into the cafetière. The water boiled and I poured it on to the coffee. I also made a piece of toast and marmalade. I sat at the kitchen table and gulped the hot, black, strong coffee and ate the toast in slow, deliberate bites. After all, what did it matter now? I had lots and lots of time.

I had woken into a new world, a world that was cold and harsh and entirely different from anything I had ever imagined for myself, and I had to think about it carefully and with clarity. I had got up this morning and been one person and now I was another. I was a woman whose daughter, aged fifteen, had run away from home. I had a daughter who had secretly gathered together a few pathetic possessions and some money and had gone out into a biting December day rather than be in this home with me. There was somewhere else she would rather be, perhaps someone else she would rather be with. Anywhere but here.

There was something I found hard to confess even to myself. It was the single most shameful thing I had ever felt in my entire life. I felt embarrassed. Gradually, the people around me, family, friends, acquaintances, neighbours, would hear that Nina Landry was a mother whose daughter had run away from home. Parents having terrible rows with their children would comfort themselves by saying, "At least I'm a better parent than Nina Landry. Relations with my children may be bad, but they haven't run away, not like that daughter of Nina Landry's." I imagined the next few days, bumping into people in the street. A look of surprise. "I thought you were on holiday." "We had to cancel—unfortunately my daughter . . ."

Gradually, as word spread, I would be met not by a look of surprise but of awkwardness, followed by a murmured word of sympathy delivered with the glint of excitement we feel about the disasters of other people.

It was awful and contemptible, but it was what went through my mind and I made myself think about it as if I were plunging my hand into boiling water and holding it there.

I poured myself another cup of coffee and sipped it. If I included the nine months of pregnancy, with its nausea, apprehension and lurching anticipation, this was the first moment for about sixteen and a half years that I hadn't known where my daughter was. I had to decide what to do. I picked up the phone and called Renata's mobile.

"Nobody's seen anything of her," she said, "but—"

"I know," I said, interrupting her. "You can come back now. I'll tell you about it."

"Don't you want us to—"

"No," I said, and hung up.

What were my possibilities? The policeman had made Charlie's departure seem like just another of those things that happen as children grow up, like birthday parties and Brownies. According to that view, I could get on with my life, with a few regrets and sniffles, and wait for my daughter to be in touch. I only had to articulate that to myself to realize how impossible it was. I had to find Charlie and talk to her, even if the only result of it was that she told me things I didn't want to know. I tried to think what other mothers would do and it just wouldn't compute. I was stuck with myself and there was nothing I could do about it. Charlie was fifteen years old, she was my child and I had to find her. Everything else could wait. So, where did I start?

My first impulse was to jump into the car, drive, stop strangers in the street and just do anything and everything until she was found. Hysteria and instant action might have made me feel better, or stopped me dwelling on things that were painful, but I needed to be effective. I reached for the pad that I kept on the kitchen table for shopping lists. It had a pen attached to it by a Velcro strip. I ripped it off and doodled as I tried to order my thoughts.

Charlie had taken a few possessions with her so

she must have run away from someone or with someone or to someone. She could have gone to stay at a friend's. The worst possibility was that, whatever Rick had said, she had up and gone alone, hitched a lift, left with no plans and no destination, just heading away. I thought of Charlie standing by a road, thumbing a lift, getting into a stranger's car, leaving us all behind, and felt a stinging in my eyes. For the first time in my life I thought of killing myself and then I thought of Jackson and Charlie and put that idea away for ever.

What was most likely was that she would be with a friend, or that a friend would know of her plans. If I could find someone to put me in touch with Charlie, I could talk to her and she could tell me what had gone wrong between us. Where to start? At some point before the party had begun, while I was out having my car fixed, Charlie had returned to the house, retrieved what she needed and gone. Her decision to leave, or at least her decision to leave today, before going on holiday, must have been sudden or she would have taken her purse and washbag to Ashleigh's. One guest after another at the party had told me how Charlie had organized it. I knew my daughter was a wonderfully strange and chaotic girl, but would even she organize a surprise party for her mother on the day she was going to run away from home?

Now a thought occurred to me. Could it have been that something had happened at the sleepover to provoke this crisis? I wondered what could have made her run away instead of coming to me. I couldn't

think of a scenario that made sense but it was clear I
had to start with the sleepover. I reached for the
phone book, then remembered I didn't need to: Joel's
home number was on my mobile. Another life, another story. I clicked on it and rang the number but it
was engaged. A voice asked me to leave a message
but I couldn't say to a machine anything of what was
needed. Rather than wait, I decided to drive over—
his house was only a couple of minutes away. I left a
scrawled note to Renata on the kitchen table and got
into the car. I drove along the front and turned right
into Flat Lane, which led inland. I pulled up outside
Alix and Joel's whitewashed thatched cottage, a
tasteful anomaly in a road of terraced houses that
could have been in the suburbs of any large English
city.

I rang the doorbell, then rapped hard with a heavy
wrought-iron knocker. Alix opened the door with the
phone at her ear, gave me a look of puzzlement and
gestured me inside. I hovered on the threshold while
she continued with her conversation. She turned away
from me, as if to keep her privacy, but I could hear
she was having a professional conversation with
someone at her practice. It sounded like a routine discussion about a rota because someone was ill. This
was ridiculous. I took a deep breath and tapped her
shoulder. She looked round, frowning. Was I really
telling her to get off the phone, as if she were a garru-
lous teenager? Yes, I was.

"It's urgent," I mouthed at her.

"Sorry, Ros," she said. "I'll call you back.
There seems to be some sort of emergency."

Alix put a sarcastic emphasis on the word "seems" but she hung up. "Karen's not too bad," she said. "I just got back from the hospital. She was seen at once because of the bleeding. She's had some stitches and the break in the arm was quite nasty. She'll have to stay for the night at least. Rick's stuck there with her, poor man. It's a greenstick fracture. Do you know what that is? It's like when you get a twig and snap and it doesn't break off—"

"It's not about that," I said. "Charlie's missing."

Alix looked at me quizzically. "Missing?"

I gave her a rundown of the events of the morning. I saw a familiar expression of disbelief appear on her face. "But it's only been a couple of hours."

"Not a normal couple of hours. We were about to leave for the airport. I know it's shocking and inexplicable but Charlie has taken her stuff and run off and . . . I don't know . . ."

There was a moment when I almost let the tears run from my eyes. I had the temptation to let go, to howl, put my arms round Alix and ask for comfort and help. But a glance at her sceptical, detached expression made me take control again. This wasn't the right shoulder to cry on. And this wasn't the time to collapse. I took a deep breath. "I'll need to talk to Tam," I said.

She looked at me for a second. Everything that was important in our relationship with each other was unsaid, lying deep and cold under the surface politeness. We both knew this, both knew that the other knew. I had had an affair—no, a brief fling—with Joel, although at the time they weren't living

together and I wasn't sure if that counted as betrayal or not. We'd never mentioned it, nor would
we, although it was in every glance we exchanged,
every word we spoke. And then, as if in a weird act
of revenge, exacted without the main players even
being aware of it, her daughter had bullied and tor-
mented my daughter until Charlie had dreaded set-
ting foot in school. Alix was certainly aware of that.
I knew that Rick had called her into school and talked
to her about it, but I never discovered how she had
responded, whether she'd been self-righteous, defensive, appalled, disbelieving, secretly pleased. We'd
never mentioned that, either, and we probably never
would.

In another life, I thought, as I stood inside the front
door, we could have been friends. She was dry and
strong-willed and I could imagine liking her. But all I
could think now was that her daughter had made mine
suffer and now my daughter had disappeared. We
were never going to be friends and I didn't feel like
pretending that we were.

"You've already talked to Tam," Alix said. "On
the phone."

"I need to talk to her properly, in person."

Still Alix didn't move. "I think she's having a
shower. Jenna's still here as well."

"I can talk to them both," I said. "Can you call
them down, or shall I go up?"

"I'll call them." She went up the stairs and I heard
her rapping at a door, then the muffled rise and fall
of voices.

"They're on their way," she said, walking down

the stairs. "You'd better come into the kitchen. Coffee? Tea?"

"No, thank you."

She led me through and gestured to a chair. The stainless-steel surfaces gleamed above the stone tiles. All the domestic appliances—the espresso machine, the food-processor, the bread-maker, the toaster, the juicer—stood in a line. The smell of toast hung in the air. There was a Christmas cactus on the table, next to a large bowl of satsumas. I could see it was a lovely room but now it felt implacable and coldly efficient. Alix sat opposite me: clearly, she had no intention of leaving me alone with Tam and Jenna.

Bullies come in all shapes and sizes. Tam was at least a head shorter than me, with a tiny face, large eyes and mouth, a cascade of dark blonde hair. She came into the kitchen all washed and brushed, curled and pampered. She wore a brightly coloured smock-top, gathered with a ribbon over her surprisingly large breasts, and blue jeans. Everything about her glowed. I felt a stab of fury and had to take a deep, calming breath. Behind Tam, her friend Jenna was large, clumsy and anxious.

"Mum said you wanted to talk to us."

"That's right. Charlie's disappeared." I watched an expression I couldn't read flicker across her face as I made myself say: "It looks like she's run away."

Jenna gave a little gasp.

"Run away? Charlie?" Tam frowned.

"Listen," I said. "I know what happened between you and Charlie last term. I'm not interested in any of that. Right now, I don't care who did what to whom. I want to find out where she's gone and I want you to tell me anything that might help. She was here last night, you were the last people I know saw her. What happened?"

"What d'you mean, what happened?"

"Was she all right? Did you all get on? Was there a falling-out, a quarrel? Did she say anything that seems odd to you now?"

"No," said Tam.

"That's all you've got to say—*no*?"

"She was all right," Tam said, with stubborn sulkiness. "There wasn't a quarrel, she didn't say anything odd."

"Tam, I don't care if there was. I just want to know about it. I need a clue."

"I think Tam is saying she doesn't have a clue to give you," said Alix. "Is that right, Tam?"

"Right. Nothing happened."

"She was excited about going on holiday," said Jenna. She was pulling strands of her long brown hair over her face and looked embarrassed.

"Did she seem troubled?"

"Not really."

"What did you do?"

"Talked, watched a movie, ate pizza . . . you know."

"And Charlie did all that too?"

"Yeah."

"Did she phone anyone in the evening, send a text, anything like that?"

"Probably. I didn't notice. I wasn't watching her the whole time, you know."

"Tam!" said her mother, sharply.

"What is all this? I wasn't particularly keen on inviting her in the first place."

"So Charlie joined in with everything, seemed fine."

"Yes."

"What did you talk about?"

"We just talked. Stuff, you know. Nothing, really."

"What time did you all go to sleep?"

"About one," said Tam, at the same time as Jenna said, with a furtive giggle and a sliding glance through her veil of hair, "We didn't really sleep much."

"So you didn't really sleep much and she set off around nine to do the paper round. Was she exhausted?"

"She seemed all right," said Tam.

I stared at her stubborn, pretty little face, her big blue eyes. "You do realize that I'm not asking you these questions for the fun of it?"

"I hope you find her," said Tam, looking away. "I'm sure she'll turn up. Have you asked Ashleigh?"

"Of course I've asked Ashleigh. I've asked the newsagent, I've asked her father, I've abandoned the holiday and I've called the police."

"The police?" Jenna's voice was high with distress.

"Yes."

"Will they come and see us?"

"I've no idea. Why?" I looked at her closely. "Is there a problem?"

"I think that's enough," said Alix, stonily. "I know you're distressed, Nina, but—"

"I'm not *distressed*, I am scared about Charlie."

"Nevertheless it doesn't give you the right—"

"Yes, it does. Your daughter made my daughter's life a misery for months. Last night Charlie was here and now she's run away. It doesn't take a genius to make the connection. Something happened."

"Tam says it didn't."

"It didn't," repeated Tam, in a high, indignant voice.

"I don't believe her. I want to know what they did to Charlie last night."

"That's enough. I think you'd better leave now."

"Was Suzie at the sleepover as well?" I asked.

"Yes, why?"

"Just wondering. She lives in that pink house near the church, doesn't she?"

"I don't know what you're trying to achieve here," said Alix, frostily. "I understand you're concerned, but if you think you'll do any good by making wild accusations, you're quite mistaken. The girls have told you everything that happened."

I stood up.

"I'm not *concerned*, I'm scared. And I'll do whatever I can to find Charlie. Listen, if you two think of anything—*anything*—you have to get in touch." I saw a Post-it pad and pen lying near the phone. I scribbled down my mobile and landline numbers. "There. Just call me."

They nodded mutely.

"I can see myself out," I said to Alix, as she rose from the table.

But she followed me to the door and shut it firmly behind me. I was already running down the path, run-

ning because I had to do something, although I had
no idea what.

I went to Suzie's house. Suzie was a languid girl
who, on the few occasions I'd met her, scarcely
spoke but always wore a half-smile that gave nothing
away. Charlie had told me she was powerful at school,
precisely because of her inscrutable passivity.

I knocked on the door and Suzie's mother opened
it, wearing an old tracksuit and washing-up gloves.
Behind her, there was the sound of a TV at full vol-
ume and, over that, children fighting. A scream like
a drill cut through the air, then someone weeping
steadily.

"Hello?" she said, then, turning her head, shouted,
"Shut up, you boys. Sorry. It's Nina, isn't it? Charlotte's mother."

And she frowned at me. Like Alix, Suzie's
mother—whose name I couldn't remember—had
been informed that her daughter was part of the group
who had bullied Charlie. I'd imagined that one of the
mothers might have contacted me to say sorry or to
talk over what had happened, but no one ever had.

"Sorry to bother you, but can I have a word with
Suzie, please?"

"What do you want her for?"

"Charlie's disappeared and I wondered if Suzie
could help me."

Suzie's mother didn't step back to let me in, but
stayed solidly in the doorway. "Why would she
know?" she asked.

Would I react like this, I thought, if Suzie had gone missing, with an aggrieved sense of my own blamelessness? I hoped not. I hoped I would lay aside all hostility and help in whatever way I could. "Is she there?"

"She went out," said Suzie's mother.

"Where?"

Even as I asked, we both saw Suzie meandering along the road towards us, and by her side an equally stringy and unhasty boy, carrying her bag.

"Suzie," I said, as she came towards us. "Can I have a quick word? It's about Charlie."

Suzie stared at me as if she couldn't understand anything I was saying to her. The lanky youth shifted his weight from foot to foot.

"It's getting cold," said her mother. "You'd better come into the hall."

So the four of us stood wedged together in the narrow hallway, among the wellington boots and coats.

"Charlie's disappeared," I said again. "I was hoping you might be able to tell me something."

"What?"

"About how she was last night. Whether anything happened to upset her."

Suzie shrugged. "She was fine."

"So, nothing at all happened?"

"Don't think so." She slid her ironic smile across to the youth and he smiled back.

"Tam and Jenna said—"

"You've been to see them and now you're here too?" said the mother. She peeled off her washing-up gloves as if she was preparing for a fight. "Why? Did they say something I should know about?"

"Not at all, they couldn't really help, but—"

"They couldn't help but you come here making all your old accusations about Suzie. I know there was a falling-out last term, but you can't go around making out that your daughter's a victim and mine's a bully. I've had enough."

"I don't care what happened last term, I'm just trying to find my daughter." I drew a deep breath. "She's run away."

"Run away? That's different from going missing, isn't it?"

"I—"

"If you ask me, you're trying to shift responsibility for this from where it should be on to my daughter. And we all know where it should be."

I turned away from her and tried to meet Suzie's gaze. "Please, Suzie," I said. "Something happened, didn't it? I'm not trying to get you into trouble, I just have to find Charlie. Please."

For a tiny moment, she looked at me. She half opened her mouth to speak.

"Out," said her mother. "And don't come bothering us again, do you hear?"

Suzie took the boy's hand and said to him, "Let's go to my room, shall we?"

The door slammed.

Sludge lay under the kitchen table covered in the sticky estuary mud, so I knew Renata and Jackson were back, and I called to them as I checked for messages on the answering-machine. There was only one, from Rory, saying, "Hello, hello, *hello*. Nina! Will you pick up?"

"Jackson's crying in his room," said Renata, as she came down the stairs.

I went to find him. He was sitting on his bed, still in his jacket and boots, which had left muddy tracks across the carpet, and tears were streaked down his flushed cheeks, like snail tracks. He looked thoroughly forlorn and suddenly much younger than eleven. I picked up his cold hands and blew on them to warm them. "I'm so sorry about all of this," I said.

I told him about the police coming to the house, about Charlie's missing things, the washbag and makeup bag, nightshirt and purse, and the inescapable conclusion that she had chosen to run away, although I had no idea why. I put my arm round his tense shoulders, pulled him close to me and said it was rotten for him that we were missing going to Florida, but that we would go, I promised, as soon as everything was sorted. Which I was sure would be very soon. I said that for a while—until Charlie was found—I was going to be busy. I told him I was relying on him to help me.

I said all these things—I heard my calm, authoritative voice, speaking whole sentences, and saw myself as I stroked his dark hair back from his forehead—but only a tiny part of me was there with my son. My brain was like a well-occupied household, activity taking place simultaneously in each of its many rooms. I was thinking about what I should do next. I was making lists and running through options. I was trying to look back over the past days and weeks to find anything, a single word or an overheard scrap of a conversation, that might lead me in the right direction. I was looking at the digital watch strapped to Jackson's wrist and trying to work out exactly how many minutes Charlie had been missing. I put my hands on Jackson's shoulders and thought about Charlie; I looked into Jackson's eyes and saw Charlie looking back; I talked to Jackson and called out to Charlie—*just come home.*

"So what shall I do to help?" he asked, in a wobbly voice.

"Think," I said. I kissed his forehead. "Think of anything she said to you. Anything you heard her say to anyone else." I hesitated for a second. "Anything your dad said to her, or she said about him to you, for instance."

"Dad? Why Dad?"

"No real reason."

"And that's all I can do, just think?"

"For now," I said. "And don't use the phone in case she's trying to call."

I left him. Downstairs Renata was back at the clearing-up. I could hear the chink of glasses, the busy tapping of her feet across the tiles, cupboard doors opening and closing. Sludge gave one short bark, and for a jolt of a second I thought perhaps she was barking because Charlie was there, but then the knowledge that she wasn't flooded through me and left me shaky and cold. I stood at the top of the stairs,

my hand on the banisters, and felt suspended in an
eerie sadness. Then I turned sharply and went into
Charlie's bedroom. I sat on her bed and picked up
the clothes that were lying there, pressing my face
into the soft folds that smelt of her, a smell I'd recognize anywhere, musky and sweet. I closed my
eyes and, for a tiny moment, let myself imagine that
she was with me, in the room, that when I looked up
she'd be standing there, with her lanky-legged
slouch, her dishevelled mane of hair, her bold gaze.

"Stop it," I said, out loud, and stood up.

I prowled round the room once more. I sat at her
desk and picked up the notebooks: an English draft-
ing exercise book, a red French book, which she'd
only just started; the first page was filled with ir-
regular verbs, accompanied by one of Charlie's
doodlings. She doodles on everything. She'll sit at
breakfast and draw spirals over the headlines of the
paper and then absentmindedly ink out the teeth of
politicians. She's defaced my address book. She
makes little notes and sketches, which I discover
when I open a notepad or pick up my shopping list.
Her school books are covered in jaunty little designs
or bold, cross-hatched words (on the French exercise book it said "Lush" in thick pink felt tip, which
had soaked through to the following pages). When
she was little, she used to draw stick men and women
running along the wallpaper above our bed, or trail
indelible pens along the sofas and armchairs. Lately,
she had taken to drawing on herself. Her palms have
beautiful symmetrical patterns on them, which
soften and spread in the heat. She drew tattoos on

her arms and thighs and little cartoon smily faces on her toes.

I picked up the uneven piles of school papers. There was her GCSE coursework on *Great Expectations*, an essay in French about the places she liked to go on holiday, which ended, I saw with a wince, on a reference to being about to go to Florida. She'd put that in, I knew, to show off her use of the future tense. Would you have written about going to Florida, if you weren't planning to go? Stop that, Nina. I looked elsewhere. There was a graph that showed how quickly something dissolved in something else, a rough draft of a piece she'd written about the history of Sandling Island, which was edged with an intricate mosaic in different colours. There was a messy sheet of algebraic workings-out, a piece of paper with several CD titles written on it, a recipe in pencil for stuffed tomatoes (with a drawing of a tomato underneath it). There was a white envelope with her name written on it, and inside a thin piece of paper, which I drew out. "Remember what Pete Doherty says . . ." Was that from a boy? A girl?

There was a notebook, which turned out to be full of scraps of messages, presumably passed round during classes. "Give me some chewing-gum!" it said. "I'm bored," and "Can u come tonite?" Then another spiral-bound notebook, which was empty except for the first couple of pages. There was a sketchily drawn picture of a face, gender unclear, with a sharp nose and a mass of scribbled-in hair, and underneath it, in Charlie's madcap scrawl: "I think he likes me!"

I flipped over the pages, and this time she had

written: "I *know* he likes me." And "I think I'll wear
my pink skirt." Then just a few scrawls, meaningless
insignia, as if she had been trying out a new pen, and
then, just a line that zigzagged down the page, and
her own name, written in elaborate Gothic script.

I put down the notebook and pulled open Charlie's
drawers, which were crammed full of lined and blank
paper, notepads, old homework diaries, playing-cards,
postcards, bits of wrapping paper, loose pens and pencils, cartridges for her printer. And then I found an
elaborate doodle, which, on closer inspection, seemed
to be made out of interlaced letter Js.

It reminded me of something. I flicked back
through the last notebook until I got to the page I
was looking for. "I think I'll wear my pink skirt."
And those swirling inscriptions. They weren't just
meaningless scrawls after all.

I phoned Ashleigh.

"Has she turned up?"

"No," I said. "Who's J?"

"What?"

"I'm desperate," I said. "I've been looking through
some of Charlie's stuff and I saw the letter J written
several times. I don't know if it means anything."

There was a silence. It was all about tactics. I could
threaten Ashleigh, but that might make her clam up
altogether. I could plead, bargain. Or just be straight-
forward.

"Ashleigh," I said, "I'm not going to be cross
with anybody about this, not with Charlie, not with
you. Maybe all of this is nothing. But I need to know

that she's safe. And maybe it isn't nothing. What I mean is that if you know anything you really ought to tell me. Just in case."

Another silence.

"Ashleigh?"

"He's a friend."

"Who?"

"Jay."

"What does it stand for?"

"No," said Ashleigh. "That's his name. J—A—Y."

"Who is he? A boyfriend?"

Another pause. It felt as if Ashleigh was sitting there with a lawyer at her ear, advising her to say as little as possible, no more than was specifically asked for and nothing that might incriminate her. Didn't she realize that we were talking about my daughter and her best friend?

"I don't know," she said. "I can't really . . . He's a friend."

"Where can I reach him?"

"I don't know his number."

"What's his second name? Where does he live?"

Another pause.

"Birche. His dad's a farmer. The one over near that big old empty building."

"The Malting?"

"That's right."

"Is there any chance she might be with him?"

"I don't know."

"Did she talk about Jay when you spoke to her yesterday?"

"Not really. You know."

This was becoming ridiculous. I couldn't tell whether Ashleigh was being so reluctant and generally uncommunicative because she had something to hide or because she was fifteen years old. I told her I'd be back in touch and rang off. I tried to think if I might know any friends of the Birche family but nobody sprang to mind. As far as I knew there weren't more than a couple of farms on the island and the farmers were in a different social league from most other people. They didn't send their children to the local schools. If you were going to meet them, it would probably be at the tennis or golf club or riding with the local mainland hunt. Clearly it would have to be a cold call. I found the number in the phone book and dialled it, feeling like a double-glazing salesman. A man answered.

"Is that Mr. Birche?" I said.

"Who's that?" the voice said abruptly, as if he was shouting at me across the island with a megaphone.

"My name is Nina Landry. Is this Mr. J. Birche?"

"What do you want?"

I took that as a yes.

"You don't know me, but I think your son may be a friend of my daughter."

"Which son?"

"Jay. I was hoping I could talk to him."

"He's not here."

I felt a spasm of excitement. Had they gone together? Could it possibly be as easy as that?

"This will sound strange but I really do need to talk to him. It's important."

"I don't know when he'll be back. He went out this morning to some sort of birthday party."

I felt a disappointment so keen that it was physical, a wave of nausea passing through me. So Jay must have been one of the teenagers in the house. He had been there and she hadn't. What did that mean? New possibilities appeared in my mind. A row?

"I've got to get hold of your son right now. Immediately."

"What's this about?" He sounded defensive, suspicious. "Has he done anything wrong?"

"No, no, nothing like that. But it's an emergency. I'm trying to find my daughter and I thought your son might be able to tell me where she is or know something."

Even at the other end of the telephone line, I could tell that he was thinking. Was this woman mad? Was she to be trusted? Was he risking anything?

"He's probably in town with friends."

"You mean on the island?"

"Yes. He hangs around the café or that dreadful coffee place. But I've got his mobile number somewhere here."

I heard paper rustling and then he came back on the line and read me the number. I thanked him effusively and rang off. But when I dialled it there was just a message. I left my number and asked him to call at once. But I knew I couldn't sit and wait—he might have left his phone at home or his father given me the wrong number.

I met Renata downstairs. She was sitting among the wreckage of the morning with a dazed expression on her face. Although she was holding the newspaper, she clearly wasn't reading it and when she saw me she put it down, as though she felt guilty to be relaxing, and looked up at me questioningly.

"No," I said. "There's no word. But it does now seem clear that . . ." I swallowed hard. "That Charlie has gone missing of her own accord. There are things missing from her room: her washbag and pink makeup bag, for instance, and her favourite nightshirt." I swallowed hard and gave a small smile. "The one that says, 'Please do not sell this woman anything.' So it looks, well, it does look like she's run away."

I held up my hand to stop Renata's questions or ward off her expressions of appalled sympathy.

"I'm going out to try to find a friend of hers. It's probably a waste of time." I was going to leave it at that but then I stopped. "Jackson's in a bit of a state. I'm sorry, Renata, but could you do something with him to take his mind off things?"

Renata looked panicky. "Of course, anything. But what shall I do? I'm not really used to children." Tears filled her eyes again.

"I don't know," I said. "Mechanical things are usually a good idea. He was messing around with our new camcorder. Perhaps you could ask him to recharge it and get rid of all the rubbish he was filming this morning. That's so, so wonderful of you."

This last was said because of the haunted look Renata gave me as she turned to go up the stairs. I pulled the door open and found myself standing face to face with Eamonn, his hand raised to knock. He looked white and peaky; his hair had come untied and hung in clumps.

"Ms. Landry, um, Nina. Mum and Dad are still at the hospital, they'll be there for ages, they said. I just wanted to know about Charlie. Has she come back yet?"

"No, she hasn't, and I can't stop now, Eamonn."

"But—"

"If you think of anything, Eamonn, or hear anything, let me know, will you? I'm going to dash now." A thought struck me. "You don't happen to know Jay Birche, do you?"

His face flamed and an odd little smirk twisted his lips. "Him? He's a turd. Thinks he's so fine. Little private-school idiot."

I was taken aback by Eamonn's outburst. "Live and let live, eh? Listen, I might come and talk to you later."

"Is he with Charlie, then?"

"I don't know. It doesn't look like it."

As I drove off, my mobile rang. It was Rory. "Any news?" he asked.

"Some things are missing from her bedroom."

"So she's staying with someone?"

"I don't know."

"Did you two have a row, Nina?"

"No."

"You mean not ever?"

"I mean that she didn't leave because of a row."

"I hear you talked to Tina."

I was at a loss for a moment. Then I remembered whom he was talking about. "Oh, yes."

"I was meaning to tell you about her."

"Rory, this isn't really the time."

"It was difficult being on my own."

"Rory . . ."

"She's been a rock for me."

I drew the car in beside the café opposite the library. As soon as I stopped, there was a tap on the window. I lowered it and saw a dark uniform.

"Excuse me, madam," said a familiar voice, "are you aware that it's an offence to use a mobile phone while driving?"

It was the policeman. Mahoney.

"Got to go," I said to Rory, and then pleadingly, "Oh, God, I'm sorry. I'm still searching for my daughter. I've been on the phone solidly. That was my husband. I'm really sorry."

"Have you heard anything?" Mahoney said.

"I'm looking for someone now. He might know."

"And you're on a yellow line," he said.

"I'll be five minutes," I said. "And please tell me if you hear anything at all."

I ran towards the café and looked through the window. Two old men at one table, eggs and bacon and a cloud of cigarette smoke. At another a young woman was sitting with a toddler. This was hopeless. He could be anywhere. I walked along the street to Beans, where you can read newspapers and drink about twenty-seven different kinds of coffee. I went inside. In one corner a group of teenage boys was sitting around a table full of oversized coffee cups, ashtrays and cigarette packets. I walked over to them. "Is one of you Jay Birche?"

A boy looked up. I immediately recognized him from the surprise party. He was about seventeen. Dark hair, pale, stubbly skin, grey eyes that were almost green, clothes worn in layers, as if he'd just got out of bed and pulled on whatever was at hand. He had about him a slouchy, unkempt beauty that reminded me at once of Charlie.

"I'm Charlie's mother." He raised his eyebrows but didn't move from his place. I started to speak, then felt awkward. "Can we have a word? In private?"

He half grimaced at his companions, as if to say, "Old people, what can you do?" then got up and followed me outside.

"I'm Nina," I said. "We've not met but Ashleigh told me you're a friend of Charlie's. Is that true?"

"What's the problem?" he said.

"She's disappeared," I said. "I don't know where she is. I wondered if you knew?"

"Disappeared?"

"We were meant to fly to the States this afternoon but she never came home."

"I haven't seen her today," he said. "I thought she'd be at your party, but you know Charlie. She's not the most reliable person in the world, is she?"

"You haven't any idea where she might have gone?"

"No."

"You don't go to school on the island?"

At this his expression broke into a half-smile. "I'm at the high school."

The private school on the estuary by Hemsleigh; that made sense. Farmer's son. I wondered where they'd met. I couldn't leave it like this. I'd got nothing. "I'm worried," I said. "She's disappeared. She's taken some of her things with her. It's like she prepared it. I need to find her."

"I haven't seen her and I think I'd know if she was going to run off. You shouldn't worry about her. Parents always worry too—"

I interrupted him: "So, are you her boyfriend?"

"I'm sorry?"

At that moment my phone rang. "Hang on," I said, and answered it.

It was Renata. "You need to come back," she said.

"Charlie?"

"There's something you need to see."

"Can't you tell me?"

"It's hard to explain. I'm not sure if I'm right. But if I am, you need to see it."

"I'll be there in two minutes," I said, and turned to Jay. "I've got to go. Something's up. Can I call you on your mobile?"

"What for?" he said.

"I don't know," I said. "Just in case."

"I guess," he said.

He dictated the number and I touched the digits into my phone.

"Good luck," he called after me, as I ran back to my car.

There was a parking ticket on the windscreen. I looked at it: 12:26. I scrunched it up and threw it on to the back seat, then turned the key in the ignition and drove home, ignoring the speed camera that flashed at me on The Street.

"What is it?" I said, as I burst through the door. "Tell me."

Renata called up the stairs for Jackson. "Your mum's here. Come on down now. Quickly."

My son bounded down the stairs, two steps at a time, nearly tripping on his laces. The camcorder bounced round his neck and his face was hectic with tiredness and excitement.

"Renata, this had better be important."

"I don't know what it is," said Renata. She had scarlet patches on her cheeks. "Go on, Jackson."

"Let me find the right place," he said, pressing rewind and watching as images jerked incomprehensibly backwards. "Yeah, here. Look, Mum."

I stood behind him and squinted at the small screen. A blur of grey-green colour moved along it. The upstairs carpet.

"I can plug it into the computer if it's hard for you to see. That's what I was just about to—"

"What am I looking at?"

"Fast-forward, Jackson," said Renata.

"No, it's here."

The camera had reached Charlie's bedroom door. It swung up to the sign that said, "Knock first!" in big block letters, then bobbed down again as the door was pushed open, presumably by Jackson. It moved in and out of focus round Charlie's room. To the window, the strewn bed, the half-open wardrobe, the sheep clock. I forced myself to stay calm as I watched the familiar objects slide past, looming in and out of focus, all the things that I'd been sifting through so recently: the towels, the flung clothes, the CDs, the pieces of paper, the ointments and lotions, the . . .

"There," said Renata.

The nightshirt, held in a blurred freeze-frame. It lay on the floor. I could even half make out what was written across it, and supply the rest: "Please do not sell this woman anything." I'd bought it for her last summer. She'd worn it the night before last. The camcorder moved on.

"Go back," I said, in little more than a gasp.

"Hang on, look," said Renata, pressed against me behind Jackson.

The camera swung over something pink and Jackson pressed pause. Out of focus, and only half in view, but indisputably Charlie's makeup bag.

"We looked for the washbag as well, and the purse, but there's nothing else. We've gone through all of it," said Jackson.

"Several times," said Renata. "It doesn't mean they weren't there, just that Jackson didn't film them. Lucky he didn't delete it all, wasn't it? And I could easily not have noticed. It was the nightshirt that did it."

"Go back a bit," I said. "Yes, stop there."

The sheep clock told me it was 11:17, and the small screen on the camcorder had the time in the bottom corner, as well: 11:17. It must have been just when the first guests were about to show up. I pressed my fists into my eyeballs and tried to think, but what I was thinking made no sense.

The things that had gone missing and that showed

me Charlie had run away were there when I came
back from Rick and Karen's. So she'd taken them
afterwards. Was that it? She'd sneaked into the house
when I was there, already worrying about her, phon-
ing her mobile, pestering her friends. But when? How
had I not seen her, or someone not seen her? Unless, I
thought wildly, she'd climbed into her room through
the window, in which case she would have had help.
Jay, I thought. I'd seen him going up the stairs. Or
Ashleigh. Or someone I didn't know about yet because, after all, I hadn't known about Jay. Images
and ideas poured through my skull, and I tried to
separate them out and consider them rationally.

Charlie had returned to fetch her clothes after
11:17. That changed the timings. She hadn't come
straight back after her paper round, while I was still
out and the house was empty, to pick up the things
she needed. She had come back a couple of hours
later, when the party she'd organized was starting or
under way, when we were soon to go to the airport.
And what had she been doing in the gap between
her paper round and then?

"Nina?"

"Yes?" I was startled. I had forgotten that Renata
and Jackson were there, waiting for me to speak.

"It's very odd, isn't it?"

"Jackson, did you move anything in Charlie's
room when you went in there?"

"No."

"Think carefully."

"It's not my fault."

"Of course not."

"I didn't touch anything. I just went in for a minute and then went out again, honestly."

I ran up the stairs, two at a time, and into Charlie's room. I had to see for myself. It looked the same as in Jackson's film, except that in the film the nightshirt and makeup bag were there and now they were gone. Restlessly, I walked round the room, touching the shelves and the bed, as if to convince myself they were real. I pulled open the top drawer of the chest next to Charlie's bed. Everything I saw felt like a jab of memory. A few foreign coins she had kept, a broken wristwatch she had never thrown away, a daisy chain of coloured paperclips, a complicated penknife that contained tweezers, several blades, a toothpick. There was the container of antibiotics for her impetigo. I picked it up and the pills inside rattled. There was a wooden elephant with a baby elephant, a ceramic plate—the first thing she had ever brought back from secondary school. I picked up the pink plastic bottle of her makeup remover. I sniffed it and the familiar astringent odour stung my nostrils.

Downstairs I dialled the number for the police station; asked to speak to Mahoney. I was told he wasn't there, but was expected back in a few minutes and they'd make sure he got my message to call me. I put the phone down and stared at it. I didn't want to sit and wait for ten minutes, doing nothing while scary images slid through my mind.

"Can I make you some tea?" asked Renata. "Or something to eat? You've got to eat. It won't do Charlie any good if you're starving yourself."

"No," I said, picking up the camcorder. "I've got to go to the police station."

"Can I come with you?" Jackson plucked at my sleeve.

"No."

"Mum—Mummy—please can I come? Please?"

"All right, then," I said, abruptly changing my mind. "Renata, I'm on my mobile. Call me if there's anything."

"I forgot—someone called Christian rang. He's stuck on the M25, can't move at all."

"Oh, well. Come on, then, Jackson."

I took his hand in mine and we ran to the police station. It was quicker than driving. Our feet smacked against the icy surface of the road and the cold wind blew in from the east, whipping our hair on to our cheeks, making our ears ache. Jackson's breath was coming in little sobs, but I didn't let up. I tugged him past houses with smoke rising from their chimneys, windows strung with Christmas lights or illuminated with baubled Christmas trees. In the distance the grey sea lay beneath the grey sky. You couldn't see the sun at all.

"Is he here yet?" I asked, as we clattered breathlessly into the station.

"Excuse me?"

The woman at the desk looked at us both suspiciously.

"PC Mahoney. Is he here? I'm Nina Landry—I called. I have to see him at once."

"He just got in. I gave him your message and he was going to call—"

"In there?"

I took Jackson's cold fingers again and marched him across to the door, knocked firmly and opened it before anyone had a chance to reply. Mahoney was standing near the window that overlooked the small car park at the back, with a polystyrene cup of coffee in his hand. He looked chilly and tired. Tinsel hung along the walls, a tiny fake Christmas tree stood on top of the metal filing cabinet in the corner, and on the desk there were several framed photographs: of him and a curly-headed woman I assumed was his wife; of a large fish at the end of a line, with glazed eye and gaping mouth; of a girl who must be the daughter he'd talked about, Charlie's age. She wore braces and her hair was tied back in a single dark brown plait.

He looked at me in surprise.

"I've got something to show you," I said. My throat hurt when I swallowed, my glands ached. I felt clammy and my skin prickled under my jacket. "Jackson, go ahead."

Jackson started fiddling with the camcorder. His hands were shaking, with cold or fear, I didn't know. I put a hand on top of his silky head and watched as Charlie's door swung open on the small, smeary screen in front of us.

"We have a patrol car looking for your daughter," said Mahoney. He coughed awkwardly. "I know it's difficult to be patient but—"

"Quiet," I said. "Look at this. Hold it there, Jackson." I gestured at the miniature screen. "That's her nightshirt. Her nightshirt that's not there any more."

"Ms. Landry—"

"Go forward, Jackson. There. That's her makeup bag."

"Yes," he said cautiously.

"Don't you see? Look, it's eleven seventeen. Go back, Jackson, show him the clock. There. It makes everything different. *Don't you see*? We'd assumed she came back after the sleepover or the newspaper round, took her stuff and then ran away. But she didn't. She waited until I was at home and then she came back. But how didn't I see her?"

"Sit down, please. Would your son like to wait outside with—"

"No." Jackson settled himself in my lap, as if he was six not eleven, and I wrapped my arms round his solid body and put my chin on his head.

"Well done," I whispered into his ear, and he leaned more heavily against me.

"Either she came back or someone came back for her," said Mahoney, slowly. He rubbed his eyes with both fists.

"Yes, yes, that's true. That's possible."

"Now." He sat at the desk opposite us, picked up a pen, pulled a pad of paper towards him. He thought for a moment. "So, where are we? We know this film was taken at eleven seventeen."

"Yes."

He wrote down the time and frowned at it. Outside the door, someone broke into a tuneless rendition of "God Rest You Merry Gentlemen."

"Charlie, or someone on her behalf, took her things away after that."

"Yes."

"But before we went into the room at, let me see, five to twelve."

"Yes."

"And you were in the house all that time?"

"Yes. I was. I got back at about eleven with Jackson and didn't leave again until after you left, when I visited one of Charlie's friends, the one whose house she was at last night."

"Who else came to your house between eleven fifteen and just before twelve?"

"Oh, God, a whole crowd of people. There was the party. You know about that. So, there was me and Jackson. And then there was, let me see." I put my fingers to my temples and tried to picture the first group at the door this morning. "Joel Frazer and his wife, Alix Dawes—Dr. Dawes. And then Ashleigh Stevens, she's Charlie's best friend. And the vicar, Tom something."

"Reverend Drake."

"Right, and there was a man called Eric or Derek, I don't know. With his wife or partner or whatever. And Carrie Lowell from the primary school, and her husband but I've no idea what his name is. I'd never seen him before."

Mahoney was looking dazed. I ploughed on: "Rick and Karen Blythe. They left early—Karen had an accident. She was drunk. She broke her arm."

"Quite a party," he said glumly.

"They went to the hospital, with Alix and Joel following them. Oh, and their son Eamonn, he was there. He's in love with Charlie, I think, but I'm pretty sure she'd never look at him. Joanna or

Josephine, the solicitor who lives in that grand house. And then, well, lots of people whose names I don't know and some I probably never even saw. Other people let them in, and it was a party that kind of went on without me. I was upstairs a lot of the time. I wasn't really in the mood—I was worrying about packing and wondering where Charlie was."

"I see," said Mahoney. He'd stopped writing and was fiddling with his pen, staring helplessly at the list of names that straggled down the page. "I see."

"And then there was Jay," I continued.

"Jay?"

"Jay Birche, but I didn't know that then. I tracked him down a few minutes ago. Ashleigh told me his name."

"You have been busy," he said drily, but he wrote down the name, then underlined it.

"He lives at the big farm near the marshes. I didn't know Charlie knew him but obviously she does. He was with a load of other teenagers, and I've no idea who they are, although some of their faces were a bit familiar."

I came to a halt at last. "What does it mean?" I asked, in a low voice.

"I know Mr. Birche," said Mahoney. "This Jay, his son, was he Charlie's boyfriend?"

An hour or so ago, I had been vehemently denying that Charlie had a boyfriend, insisting that I would have known. Now I stared at Mahoney across Jackson's head. "Maybe."

"What was your daughter wearing when you last saw her?"

I could see her now, as vividly as if she was standing at the door and looking back at me. I had the strangest sensation that I could reach out to that memory and pull her back, stop her walking away from me into the gusty winter night. "She was wearing faded blue jeans, a leather belt with an ornate buckle, turquoise and pink. A bright pink T-shirt, scoop-necked and long-sleeved, with scribbled patterns in different colours on it. A scuffed-leather bomber jacket that had belonged to her father but that she'd taken over. It's black, with a torn pocket. Flat suede boots with beads on them. She had a scarf thing—blue and pink and silver, with sequins; she sometimes ties it round her hair, but when she left it was round her neck. And she took a hoodie with her in case it got cold. Grey, with ragged cuffs. She always chews her cuffs. A small leather shoulder-bag. Chunky beads in all different colours . . ."

"That's probably enough," he said gently, and I looked away. I wasn't going to cry; I mustn't. I could cry later, when Charlie was safe again.

He tapped his pen on his pad, gazing down thoughtfully at the long list of names. "All I can say to you is what I said before. You should go home and wait by the phone. There's a patrol car keeping an eye out for her. From what we now know, it seems possible that your daughter is not acting alone."

"I can't just wait. Every minute counts, that's what I keep thinking. We've got to find her now."

"I know it's hard, but I've dealt with more cases like this than you'd believe, and they usually come home."

"Something's wrong," I said.

"You don't know that."

"And it's so cold outside."

Jackson let me hold his hand again as we walked home but we didn't talk. My mobile rang several times and each time I answered it with a terrible lurch of hope. First it was my friend Caroline, but I cut her short after three or four words and said I'd call her when I could; then Rory saying he was nearly there; then Christian, at a standstill on the M25 because of an accident—a lorry had fallen sideways and tipped its load across both carriageways. I was curt with each of them. I didn't want to talk to anyone unless it was Charlie or someone who could tell me how to find her. Everything else was noise, an irrelevant hiss and rumble from a world to which I no longer felt connected. I looked around me constantly, thinking I might glimpse some tiny sign of Charlie if I was alert enough, if I was looking in the right place. Behind the hedge, down the alley, in the car, up in the lighted first-floor window of the gabled house, going into the shop, disappearing round the corner like that dog-walker now, in the ploughed field that in summer was golden with wheat, among the boats that stood in the yard, halliards tinkling and tarpaulins flapping. I was terrified of looking in the wrong direction, terrified that she might be just behind me or just in front and that I would miss her because I wasn't alert enough. My eyes zigzagged along our route, until everything I saw seemed surreal, plucked out of its everyday context.

"Mum, Mum." Jackson was saying something, tugging at my hand.

"Mmm?"

"Why's she here?"

I looked up and saw, walking very fast and very upright towards our house from the opposite direction, Alix. Stranger still, she was gripping Tam's upper arm, pulling her forcibly along. Tam was half stumbling; her head was down, her hair flapping in the wind. Behind them came Jenna in an ungainly jog, openly crying. I quickened my pace and we met at the gate.

"What is it?"

"There's something you have to know," said Alix. Her face was stern and pinched. She did not release Tam's arm. "Can we come in?"

I opened the door, noticing that the key shook in my hand. Sludge hurled herself at us as we entered, but I didn't touch her, just told Jackson to throw a few sticks for her in the back garden.

Renata was on the phone, but she shook her head at me and quickly ended the call, saying we would ring if there was any news.

We went into the kitchen. I didn't take off my jacket and didn't offer tea or coffee, just gestured at the chairs. It was curiously silent for a moment. I could hear the sound of my own breathing, and the clock on the wall ticking. I glanced up at it and then away, although I could still hear the awful metronomic sound.

"Tell me," I said.

"Tam," said Alix. It was an order.

Tam looked up at last through her snarled hair. Her eyes were red. "We didn't mean anything," she began, and beside her Jenna stifled a sob.

"What happened?"

"It was meant to be a bit of fun—"

"*What happened*?" I had no time for excuses, and this time Alix didn't interrupt to defend her daughter.

"Last night," said Tam, "about one o'clock maybe, after we'd watched the film anyway, we—" She looked at her hands, then back at me, and finished the sentence in a rush. "We put vodka in Charlie's orange juice."

"Without Charlie's knowledge," added Alix, in a clipped voice.

"How much?"

"It wasn't that much," said Tam, "but she drank it more quickly than we'd expected, all in one go."

"Was she drunk?"

Jenna gave a terrified giggle, then clamped a hand over her mouth.

"Yes," said Tam.

"How drunk?"

"Kind of floppy and quiet at first."

"Was she sick?"

"Yeah," mumbled Tam.

"After she vomited, she passed out," said Alix, quietly but clearly, looking straight into my eyes. There was still enough space in my teeming brain to admire the way she was making no excuses for her daughter or herself. After all, she had been the adult in charge. "As far as I can tell, she was unconscious

for a while, but then she came to and vomited again.
Is that right?"

"Yes," said Tam, tonelessly.

Jenna snuffled again and put her face into her
hands. "We didn't know it would be like that. It was
just a laugh. But then she got ill. At first we couldn't
wake her up and when we lifted up her eyelids, her
eyeballs just rolled back in the sockets and she
made this groaning noise. It was horrible. We got so
frightened. We didn't know what to do about it. We
thought she was dying and we'd killed her."

"We were asleep in bed," said Alix, quietly. "I
had no idea. I should have suspected something was
up when I found they'd opened the bedroom windows and washed the sheets."

I forced myself not to imagine Charlie, wretchedly
sick in the house of the girl who'd bullied her, vomiting and crying and falling unconscious and waking
up again and not calling me, not asking me to come
and get her and take her home where she'd be safe,
and instead concentrated on the stark facts: "She was
sick and she passed out and then she was sick again.
What time was that?"

"Three or four in the morning," said Tam. "I didn't
look at the time. But she got better," she added. "We
told her how sorry we were."

"We made her have a shower," added Jenna. "And
Tam gave her some extra-strong coffee and she drank
it and I made some toast for her but she wouldn't have
that."

"She still left at nine to do her paper round?"

"Something like that."

"Feeling like death?"

"She wasn't so bad," said Tam, defensively.

"What did she say?"

"You mean, in the morning? Not much. I don't remember."

"She said I was weak and Tam was vicious," said Jenna. "She said she was sorry for us because we had such manky little lives that spiking someone's drink was our idea of fun." That sounded like my Charlie.

"And then she left. On her bike?"

"I think so."

"You didn't offer to help her with the paper round, given the circumstances?"

They didn't answer.

"I'll take that as a no. And you haven't seen or heard from her since?"

Jenna covered her face with her hands. Her hair streamed down on to the table. She said, in a muffled sob, "It'll be all right, won't it? We didn't mean anything to happen, it was only a joke. We would never have done it if we'd known, Ms. Landry, you have to believe that—"

"Shut up," said Tam. "Just shut up."

"I thought you should know immediately," said Alix.

"I've got to ring the hospital," I said. "She might be there."

"I'll do that for you. I know people there. Is there a phone in the living room?"

"Yes."

"You two can go home now," said Alix, to Tam and Jenna. "Get Joel and tell him what's happened."

"But, Mum—"

"Tell your father," she said. "And you, Jenna, you'd better tell your parents as well. If you don't, I will."

The girls left, and I saw them walking down the road several yards apart, their feet dragging against the pavement.

I could hear the rise and fall of Alix's voice from the living room although I couldn't make out the words, then a pause while she waited. Outside in the garden, Jackson was standing wretchedly by the wall while Sludge was charging around wildly with a stout stick forcing her jaws open into an idiotic, pink-tongued grin. My hands were clenched in my lap. I opened them out and stared at my palms, my ringless fingers, the scar along the left thumb, my life line. Charlie's hands were whiter and smoother than mine, her fingers long and elegant. She wore a glass thumb ring and round her wrist a thin leather bracelet. I hadn't told Mahoney that.

"Nothing," said Alix, coming into the room. "So that's good news."

"Is it?" I said. "The problem is—*one* of the problems is—that I go over things in my head repeatedly and I've stopped being able to tell what's good and what's bad and what things mean." I halted. It was as if I knew there was something out there in the darkness and I had to feel for it. Yes, that was it. "For instance, I've looked through Charlie's room. She seems to have taken her washbag and her nightshirt, the things that were lying on the floor. But then I opened her drawer and there were other possessions—like her antibiotics—that were just as important."

Alix nodded in recognition. "Yes," she said. "She was very self-conscious about her impetigo. She asked how quickly the rash would go."

I looked at her sharply. Alix was so super-discreet about her work as a GP, about her knowledge of people's secrets, that it was a shock to hear even so guarded a comment as that. "You don't know something, do you?" I asked. "Did she tell you anything? I mean, that might throw any light on why she would run away?"

Alix's expression hardened. "If I did, I would tell you, or the police."

I paused. Clearly there was no point in pressing her. "But do you see?" I said. "Isn't it strange?"

"I don't know," said Alix, uneasily. "I suppose so. But if you were running away, you wouldn't be thinking very clearly, would you?"

"It's as if . . ." I was struggling to make myself clear, when I wasn't even clear in my own head ". . . as if she could only take the things she could see."

"I suppose she was in a hurry," Alix said.

"But to forget her medication. Or take her makeup bag but not the makeup remover. Maybe it means that she sent somebody to get the stuff for her, somebody who didn't know where everything was."

"I'm going to make you something to eat now."

"No. I've got to go."

"Where to?"

"I've got to go," I repeated. "I'll let you know if anything . . ."

It was a sentence I couldn't complete. Images swirled in my mind and I made myself focus on the tasks ahead. Before I could leave there was Jackson.

"Renata!" I called up the stairs.

There was a muffled groan, then silence. I ran up the steps, two at a time, and knocked on my bedroom door.

"Yes," came her faint voice, and I pushed open the door.

She'd closed the curtains and at first I couldn't see her. Gradually I made out a humped shape in the bed, and shook it gently where I thought her shoulder might be. "Renata?"

"Whassit?"

I pulled the duvet back. She was fully dressed under it, but half sat up. "I don't feel very well," she said. I could see she had been crying. Her mascara had run in smudgy streaks down her cheeks. "I'm sorry, Nina. Maybe I ought to leave. I'm no use to you—I'm just in your way."

"You can't leave," I said. "You have to stay here and make sure Jackson's all right. I'm going out to look again. Up you get."

"I feel a bit sick."

"Here, up. Make yourself some coffee, help yourself to food. Keep an eye on Jackson. Thanks. I'll call you."

I didn't wait for a reply, but ran down the stairs again. Alix followed me out of the house, looking awkward. She began to say something but I got into the car and drove away, with that rattle still there, not knowing where I was going.

For the moment I had done with rationality. Now I had the wild idea of searching randomly. Perhaps I would find her lying injured beside her bike, or spy her walking by a distant shore. I drove along The Street, quickly passing the shops, the bungalows, the bowling-green and the playing-fields and then I was in open farmland—The Street becomes a country road that bisects the island. After a few hundred yards I turned right on to a road that leads directly to the sea. At the end there is a youth camp where children come in the summer to swing from ropes, play football and canoe, get fresh air and get drunk, smoke and steal from local shops. But now it was deserted. I parked in front of Reception, a green wooden hut. I had thought of asking if anybody had seen Charlie but I didn't even get out of the car. The car park was empty, the hut door padlocked. A cat lay on the step and peered at me suspiciously. A couple of seagulls stalked round the bins, steadying themselves in the breeze with their huge wings. Was it worth walking along the sea wall? I decided I was better off in the car. I turned round and drove back to the main road, then right, heading for the less populated end of Sandling Island.

On my left I saw a sign for Birche Farm. Jay. Did I need to get back in touch with him in the light of what I had learned? I felt my brain was working slowly when it needed to be quick and nimble. I had thought Charlie had made it up with the girls who had been bullying her but they had spiked her drink and she had vomited. I thought she had planned to run away. Now it seemed as if it had been more of an impulse, and that someone had helped her. Who could that have been? Jay was an obvious candidate, but would he help her and not go with her? Was there someone else she hadn't told me about?

The road narrowed into a lane and then into a rough parking area. It was hard to believe that in the summer there was often a jam even to get into it but now only two cars were there. Dog-walkers. I stopped, got out and ran across the rough grass that led to the sea wall. In the distance I could make out a small group of people. As I got closer I saw there were three of them, an elderly couple in conversation with a white-haired woman. Two small dogs scampered and yapped at their feet. They turned as I ran up to them, panting with the effort.

"I'm looking for my daughter," I said. "Have you seen anybody?"

They shook their heads.

"We just got here," said the man.

"I've walked along the sea wall to the marsh," said the white-haired woman. "There's a man picking cockles on the sand. I didn't see nobody else."

I ran past them to the edge of the path. The tide was still quite low, shingle, sand and mud. The water between the island and Frattenham on the mainland was just a hundred yards or so wide. I was standing on the point, the easternmost tip of the island, and from it I could see along the path a mile to the north and almost as far in the other direction, to the south-west, until the path disappeared from view round the gentle curve of the sea wall. North, I could only see one figure, the cockle-picker, on the sands. Southwest, there was nobody. A small crane stood in the distance, where the sea wall was being repaired, but even that was still and unused at the weekend.

As I turned back towards the car, I passed the three old people again.

"She's a fifteen-year-old called Charlotte," I said. "If you see her, ask her to call home."

They didn't speak. If I had chatted with them about the weather, or asked them the ages and names of their dogs, they would have been content and polite. But they were uncomfortable with a strange woman in search of her daughter.

It was impossible to drive north of the road except for a couple of tracks that led directly into the yards of the two main farms on the island. The north of the island that faced the mainland was much less accessible than the south, arable fields that gradually wettened and dissolved into marshland, reeds and disused oyster beds, then the sea and England. Of course Sandling Island was England as well, but it didn't feel like that. It had just about clung to the mainland for centuries, but its grip was loosening and I sometimes imagined that one more storm would wash it away.

On the way back, the grey sky started to break up and widening patches of blue appeared. An idea occurred to me, and instead of heading back into the town I turned right on the road that led to the mainland. The island is almost flat, except for a few hillocks, bumps and sandbars, and one prominent reminder of the island's ancient past, a tumulus beneath which is a large burial site. It must have been chosen because of its vantage-point, the views it gave of potential threats, whether from the North Sea or the two channels running round the island or the mainland. Now it was a grass-covered anomaly in this otherwise flat landscape.

I parked the car and made my way up the slope. It was really nothing more than a large knoll but it gave a view of much of the island and across the sea to the mainland beyond. I could see the town to the far west and then I let my gaze follow the line of the coast, past the caravan park, then a mile of marshland and grass until it reached the causeway, which stood well clear of the water and the mud, now that the tide was still only half-way in. Once, years ago, there had been a path round the whole island but there had been a winter of terrible storms ten years earlier and the sea wall had collapsed under the onslaught. Now, just down from where I stood, there was a treacherous series of creeks and salt marshes, old concrete emplacements, pillboxes, and paths that led nowhere. As I turned, clockwise, the land seemed to firm and harden, and the path between the marsh and the mud reappeared. The far end of the island was difficult to make out in the haze of the winter day and the south side of the island I couldn't see at all, hidden as it was by lines of pine trees, planted for some obscure tax reason back in the seventies and now left, unmanageable and unsaleable.

I took a deep breath and felt the cold wind and the cold sun on my face. Either my daughter had passed

across that causeway and was gone, or she was somewhere within my gaze on this island. But where? And
what should I do? I looked up. Far, far above I saw a
trail of smoke in the sky and at the end of it a plane,
small as the point of a pin, spilling out the smoke in
its wake as it headed away to Europe, the Far East or
Australia. People inside that pinprick were settling
down to their bloody Marys and miniature bags of
salted nuts, their trays of food and their in-flight
movie, anticipating the beach or the ski slope. I remembered that we could have been among them and
the thought made me gasp as if I'd been struck in the
stomach.

I looked beyond the silver plane at the growing
blueness of the sky and thought of the stars and the
light years of cold, empty space, and I closed my
eyes and prayed to the God in whom I didn't believe.
Give me my daughter, I said. Give me my daughter
back and give me my son and you can have anything. I'll do anything. I had uneasy memories of a
teacher at school telling us that we shouldn't bargain with God. But then I had gone away, read the
Old Testament and found that it was full of bargains.
I remembered a recent walk along the sea wall with
Charlie and Sludge, on just such a day as this, bright,
windy and cold. I remembered her wild eyes, her
growing body leaning into the wind, Sludge leap-
ing up at her, tongue flapping in happiness. Charlie
had looked at me with her hair blowing across her
face. Give that moment back to me. I'll do anything.
I'll go to hell for all eternity if you make my daughter safe.

And I remembered her in the summer, the impossibly distant heat of last August. I had gone to collect her on a late Saturday afternoon when she had been—what was it? Kayaking? Canoeing? Sailing? I had seen her from a distance with a group of people her own age who were too far away to identify. But I could recognize Charlie's profile anywhere. At that moment I had thought, She's becoming a woman. And, She has friends I don't know anything about. At the time it had made me feel happy, complicatedly happy. I remembered how I had seen her throw back her head and laugh. That lovely, carefree sound carried to me over the months that had gone and I could hear it again now as I stood on the barrow in the icy winter silence: a peal of mirth so clear and fresh that I stared wildly around as if Charlie would suddenly be standing in front of me and I could run to her and put my arms round her lean body and hold her safe against me. Of course, no one was there, nothing, and I was alone on a solitary hill.

What now? I wondered if I should go home and wait for the phone to ring. But even if I should, I couldn't. There was one more thing.

I ran back to the car. As I reached it my mobile rang. Once more, I felt a wave of hope, quickly followed by despair. It wouldn't be Charlie. I knew that.

"Yes?"

"It's me. Rory. I'm nearly there."

"No Charlie yet. Listen. When you come, wait with Jackson. Try to cheer him up. Keep him occupied. I'll be back soon. There's something I've got to do."

"I'm here to find my daughter, not to baby-sit my son." He was practically shouting down the phone.

"I know. Look, I'll call later." I cut him off before he could say anything else and, very briefly, put my head in my hands, trying to collect my thoughts. Then I drove back the way I had come, and turned at last on to the main leg of The Street, where most of the shops were. I drew up outside Walton's, the newsagent, and leaped out.

"Hello," I said, pressing up against the counter and ignoring other customers. "I'm Nina, Charlie's mother. I phoned earlier to ask about her newspaper round."

"Hold on a minute," said the woman behind the counter. She was counting ten-pence coins into a small plastic bag.

"No. I can't hold on. It's important."

The woman didn't answer, but carefully sealed the little bag. "How can I help you?" she said, chilly disapproval in her voice.

"I have to know who's on Charlie's paper round. At once."

"What for?"

"Oh, for God's sake. She's missing. I've got to have those names."

"We don't just give out customers' names to anyone, you know."

"Why not? You're not a doctor or a priest."

"There's no need for that tone. You're still quite new round here, aren't you?"

"Sorry. Sorry. Sorry. I'm doing this wrong. It's

because I'm worried. So please—*please*—can you give me those names?"

"I'll have to ask my husband."

I gritted my teeth to stop myself howling in her face. "All right." But she didn't move. "Is he in the back?"

"He's out on a delivery."

"What? Out?"

"I'll ask him when he gets back. It shouldn't be long."

"But I need the names *now*!"

"I'm afraid you'll have to be patient."

"You don't understand—"

"Excuse me, I've got work to do."

She went into the back of the shop, the bead curtains parting to let her through and dropping back into place. In despair, I banged hard on the bell on the counter, but she didn't reappear.

So I left the shop, barging past customers, stumbling over the threshold like a drunken woman. I could feel fear rising in me inexorably, and I knew that if I let it, it would engulf me. I stood outside the door and closed my eyes, feeling the throb from my temples in the tips of my fingers. In the darkness, I searched for a way forward, a pinprick of light that I could follow.

"Where are you?" I whispered. "Where are you, my darling one?"

"Here. This is what you were after."

My eyes snapped open and the world loomed back into view. "Joel. What are you—"

"The names you were after." He held up a sheet of paper.

"Were you in the shop? I didn't see you—how did you get them?"

"I know Janet. It's a matter of asking her in the right way." He handed me the sheet of paper. "Tam told me what happened last night." He put his hands on my shoulders and gazed at me. "I'm so terribly sorry, Nina. And ashamed. I don't know what to say to—"

"Never mind that now."

Together, we looked at the list. There were nineteen names, with the titles of newspapers and addresses next to them. Unfortunately, they weren't all on the same street, but were scattered through the east side of the town and out towards the coast.

"Which route would Charlie have taken? Which one is Pleshey Road?"

"Let's see." He frowned and followed his blunt, calloused finger down the page. "We need a map for this. Hold on, Nina."

Once more he headed into the shop, but this time came back empty-handed.

"No maps in stock," he said. "We'll have to draw our own. Let's go in here." He didn't wait for my reply but, holding me closely by the arm, drew me into the coffee shop next door. "Sit down," he said.

I sat at the table next to the window, so that I could see whoever passed by. I was still buttoned up in my jacket and perched on the edge of the seat, ready to jump up at any time. Joel turned over the sheet with Charlie's paper round on it to give him a blank space, and pulled a pen out of his overall pocket. He handed it to me. "Get started on this. I'll get us coffee."

"I don't want coffee."

"It's going to be all right, Nina. And I'm going to help you. It's the very least I can do. You're not alone."

At that point, I knew Joel was still in love with me, that Alix was right to be jealous and bitter. But I didn't care, if it meant he would help me. "Thank you," I said.

He smiled down at me, laying his large warm hand on the crown of my head for a moment, and was gone. I drew the approximate shape of the island, like a clumsy boot, its toes facing out to open sea, then sketched in The Street, running from the causeway towards the south coast, then veering inland.

"Drink this. Here, let me." He took the pen from my hand. "This one's Low Road, and Barrow Road goes here."

"The roads that Charlie had to go down were . . . Hang on." I turned over the page. "Tippet Row, East Lane, Lost Road and Pleshey Road."

"Pleshey Road's the small one that connects East Lane and Lost Road. Approximately like this."

"Right."

"Now look." He drew the pen in a wavering line down a pattern of roads. "Charlie'd probably have gone this way, starting on Tippet Row, up Cairn Way, then East Lane, Pleshey Road and ending up at Martin Vine's house at the far end of Lost Road, here. It's the obvious route."

"Right," I said. I stood up and took the paper from the table. "Thanks, Joel."

"You haven't touched your coffee. Anyway, I'm coming with you. We'll find Charlie."

I didn't have time for niceties. "I hope so. And I'm grateful."

"You don't need to be. I feel responsible, and anyway . . ." He stopped himself.

I pushed at the door and the wind stung our cheeks. We stepped out into the cold and my hair blew over my face, half obscuring my vision.

"We should start here." Joel jabbed his finger at the map.

"Right."

"Or this is a better idea. Let's miss out the first . . . let's see . . . the first six or seven houses that are very spread apart, and start here, with the Gordons. I know them—I chopped down their old elm last month. We can take my truck. It's a few blocks down. If they haven't received their paper, we can go backwards instead of forwards."

He linked his arm through mine and pulled me close to him.

"Where do you think you two are off to?" Alix was standing in front of us, a hat pulled down over her head and her eyes bright in the cold wind. "I saw your truck and wondered where you were," she said.

"We're trying to find Charlie, that's all. We're going to follow her newspaper round."

"We are, are we?"

I didn't have time for this, but Alix laid her hand on Joel's arm. "You promised to take Tam into town for her Christmas shopping," she said.

"Do you really think Tam deserves to go shopping? Anyway, I'm not taking her."

"You are."

"This is an emergency. And I'm going to help Nina."

"No. I'm going with Nina," said Alix. "You're staying here."

"I don't think so."

For an awful few seconds they stared at each other, but the winner of the battle of wills was never in doubt. She turned to me. "Come on, Nina—it would be better if we went in my car. I'll drive and you can direct me."

At any other time I would have left them there together, tied up in the bitterness of their marital discord. Not now. I shrugged at Joel and turned away, leaving him disconsolate in the road. Alix and I hurried down the street towards her car. My eyes were watering in the cold; I held the sheet of paper fluttering in my hand. I climbed in and sat in the passenger seat, leaning forward anxiously, seat-belt undone. After I'd given her the address of where we were going first, neither of us spoke.

When we arrived at the seventh address on Charlie's list, I leaped out and rang the bell of the Gordons' house (23 East Lane, the *Daily Mail*), heard it sing a clanky little tune deep in the house. I heard footsteps and the door was pulled open. The young woman who stood there was holding a tiny baby to her breast. Its red, wrinkled face peered out of the white blanket. There was a milk blister on its lip. A smell of washing and baking wafted from the kitchen. Life was going on.

"Mrs. Gordon?" I said. "My name is Nina Landry and I just wanted to ask—"

"Come in. I don't want to stand in the cold with Eva. She's only a few days old and—"

"I only wanted to ask if you received your *Mail* this morning?"

"My *Mail*?"

"Your newspaper. Did you get it all right?"

"Why?"

"My daughter—" I started, then stopped and collected myself. "There have been a few queries about the papers this morning and we were simply checking that they'd all arrived safely."

"It's here. I haven't read it yet, though. No time. We only came back from the hospital a few—"

"Thank you," I said, and stepped away from the door, hearing her voice following me down the path.

Next was Sue Furlong, whom I knew vaguely because her black Labrador was Sludge's sister. The two sometimes had wild chasing games on the sea wall. Indeed, as I knocked at the door of her rather shabby terraced house, I could hear the dog barking frantically inside. But no one came. I pushed open the letterbox flap and peered inside. There, on the mat, lay her chewed and muddy newspaper, beside a pile of mail.

The Gunners (Honey Hall) had received their

Guardian; Bob Hutchings on East Lane his *East Anglian Daily Times*. I could hear the radio from his kitchen: the news had just ended. Down Pleshey Road, and Meg Lee had her paper. She'd even glimpsed Charlie as she cycled up the short drive. The teenage son of the Dunnes didn't know if his parents had received theirs, but I pressed him. He sighed, irritated, then went into the kitchen and came back to tell me it was there, opened on the table.

The houses were more scattered here. Charlie had only just started doing the paper round so she had the least desirable route, which took her twice as long as the ones that covered the centre of the town. Alix and I drove from Lost Road to the coastal road that led along the crumbling sea wall. We didn't speak. The tide was drawing steadily nearer, rivulets of water running up the mud ditches. The long grass in the distance shimmered like a mirage in the chill breeze. It was probably not more than half a mile, but the flat road stretched ahead of us and we seemed to be getting nowhere, stranded in a monotony of scrubby grass, mudflats and oozing ocean. There was a faint streak of light where the sea met the sky, and I kept my eyes on that. I tried not to think of how we were probably wasting our time, going in the wrong direction, further away from the truth, further away from Charlie. I used to think that if she or Jackson needed me, I'd know it and know where to find them, as if they could send out some radio wave of distress that only their mother could pick up. Not any more.

Christian called and I cut him off. Rory called

and started saying something about how it was my fault Charlie had run away. I cut him off too. At last we bumped down the drive to where the Wigmores lived: it was a ramshackle cottage, with a sagging roof and stained, ancient walls. Small white lights festooned the tree at the front door. I knocked, and after a while an elderly man came to the door, wearing an apron, his sleeves rolled up. His face was whiskery and shiny and he was annoyed at being interrupted. "What is it?" he said.

"Did you get your paper this morning?" I asked, without preamble.

"Eh?"

"Your newspaper, did you get it?"

"My paper? I'm making the Christmas cake now. I'm putting in the glacé cherries. You could have asked me before."

"Sorry?"

"That's all very well."

I exchanged a dispirited glance with Alix.

"Did you get your paper today, Mr. Wigmore?" she enunciated loudly, clearly, and he scowled.

"I can hear as well as you and I got it all right, but it was missing the sports. I like my sports pages on a Saturday."

"Thanks," I said, backing away, past the ancient tractor, the pile of wire netting and old doors.

The next house was half a mile further on, a red-brick townhouse that looked built for a residential road in a northern town, but had been plucked out of context and set down unprotected on this bleak spot, in the path of the wind and rain. Its square windows overlooked the sea in one direction, and toughened grassland in the other.

As she parked, Alix said, in the same voice she had used to Mr. Wigmore, as if she were teaching elocution: "You weren't the first, you know."

"What's that?"

"I said, you weren't the first." It was almost a shout. "With Joel."

"Oh," I said. I opened my door and swung out my legs. "No, I didn't know."

"He likes women. Usually younger than you, though."

"I'm sorry," I said, although it wasn't true. I didn't care about what had happened between me and Joel, and I didn't care if there had been others before me. I knew that later these things would mean something again—unless, of course . . . My mind shuddered to a halt right there.

As we approached the door, Alix hesitated. "Is there a point in this?" she said. "I mean, Charlie delivered the papers. Is this telling us anything?"

"I don't know," I said. "We're retracing her steps. Someone might have talked to her. What else can I do?"

Alix nodded and rang the bell, then rang again. We both waited, our faces stiff with cold. A woman answered the door. She was wearing a blue housecoat. There was a mop in her hand.

"Yes?"

Suddenly it all seemed ludicrous, hopeless, a meaningless charade. I could hardly bring myself to speak the string of words. I glanced down at the piece of paper. "Hello. It's Mrs. Benson, isn't it? I was wondering if you got your newspaper this morning."

She looked puzzled. "My paper? Sometimes it comes late on a Saturday, so I don't usually get too bothered."

"You mean it was delivered late?"

"They sleep in late on Saturday, the young kids, don't they? Once it was delivered with the Sunday paper."

"So it was late?" I said.

"Have you brought it?" she said.

"No," I said.

"I thought you were bringing it," she said.

"No."

"Will you tell them at the shop?"

"You mean the paper wasn't delivered?"

"No."

"You're really sure. You're absolutely sure?"

Mrs. Benson seemed confused. "It makes a noise when it comes. I hear the flap of the letterbox. I get it from the mat here."

"You might have forgotten," I said.

"Come on, Nina," Alix said.

I made myself thank Mrs. Benson, say goodbye like a normal person, and we hastened back to the road. The ground felt unsteady under my feet. We got back into the car.

"What now?" asked Alix.

"Now we know that the paper was delivered to Mr. Wigmore but not to Mrs. Benson."

"We should double-check, though. Who's next on the list?"

A few hundred yards further on an Andrew Derrick was out at the front washing his sports car. No, his paper hadn't arrived and he wasn't at all pleased about it.

Alix and I stared at each other.

"Well?" she asked.

"Got to think. Now we know something. Charlie started her paper round. She did the first—what?—twelve houses. She delivered the paper to Mr. Wigmore back there. The next house on her route was Mrs. Benson's. She never delivered it." I could feel the blood pumping through my body, I could feel it along my arms and up in my head, the veins pulsing with it. I felt that, if I let myself, I would faint. But I couldn't. I had to be calm and think clearly. It helped to talk. It helped to have cold, rational Alix there. "Now, if you're fifteen years old and you're going to run away from home on the day you're meant to be going on holiday, you might skip your paper round, because that really is the least of your worries. Or, if you're feeling some peculiar sense of obligation, you might do your paper round and then leave home. But what doesn't make sense is to do half your paper round and run away."

We stared at each other, thinking furiously.

"Could she have had an accident?" said Alix.

"You checked the hospital."

"She might . . ." She paused, not wanting to say the words. "She might still be there—between the houses."

"Quickly. Back to the Bensons," I said.

Once there, we got out of the car again and together we began to stumble along the road, looking
carefully to either side. The road was black Tarmac.
There were some patches of clay on it that had fallen
off the wheels of farm vehicles and tracks of car
tyres across them but I saw no sign of bicycle tyres.
On the left side of the road there was a ditch and
some small, scrubby bushes, twisted by year after
year of wind off the sea. Beyond them rough grass,
like seaweed, dipped down and led towards the mud
of the estuary. On the right-hand side there was a
hedgerow and some trees marking the boundary of a
large field that had just been ploughed so that it
looked like a frozen brown stormy sea.

"We'll look as far as the Wigmores' house and
then—"

I stopped because I didn't know what to say. And
then what? I couldn't bear that thought now. Leave it
for later.

There are a lot of things on an empty road when
you walk it slowly, staring at every inch. The rem-
nants of damp leaves from the autumn, a cigarette
packet, beer bottles, a torn shopping-bag, a soggy
tissue, a sodden newspaper, a polystyrene container
with some unrecognizable remnant of takeaway food
stuck to it.

"What are you looking for now? Lost something?"
said a voice.

It was Mr. Wigmore, a strange tweed hat on his
grey head.

I didn't have time to explain properly. I waved a

hand in his direction and said, "My daughter. She delivered the paper to you but not to the Bensons. I need to find her."

"She never delivered the paper to me."

I straightened up. "What?"

"She never delivered it," he repeated.

"But you said—"

"I collected it myself. I thought you understood. It didn't arrive so in the end I had to go and get it. But it didn't have the sports section."

"Why didn't you tell us it hadn't been delivered?"

"You asked if I'd got my paper. I did get it. I got it myself."

"All right, all right," I said. "My mistake."

Mr. Wigmore walked off, still muttering to himself about his paper.

"Let me get this straight—" started Alix, but I interrupted her.

"It means we're looking in the wrong place," I said. "It's between Mr. Wigmore's house and the Dunnes' that she disappeared."

I took her by the sleeve and pulled her, half running, back to the car.

Once more, we retraced our route and stopped by the side of the road, just beyond Mr. Wigmore's shabby cottage with the Christmas lights twinkling under the winter sky. Once more, we trudged along the road, one of us on either side, not knowing what we were looking for. The day deepened. The light was changing and thickening. The tide was coming in.

Something caught my eye. A newspaper. I shouted at Alix, who was ahead of me and ran back.

It was a copy of the *Daily Mail*, wet, spattered with
mud, lying in the grass, half hidden. I picked it up. I
opened it and a magazine wrapped in polythene fell
to the ground, along with a clutch of cards advertising insurance and conservatories. I showed it to
Alix.

"That may explain it," she said. "Charlie must
have dropped it without realizing. On a windy day
like this, newspapers could easily have blown from
under her arm or however she was carrying them."

"There's only one here," I said. "She didn't deliver the paper to the second house along either."

Alix looked a little less sure of herself. "She may
have dropped other papers too. They could have
blown away."

"Maybe," I said.

I knelt down and looked closely at the ground. At
the edge of the road where the Tarmac ended, it was
muddy, messy. "Alix," I said, "does the ground look
churned up here?"

"I don't know," she said. "It's pretty muddy everywhere. There's been a lot of rain."

"I know, I know," I said. "But this is all we've got.
This spot. Before we move on, can we make a circle
about twenty yards round it and look very carefully?"

There was just the tiniest hint of a pause. I was a
person about whom Alix had mixed feelings—to put
it mildly—and she was a busy doctor on a free day,
but she was wandering along this road in the wind
and cold, and there was probably no point in it, and
there must have been a million things she would

rather have been doing. I could see a silent internal sigh of resignation.

"All right," she said.

Alix had walking-boots on so I pointed her into the thicker undergrowth.

"How far shall I go?" she asked.

"Just look for twenty yards in that direction. I'll do the same across the road."

Alix had got the worst of the deal. I took slow steps across the road, just a few inches at a time, staring at it so closely that I was almost on my hands and knees. But Alix had to clamber across the ditch and although she was wearing boots, I saw that her jeans were dark with damp from the long grass.

I looked at every twig, every loose stalk, but there was nothing. I walked off the road on the coast side. Twenty yards through that long rough grass was quite a long way. How was I going to search it? With my fingertips? Was there any point? Was it merely a form of neurotic activity? As I was pondering this I heard my name shouted. I turned but I couldn't see Alix. She was on the other side of the hedge. I spotted a gap, which had allowed her through.

"Are you all right?" I cried.

"Come here quickly."

"What is it?"

"Just come. Now."

I couldn't move. My skin went hot. There was a heaving in my chest and stomach. I gulped and thought I might vomit. And then, slowly, like a dead person, I made myself walk, one foot in front of the other, as if I had never done it before. I had to step precariously over the ditch and through the gap, like a doorway, in the hedge and into the field. Alix was standing there, gesturing with both hands. At her feet, half leaning against the hedge and hidden from the road, was Charlie's bicycle. On top of it was the bright orange bag in which she carried the newspapers. I ran forward but Alix stepped in my way so I couldn't get at it. "You mustn't touch it," she said. "We must call the police. Now."

"Yes," I said. "Police."

She took a mobile phone from her jacket pocket. She held it for a moment and then she dropped it. She picked it up. Her hands were trembling. "I'm sorry," she said. "It's stupid. I can't."

"That's all right." I took the phone from her and punched in the three digits.

A lix wanted to wait in the car, but I couldn't be inside. I stood on the road, paced up and down it, tipped my head back to see the sky. Sullen, heavy sky. Alix was beside me, her hands deep in her pockets, face raw with cold. "Nina," she began.

"Don't say anything."

I turned away from her and faced out towards the expanse of grey, inhospitable water. The sea was spreading and the island was shrinking.

I saw the police car, with its glowing orange stripes, from half a mile away, trundling towards us like a toy. Alix and I stood awkwardly, almost embarrassed with each other, waiting for it to pull up. PC Mahoney was alone. There were no pleasantries when he got out. We had met too often today for that.

"Where is it?" he said.

I nodded at the gap in the hedge. He walked through but we didn't follow. We knew without being told that we shouldn't trample over the scene.

"And in case you're wondering," I said, "I'm absolutely sure that it's Charlie's bike, and that's the bag she uses for delivering the papers."

I could see Mahoney in the field, standing and staring. When he walked back he seemed almost puzzled. "Is there any possibility that she could have loaned the bicycle to somebody else? To a friend?"

At that moment I had to control my emotions. Getting angry, shouting at a policeman, would make a bad situation worse.

"No," I said, with exaggerated calm. "We're sure. We talked to the woman at the newsagent's. Charlie arrived, collected the papers and set off."

As briefly as I could, I described how we had followed her route and what we had found out. He again seemed baffled as I told our story and I had to stop myself saying that we were only doing what he should have been doing. When I had finished he nodded. He told us to wait a moment, returned to his car and began to talk on his radio. I couldn't make out what he was saying but it went on for several minutes and it was evident that much was said on both sides. At times he was silent, nodding. He said goodbye, or over and out, whatever people say on radios, then sat there for a few seconds before joining us.

"I talked to the boss," he said. "This is more than I can handle. There'll be people coming over from the mainland."

"But what do we do now?"

"I'd like you to sit in your car. I've got to secure the scene."

"We're all right where we are," I said.

"Then I must ask you to stand back."

"Stand back from where?"

"It's important that nothing is disturbed."

It was crazy but in the midst of all that I had the memory of once when I was a small child and we were going to a fair that had come to a nearby park. I had seen the ferris wheel, the roundabouts and the stalls being constructed on my way to and from school all that week. I was desperate to go, but before we left my mother suddenly announced that she needed to get changed and couldn't decide on the right clothes, and she made me a sandwich to bring and she had to clear up, and I stood by the door hopping from one foot to the other, thinking of all the time that was being used up, all the fun that was being had, while my mother found things to potter about with.

That was the thing with Mahoney. When it hadn't been important, when he was sure that nothing had happened to Charlie, he could take notes, give bits of advice and tell me not to worry. But now that we were facing the sickening possibility that something *had* happened, it made him feel safe to fall back on a narrow form of procedure that would use up precious time.

He opened the boot of his police car and returned with a pile of traffic cones, stacked one on the other like paper cups for a children's party. With a great show of solemnity he arranged them in a half-oval shape on the road adjacent to the gap in the hedge. Then he went back to the car and returned with what looked like a bundle of canes and a giant roll of tape. He stepped through the cones and the gap in the hedge. He detached the canes, one by one, and stuck them into the ground at intervals, then disappeared from sight. When he emerged into view we saw he was unwinding the tape and connecting the cones to form a symbolic barrier round the area where the bike and the bag were lying.

I walked over to Alix. "Do you think this is necessary?" I hissed. "It's not as if there's a crowd of people likely to disturb the crime scene. Have we seen a single car all the time we've been here?"

She looked across at Mahoney, who was now sitting on the driving seat of his car with the door open and his feet resting on the road. He seemed to be filling in a form. "I'm sure it's required," she said. "It shows how seriously they're taking matters. The important thing is that people are coming who know how to deal with things like this. They'll sort it out quickly, I'm sure of it."

I didn't share Alix's faith in the authorities. I walked over to the car. He was scribbling busily in large, almost childlike handwriting and didn't notice me at first. When he saw me, he became self-conscious. Perhaps he was worried that I might be reading what he had written.

"I'm sorry," I said, "but nothing seems to be happening. Nothing!" And I waved at the empty road and the empty sky. My voice was cracked.

"I told you, Ms. Landry, officers are on their way."

"But look at what we've found. Not only is my daughter gone but her bike had been hidden behind a hedge. Which suggests that somebody put it there. Which suggests that she is with someone against her will. In which case, the situation is terribly, terribly urgent. Do you agree with that?"

"Ms. Landry, if there was anything I could do, this moment, that would help find your daughter, I would do it. What we have to do is wait for the officers to arrive. It's their job now."

"You should have called them at once."

"Ms. Landry—" he began, but I interrupted him.

"Don't say it. Don't say anything. How long will they be?"

"Not long. No more than half an hour."

I looked at the time on my mobile. It was twenty minutes to two. How long is not long? Oh, they were a long time. Each second was a long time, an agony of trying not to think and thinking all the time, of trying not to see her face and seeing it all the time, hearing her voice call out for me and I couldn't help her, couldn't go to her. I could feel the seconds ticking by, turning into minutes. I felt I was burning up with the need to act and the impossibility of doing so.

A quarter to two. I clenched my fists, dug my nails into my palms until they hurt, walked up and down the road, the icy wind raw on my skin, like being rubbed with sandpaper. I tried to think over everything that had happened, get it all in order so I could be ready for the police: not the order of things

as I had experienced them, moments of scrappy revelations, but the order of things as they must have
happened. Charlie had gone to a sleepover. She had
had her drink spiked, by girls who'd previously bullied her, and got horribly drunk; she'd left for her
paper round at about nine but only got as far as this
lonely spot.

And then there was the fact, incontrovertible but
inexplicable, that her things had gone missing, but
must have been taken around the time of the party, a
full two hours or so later than the time that she was
here. What did that mean? What could it mean?

I phoned home and talked to Renata, who told me
what I already knew: that there was nothing to report. I talked to Jackson and tried to sound reassuring, but half-way through he started weeping and
there was nothing I could say to comfort him. I told
him he had to write down anything he could think of
that Charlie had said to him recently, or that he had
overheard, that might provide a clue. I had no hope
he would come up with anything, but I knew I had to
give him a task, a purpose.

I called Jay, noting as I did so that the battery on
my phone was running low. I said that I very much
needed to meet him and that as soon as I was free I
would call. He sounded jumpy, but agreed to stay on
the island and wait for my call. I rang Ashleigh and
said I needed her to help me by calling all of her and
Charlie's friends and mobilizing them. I wanted them
to contact other people, who should in turn get involved in the search for Charlie. I wanted to cast the
net as wide as possible. Perhaps someone had seen

her that morning, or heard something about her, or could offer a lead that I didn't know about.

Ten to two. I went over to Alix in the car and asked if her phone charger was compatible with my phone, and if so would she charge it a bit for me now. Every minute of extra power would help. She turned on the engine and plugged it in, then said something comforting and platitudinous but I couldn't reply; I literally could not bring myself to speak the words. Stones in my throat. I just stared at her through my stinging eyes and turned away. What should I do now? I had no phone, nothing to busy myself with, and the horizon was empty. My gloveless hands were freezing, my fingers numb.

A tractor passed, the driver sitting up high in the cab, staring down out of his meaty red face. A woman on her bike, her hair tied back in a scarf and her coat billowing around her. She seemed to take ages to cycle by. Mahoney sat stolidly in his car. I scoured the landscape for signs of the police who were arriving from the mainland, but they didn't come. They couldn't get here that quickly. It was five to two.

My mobile rang in the car and Alix called me over, but it was just Christian again, his voice breaking up. He was still stuck. I cut him off after a few words. I pictured Charlie lying in a ditch somewhere; I pictured her in a van, screaming for help. I tried to stop the nightmare images that were bombarding me. Maybe she was standing on a road on the mainland in her characteristic, hip-jutting slouch, thumb out for a lift, or sitting in a warm café with a stranger, someone else she hadn't told me about.

A sailing-boat appeared out of the estuary from inland and began to make its way round the point. The large white and blue sail billowed out in the wind like a puffed cheek. I'd thought all the leisure boats had been safely tucked up on shore for the winter and this boat almost had the sea to itself, except for a small lumpy fishing-smack further down the coast, and far away, dim on the horizon, a container ship making its way to Harwich or Felixstowe. From where? China, probably. The dentist I had started going to on the island had holiday postcards pasted on to his ceiling, so that you stared up at them as you lay back in the chair and perhaps thought of something other than what was going on in your mouth. The last time I went there a profusion of things had been happening in mine—sounds, smells and sudden sensations, even through the anaesthetic—and I had looked at the postcards carefully, one by one, as if I was interested, as if that would fool the pain. I had gazed at the hackneyed scenes of Hong Kong harbour, the Sydney Opera House, a temple on a lake in Thailand, New York City with no Twin Towers, the Eiffel Tower, a beach somewhere.

Now I did the same with that sailing-boat. I scrutinized it as carefully as I could, counting the sails (there were three), trying to identify the ropes and how they fastened the sails and what their purpose was. I looked at the two people on board, one in yellow, the other in blue. There were numbers on the side and a name, but the boat was too far away to make them out. If I could concentrate enough and make myself see as many details as possible, the person in blue holding the large silver steering-wheel, the one in yellow doing something with a rope, maybe I could stop myself thinking about what didn't bear thinking about and maybe this dead time would pass more quickly. So I looked at the little green pennant fluttering at the top of the mast and the portholes and wondered if you could sleep on board. I felt as if I were holding my breath, and then I couldn't hold it any more. I turned to Alix.

"Have you got the time?" I said.

She looked at her watch. "Just gone two," she said.

"You should go now," I said.

She looked awkward. "You know, I'm sorry . . ."

"Of course," I said.

"It's just that there are things . . ."

"Absolutely," I said.

"You've got my number?"

"Yes."

"If there's anything at all I can do . . ."

"You've done a lot already," I said.

"I'm sure Charlie will . . ." Alix began, and stopped, because what could she possibly be sure about? What possible comfort could she offer? She gave a helpless shrug and handed over my barely charged phone.

"Can I borrow the charger?" I asked.

"All right."

She passed it out of the window, then turned and drove away. I watched the car dwindle, then disappear.

I walked across to Mahoney with the phone and the charger and asked him to plug it in for me. He asked if I would like to sit in his car, to keep out of the cold, but I thanked him and said I preferred to stay outside. I turned my back on him and stared at the empty road. Out of a distant past came a fragment of poetry I hadn't known I remembered, and I hung on to it and recited it in my head, over and over: "Build me a willow cabin at thy gate, and call upon my soul within the house . . ." I tried to concentrate on the syllables. "Let the babbling gossips of the air cry out." Inky fingers and the sun shining in thick, dissolving shafts through the windows. Surely they must come now. Surely. I walked back and forth, back and forth. The cold burned in my eyes, the horizon wavered and warped in the winter light. The sun was dipping towards the sea on its shallow arc. The waters rose and swelled as I watched, beads of spray riffling off the grey surface.

Like a dot, a car appeared, driving towards us on the road from the mainland. I held my breath as it came closer. It wasn't a marked police car. There were no flashing blue lights or sirens. And now I could make out two people inside it.

It pulled up behind Mahoney's. He stood up awkwardly, blowing on his fingers to warm them. A youngish woman and an older man got out and I watched them intently: these were the people who were supposed to find Charlie. The man was tall and stringy. He had a balding, shiny head and a neat grey beard thickly fringing his chin, so that for a moment his head looked upside-down.

"Ms. Landry?" he said, as he came towards me, holding out his hand and giving me a firmly vigorous shake. Grey eyes, with deep wrinkles radiating out from them as if he'd smiled a lot through his life; corrugated wrinkles on his high forehead, as if he'd frowned a lot; brackets round his mouth that gave him a lugubrious air. But his lived-in, furrowed face gave me a feeling of hope.

"Yes," I said. "Nina Landry. My daughter—"

"I'm Detective Inspector Hammill. This is Detective Constable Andrea Beck."

The woman was shorter than me, and boxy. She had thick, light-brown hair in a high ponytail, with a fringe that fell below her eyebrows, making her blink continuously, which irritated me. She, too, shook my hand, smiling sympathetically at me as she pressed my fingers.

"Thank God you're here," I said, pulling away my hand and stepping back. "Something terrible's happened to my daughter."

"In a minute a constable will arrive to secure the site," said DI Hammill. "Then we will go with you to the police station and you can tell us everything you know."

"I've told everything already. Everything. Twice. It's all written down. But that's her bike over there. Look. Lying there with the newspapers. She's in danger and you've got to find her now. What about sniffer dogs or helicopters or something? Not just more words, for Christ's sake."

"We're here to help, Ms. Landry. I know how very anxious you must be. Here's Constable Fenton now."

Obviously there was a proper way to do everything; there were rules and appropriate procedures. The detective inspector talked to Mahoney and the detective constable talked to the constable, who had cropped hair and a blunt face and looked hardly older than Charlie. They walked over to the bike and studied it. And I stamped my feet and rubbed my hands together and damped down the great howl rising in my chest.

"Right, Ms. Landry. Forensics will be arriving in a few minutes, but Kevin's staying here to wait for them and we'll go to the station now. You haven't got your car with you, have you?"

"My car? No. It's—" What did it matter where it was? "I came with a friend who's gone home."

DC Beck drove slowly and blinkingly, as if minding the speed limits. DI Hammill sat beside her, not speaking but frowning in deep thought. Every so often he tapped a rhythm on his knee with his large, bony fingers. I hunched forward in my seat, eyes flickering over the landscape.

"Will you send lots of people out looking?" I asked, at one point. I was thinking of those pictures seen on television documentaries, police in a long line, each one at arm's length from the next, heads down, inching carefully forward, searching for clues.

"Well, now, Ms. Landry, or can I call you Nina? Nina, first we have to assess—" began DC Beck.

"Assess? *Assess?* What do you mean 'assess?' What's there to assess? Don't you get it? You don't need to assess anything, you need to do something. Charlie's disappeared. She's not run away, she's not at a friend's house, she's not in a hospital. Her bike's lying in a field half-way along her newspaper route. We were supposed to be going on holiday today, do you hear me? She was excited. She arranged a birthday party for me. Assess?"

DC Beck slid a worried glance to DI Hammill, who continued to stare imperturbably out of the window. "Nina . . ." she began.

"Don't speak to me like a child. I know my daughter and I know something terrible is happening to her right now. *Now*. At this very minute—while you're talking about assessing the situation and minding the speed limits and the ruts in the road."

"First of all, we need to have all the information that will enable us to . . ." She was speaking as if by rote and I sensed she was waiting for her boss's approval. He, however, remained silent.

"I know something else too. I've read enough newspapers and I've watched enough television. It's the first few minutes that count, isn't it?"

"Every situation is different. Your daughter isn't a young child."

"I'm right, aren't I? If you don't find the missing person quickly then the chances of a *favourable outcome* decrease dramatically, don't they?"

"Yes, they do," said DI Hammill, suddenly.

"Thank you."

"We'll do everything we can to find Charlie," he said. "First, we have to ask for your help. All right?"

"All right. Just get her to drive a bit faster, will you?"

*   *   *

A t the station, I was shown into the room I'd been in with Mahoney before. The same tinsel, the same smiling photo of him and his wife, of his teenage daughter who was the same age as my teenage daughter. But on the desk there was another photograph as well: the one I'd given him earlier, of Charlie and Jackson standing together and smiling. I stared at it for a few seconds, then turned away.

It was stale and warm in the room, and my numbed hands started to throb as the feeling returned to them. DI Hammill asked me questions, and DC Beck took notes, and sometimes asked me to repeat or clarify what I'd said. They were insistent on exact times. Mahoney sat at the side of the desk in a chair that was too small for him. Perspiration ran down his face. I could hear the scratch of the pen on paper, the rustle as the pages were turned over, the hum of the radiator and, outside, the creak of the trees.

I had said these words too many times before. They were starting to sound unreal, with the tinny resonance of a performance. I was an actor repeating lines, listening to my voice as I spoke, noting the effect of my words on the faces opposite me. Even my anguish and dread were second-hand emotions. I knew that I was feeling them but could no longer *feel* that I was feeling them. The events of the day had become a story I was telling to a captive audience: the empty house, the untidy room, the surprise party, the missing belongings, the sleepover that had sent Charlie stumbling, wretchedly hung-over, out of the house of her so-called friend to do her paper round, the stranded bike, the way the times didn't add up, yet couldn't be argued with. I spoke quickly, clearly, and I watched them as I did so, and I thought I could see on their impassive faces what they were really thinking.

I described everything: not just the chronology of the day, but the context surrounding it. I knew everything they wanted to ask me before they framed the questions. I told them about Charlie's father, about my affair with Christian and Charlie's initial disapproval of it, about her hard time at school. I described my relationship with my daughter as honestly as I could. I heard myself say that my daughter was recalcitrant, volatile, emotional, romantic and intense. I saw the way they exchanged glances when I told them about Jay, about Rory. I wanted to make them realize this story was different from all the other stories like it that they must have heard in their jobs.

At the same time, my dissociation and my obedience filled me with a new, cold terror, like an icy wind blowing through me. It was as if I had, for those few moments, half given up on Charlie. By letting go of the urgent sense that I could rescue her if only I tried hard enough, thought clearly enough and loved strongly enough, I felt I was allowing her to slip further from me. Somewhere out there, in the cold and the wind and the inhospitable wilderness where sea and land meet, was my daughter, my lovely, darling, beautiful, kind and precious daughter, and I was sitting in that warm little room, an untouched mug of coffee at my hand, reciting the precise events that had led to her disappearance and

even attempting to describe her character and behaviour as if that had anything to do with this sudden loss, this fall through a crack in the world.

I leaned forward suddenly, half spilling the coffee.

"CCTV," I said.

"Sorry?"

"Is there CCTV on the causeway? Because then
we could see if Charlie's been taken off the island
or not."

DI Hammill looked doubtful. "Mahoney? Do you
know?"

He thought for a moment, then shook his head.
"No CCTV."

"Why the hell not?"

"CCTV is really for town centres and shopping
arcades," said DI Hammill.

"For important places," I said.

"It's not about importance," said DI Hammill. "It's
about places where crime happens—" He checked
himself, realizing what he had said. "Where crime
normally happens."

"So she could be anywhere."

I heard the break in my voice. She could be anywhere, with anyone, as far from here as five hours
could take her; as inexorably and eternally far from
me as it was possible to be. I made myself think it,
and it was as if my own heart almost stopped beating while I did so. In the hidden cinema of my mind,
I glimpsed a series of pornographic freeze-frames:
Charlie raped, Charlie tortured, Charlie screaming,
Charlie dying. I saw her coppery curls spreading
across the muddy grasslands, her fingers stretching

out for help, and once more I heard her cry out for me, calling me "Mummy" the way she never did nowadays. I gripped the table with my fingers. "Is that all?" I asked. My voice was strong and steady now, someone else's voice.

"You've been very helpful," said DI Hammill.

"And what now?"

"We're here to evaluate the situation."

"I'm sorry," I said. "I thought you were here to find my daughter."

He looked up at the clock on the wall. Twenty to three.

"It hasn't been much more than five hours since your daughter was last seen. It's still most likely that she's safe and well and that she'll be contacting you."

"That is what people keep trying to tell me," I said. "I was trying to make myself believe it as well, until we found the bike. If Charlie were an eight-year-old, you wouldn't be here 'evaluating the situation.' There'd be helicopters and roadblocks and people walking in lines across fields."

"An eight-year-old is different from a fifteen-year-old," said Hammill.

"What about the bike?"

"I'm trying to keep an open mind about the possibilities."

"There's only one possibility."

"That's not necessarily true."

"What else could have happened apart from her being snatched?"

DI Hammill sat back in his chair. "Every case is different, of course," he said, "but I deal with a lot of young people. An abduction of the kind you're describing is extremely rare. Teenagers running off is relatively common. In this instance, she might have encountered someone she knew, abandoned her bike and departed with him or her. It might have been a previous arrangement or a decision made on the spur of the moment."

"Who the hell would do that?" I said.

He paused for a moment, drumming his fingers on the desk.

"An obvious possibility is that it was whoever took the things from her bedroom. Your daughter may have arranged to leave with someone. She could have told him—or her—to collect some possessions from her room."

"Why didn't she do it herself?"

"She might have been nervous about encountering you. I'm sorry. That's a painful thing to say but it may be true."

"There was a party going on at the house," I protested. "Charlie knew that. She arranged it."

"She might have asked the person because she knew they were going to be at the party. This is the sort of possibility we need to eliminate in our inquiry."

"The problem with this way of thinking," I said, making an immense effort to sound calm, "is that by the time you're convinced that she's genuinely missing, it may be too late. Or, at least, valuable time may have been lost."

DI Hammill looked at me gravely. DC Beck had an intensely sympathetic expression on her face that made me want to slap her. Probably a woman had been sent along because women are supposed to be better at dealing sensitively with such situations. Except that I didn't want the situation to be dealt with sensitively. I didn't care whether it was the most sympathetic woman in Britain or the most oafish thug. I didn't care so long as they got Charlie back.

"We're not going to waste time," Hammill said. "As soon as this conversation is over, we'll be contacting the people whose names you've given us and ascertaining your daughter's state of mind over the past days."

"Then we'd better get the conversation over with, hadn't we?" I said.

"Indeed. But first of all, I want you to give me a thumbnail sketch of your daughter. Not just her appearance, her character."

"What?"

"Describe her to me."

"Why?"

"Bear with me, Ms. Landry. I need to know who I'm looking for."

Like an obituary, I thought. Charlie's life and times in a few choice phrases. I took a deep breath.

"As you know," I said, rather formally, "Charlie is fifteen years old, nearly sixteen. You know what she looks like. That's a good photo and very recent. It was taken only last Sunday. She's grown quite a lot in the last few months and is about my height now. Slim, lean. Maybe because she's my oldest child, I've always worried about her. She had lots of tantrums when she was younger, and often got into trouble at school, not for big things, but she was always a bit of a fighter. She hates injustice and was always standing up to teachers if she thought they were being unfair. She's always had good friends, but she's always had enemies as well. She quarrels with people, she has fierce opinions. She was bullied at her new secondary school, maybe because she was an outsider. I don't think she's ever been a bully, though. She's always been protective of Jackson, her younger brother.

"She likes . . ." I stopped and cleared my throat. I was flooded with memories of Charlie as a yelling baby, then as a toddler, sweet and grumpy, Charlie learning to talk, to walk, to ride a bike, her first day at school. But I needed to focus on what might be important about her for DI Hammill. "She likes weird bands whose names I can't begin to tell you, and strange fashions. She likes Japanese films. She reads modern novels. She's good at art and drama. She spends a lot of time on MSN with her friends. She loves sailing and kayaking, things that make her feel free. She's quite political, but more about single issues, like the environment. She only works hard at things she's interested in. She's very keen on not following the crowd. She draws tattoos on herself. A few times last term I noticed she'd cut herself a bit. Not seriously, but the way teenagers do at the moment, little grazes done with the blades from pencil sharpeners. I asked her about it and she said it was nothing, just a stupid thing. She seemed a bit embarrassed by it, and I don't think she ever did it again.

"The trouble with me telling you all this is that I used to think I knew everything about Charlie and now I'm discovering that she probably had many secrets. Well, of course, she's a teenager. I don't think she smokes except the occasional cigarette at a party, but she might. I don't think she takes drugs, but again, she might. I don't think she drinks much, though she has got horribly drunk once or twice. I don't think she's sexually experienced, but maybe I'd be the last to know. I think she's close to me, although we quarrel. I think she's close to her father too, but she's become very critical of him since he left, and can be scornful. She was a bit upset, or maybe angry is a better word, when I started going out with Christian, but recently she's seemed much happier about it. They get on well together. I think they do anyway."

I stopped for a few seconds and looked at my daughter's face on the desk.

"What else? She was horrified when we left London and came to live here, but when Rory left she was worried that we might leave too, so I think she likes it here after all, although she says real life happens in cities. Sometimes she seems very grown-up, far older than fifteen, but then she can seem like a little child. I don't think she'd ever get into a car with a stranger. I think that if someone tried to grab her, she'd resist. She hates waiting and inaction. She's a fighter. Is that enough?"

"Thank you," said DI Hammill, writing a note as he spoke. "We'll keep you constantly informed." He took his wallet from his jacket and produced a card. "This has my mobile number on it. Call me any time you want. And now we'll drive you home."

"No, no," I said. "Please, get on with your work. It's just as quick for me to walk."

"I insist," he said, and nodded at PC Mahoney.

It really did take longer. Mahoney rummaged in a drawer for the car keys and led me out to the dinky little car park behind the station. He had to turn the car round and drive left and right along residential streets and left on to The Street to reach the front of the police station and then to the seafront and along to my house. He pulled in and leaned across to open my door. "Just ring us if you need any information," he said.

"You must keep me informed," I said. "Please let me know if you find out anything at all. Anything. Even if it's . . ."

"You're in good hands," Mahoney said.

"We'll see," I said, then felt guilty. "Sorry, that was rude."

I got out and Mahoney began the two-minute drive back to the police station. We should both have been charged with wasting police time. I walked up the short path and put my key into the door. As I did so, I felt a hand on my shoulder. There was something familiar about the feel of it and before I turned I knew. I just knew. "Rory," I said wearily.

"Are you going to ask me in?" he said.

He looked different from when I had last seen him. His coppery hair was cut shorter, so that it stuck up on top. He was unshaven and the skin under his eyes was dark, as if he had missed a night's sleep. He was wearing a thigh-length leather jacket, blue jeans turned up at the bottom and scuffed brown suede shoes. I breathed deeply. He was Charlie and Jackson's father. This man had sat beside me, held my hand and mopped my face with a cold flannel as they were born. But now when I looked at him, I could believe he had done something to Charlie. I didn't trust him. I didn't trust anyone.

"Rory, I know all that's happened between us. There's bad things. God knows, there were faults on my side as well. But if this is something you've done to get at me, or if it's a kind of joke or if you know something, just tell me, I implore you on my knees. Tell me and I promise I won't do anything. I'll try to protect you . . ."

"Nina," he said, in the sorrowful tone that used to make me feel so helplessly angry, "how can you think that?"

"And if it turns out that you were involved in some way, I swear that I'll make sure you go down for it."

"We've started well, haven't we? Our daughter's missing and you're accusing me. I'm here to help. I came as soon as I could and I don't see why I should stand here and listen to you insulting me. It's freezing. Can we please go in? It's still my house in a way."

I bit back a reply because, after all, he was right. I turned the key in the door and opened it. Rory pushed past me. Within seconds I felt like I was suffering from a migraine and a heart-attack simultaneously. Jackson ran to Rory and pressed his face into his stomach, sniffling, while the hysterical Sludge jumped wildly up at them, then ran round the room barking. Meanwhile Renata was sitting in the corner of the room with one foot up on a stool. She explained to me that she had been holding Sludge on the lead when the dog had seen another Labrador and leaped forward, pulling her over.

"It's my ankle," she said. "Now I can't put my weight on it."

I apologized profusely on behalf of my dog. Or, rather, strictly speaking, Rory's dog. I said I'd make her tea and retreated into the kitchen. I filled the electric kettle and switched it on. After a few seconds I touched the surface with my fingers. It was still cold. What proportion of our lives do we spend waiting? For kettles to boil. For lifts to arrive. For people to answer a ringing phone. To see Charlie.

I made myself consider the situation. The police had arrived. The professionals had taken over. What I ought to do, as a good citizen, was wait for them to apply their specialized skills. There was nothing for me to do now. By the time I had felt the kettle once more and found it was lukewarm, I had dispensed with that defeatist nonsense. I had to do something. Anything.

I thought of some advice I had once heard or read about for when you've lost your keys while walking home in the dark. You should look under a lamp-post, not because they are any more likely to be there than anywhere else, but because if they happen to be there, it's the only place you'll be able to see them.

I needed to think rationally. What were the possibilities? Where were the lamp-posts? Or, rather, where *weren't* there lamp-posts? Charlie could be dead. I gulped at the thought. She might have left with someone and be off the island and far away from me, where she wanted to be. If she had been snatched against her will, she might have been driven in a white van across the causeway and on to the mainland. In any of those cases, there was nothing I could do.

I had to act on the assumption that she was still on the island, still alive.

The kettle was boiling.

Rory had this idea that if he gave Sludge something of Charlie's to smell she'd act like a sniffer dog and trace her from that. I collected an unwashed T-shirt from the floor of her room. It was yellow, with short sleeves, and when I pressed it against my face I could smell our daughter's sweat, deodorant and perfume. We went downstairs and Rory gave it to Sludge. She dribbled over it dutifully and ran round the kitchen holding it in her drooling, happy jaws, thinking it was a game. When Rory tried to take it back, it ripped.

"We're ready, I think," said Rory. He put on his jacket and picked up the lead.

"Take Jackson," I said.

"Right. Jackson, Sludge, let's go. We'll take the car down to the beach and walk from there. You don't need your Game Boy."

"I want it."

"Leave it here."

"I want to take it with me."

"Jackson—"

"Let him," I said. Rory glared at me, then shrugged.

"Can I lie on your bed again for a while?" asked Renata, as they closed the door. "I don't feel too good. I think I might be coming down with something. Unless you need me."

"Sure." I wanted her out of the way.

The phone rang and I picked it up. "Yes?"

"Nina." It was Ashleigh. "I did what you said and rang lots of people and they're ringing people now."

"Thank you," I said wearily.

"The thing is, there's this girl. She's not really a friend of ours. She's in the year below us. Anyway, she's got a friend who lives on Grendell Road, and she was staying over last night. Or, at least, I think she was staying over, she didn't actually say that, I just assumed—"

"Yes? Go on."

"This morning she thinks she saw Charlie."

"When? Where?"

"She's rather vague about it. I didn't know whether to bother you with it. Shall I give you her mobile number? She's expecting your call. Her name's Laura."

"Thanks, yes."

She read it out and I wrote it down, repeating it to make sure I'd got it right. I put down the phone and immediately rang the number. "Laura?"

"Yes."

"This is Nina Landry, Charlie's mother."

"Charlie? Oh, right, Charlie."

"Ashleigh told me you saw her this morning."

"Right."

"What time was that, Laura, and where? It's very important I should know."

"Is Charlie in trouble?"

"What time was it?"

"I dunno, really."

"About what time?"

"I'd had breakfast."

"Yes." I squeezed the phone hard in my hand and tried to keep calm. "What time did you have breakfast?"

"We didn't have to get up for anything. It's holidays and everything."

"Nine? Ten?"

"Maybe. Between that. No, I know, it was nearer half past nine, twenty to ten, because Carrie's mother said she needed to get to the shops before ten. They were going to Carrie's gran for lunch and she needed to get something. I dunno. Anyway, we were going to go with her and buy some crisps, but then Carrie said we should bike over towards the oyster beds because there's this boy she fancies lives near Lower Meadow Farm down there and we might see him." She giggled.

"Go on."

"I thought I saw Charlie. I know her from school."

"Where did you think you saw her?"

"It might have been someone else but I think it was her. It was from a distance, you see, and we were at the top of the long hill. Lost Road or something funny like that. She was at the bottom. She had a bike."

"She was riding her bike?"

"No, she was standing with it and talking to someone in a car."

"Listen, Laura, did you see who she was talking to?"

"No."

"Or what kind of car it was?"

"It might have been a van."

"What colour was it?"

"Red," she said. "Or maybe blue. It wasn't white. Definitely."

"Red or blue?"

"Or that silvery colour all cars are."

"Red or blue or silver?"

"I dunno, really. I didn't think of it."

"But you think it was Charlie?"

"I didn't think so at the time, but when Ashleigh called Carrie and then Carrie told me, I thought I remembered."

"Did Carrie see it too?"

"No. She was talking about something. She wasn't paying attention. Maybe it was someone older."

"That Charlie was talking to?"

"Maybe. They had their head out of the window. They didn't look young."

"Man or woman?"

"You're asking too many questions. I don't remember anything. Maybe a man. It was a long way off. Maybe it wasn't Charlie anyway. I didn't know I was meant to be keeping an eye out or I'd have noticed more. You don't notice things if you're not trying to."

"OK, listen to me. I'm going to give you a number to call. You want to speak to Detective Inspector Hammill, and tell him what you've just told me. Do you hear?"

"Detective Inspector Hammill," she repeated.

"This moment. Do you promise?"

"Yeah, all right."

"Everything you remember, tell him. Don't wait. If he's busy, hold on."

She promised and laboriously wrote down the number as I dictated it but I was doubtful of her managing it, so I phoned DI Hammill and told him what she had said and gave him her details. There. Let him do some detecting.

I went into Charlie's bedroom once more, my head buzzing. Charlie talking to a man. It seemed like important information, but even when I was talking to Laura I had thought of a snag. I believed that Charlie had been snatched by a man and here was a witness who had seen her talking to one. But it had been too early. With my day of driving around, I had a map of Sandling Island inside my head and I could picture exactly where Laura had been when she saw Charlie and where Charlie had been, and she was at the beginning of her paper round. Whoever the man was and whatever their conversation had been about, Charlie had gone on to deliver half a dozen more newspapers. So who had he been?

The sheep clock told me it was twenty past three. In a couple of hours or so we should have been boarding the plane to Florida. I sat on the floor, among the mess, and once more stared around. Perhaps Charlie had been snatched randomly, and there were no clues or patterns. Or perhaps I would find, among the clutter of her teenage life, some sign. I began with the drawers of her desk. One by one I opened them and tipped out their contents. I picked up each object and looked at it before replacing it in the drawer.

A lightbulb, a tiny velvet cushion in the shape of a heart, several coloured crayons of various lengths, metal and plastic pencil sharpeners, notepads with nothing in them except blank pages, certificates for swimming and hurdle-jumping, a head teacher's merit award I'd never seen before, for an excellent essay on *Great Expectations*, an empty bottle of perfume, a crumbling bath bomb, several tangled necklaces, a box of broken pastels, ink cartridges, sanitary towels, tampons, ancient catalogues, last year's birthday cards from friends—I looked through each one—Thinking Putty, dried-up Pritt Sticks, her old mobile phone minus its SIM card, a canister of safety-pins, a half-full pack of Marlboro Lights, two small boxes of matches, a bookmark she'd made in primary school with cross-stitch embroidery, a few old glossy magazines, a large shell, a battered copy of *Lord of the Flies,* another of *The Outsider*, a small torch that didn't work, scented candles that had never been lit, hairbands, a thin white wristband with the message "Make Poverty History," a travel sewing-kit, some knickers (clean), gel pens, cartridges for her printer, an ancient Beanie Baby she'd had as a small child, a watch that had stopped working long ago, a bright cotton scarf with an inkstain at one fringed end. There were folders full of GCSE work, and I leafed through every sheet of paper, just in case there was something among the algebraic formulae, the scientific data, the graphs and maps, dates and jottings that would point me in a new direction.

I rifled through the scattered possessions on her desk once more, then stopped abruptly. Her laptop.

I pulled out her chair, threw the hoodie and the old jeans on to the floor, and sat down. I turned it on with a ping and waited for it to load up. Rory and I had given Charlie her computer on her last birthday. I didn't know how to find my way round it: it was a different make from mine, with different software. Like her room, her virtual desktop was in a state of total disorganization. I found essays for drama, history, science, English, art and French. I found various quizzes, articles that she had downloaded. There was an MSN icon. But what I really wanted was to go through her emails. I knew Charlie used Hotmail, and I assumed her user name was Charlie, but I didn't have a clue what her password was. I tried "Charlie" and "Charlie1" and "Charlie2," "Charlie3," "Charlie4." I tried "Landry" and "Oates" and "Landry Oates." I tried the road we'd lived on in London (Wiltshire), then added our old phone number and tried again. I tried "Sludge," then the name of her beloved rabbit, who had died when she was eight, "Bertie." Despairingly, I keyed in several of the bands or singers I knew she liked. I rang Ashleigh and asked if she knew Charlie's password and she didn't.

I nearly gave up. I typed in "Hope" (my mother's maiden name), and "Falconer" (Rory's mother's). I remembered that a year or two earlier Charlie had wanted to give herself a middle name: Sydney, of all things. I tried that.

And I was in.

Charlie was fiercely protective of her privacy. I had to knock on her bedroom door and wait for her to tell me to come in. If I happened to glance at what she was reading or writing, she would cover it with her hand and glare at me. If she received a letter, she would often take it to her own room to read it. Now I was here in front of all of her emails. There weren't very many, once I had discounted the junkmail and technical updates. Most of her communications were done in MSN chatrooms or by text. But there were enough for me to get an illicit glimpse into her private world. For a start, there were several messages from her father. If I hadn't known who Rory was I might have thought they were from a boyfriend, for in them he told Charlie how beautiful she was, how special, how she shouldn't grow up too quickly, how he would always love her. I read them quickly and closed them down.

There were a couple from Ashleigh, in text language so I could barely decipher their meanings. "LOL & CU l8er?" said one. Another sent her the entire text of the song "My Favourite Things."

A boy called Gary had sent her several emails, rather formal and jocose, with articles he'd cut and pasted from various current-affairs websites. There was one about George Bush and his connections with oil companies, and another about fossil fuels. I didn't stop to read them.

There was one message from Eamonn saying simply, "Parents suck. This is the piece I told you about," followed by an incomprehensible article on some musician whose name meant nothing to me.

And just one brief message from Jay: "My phone's buggered, so this is to say you should meet me in our usual place at 2. I'll bring the stuff. Jxxxx." What stuff? What place? I put my head into my hands and closed my eyes for an instant.

I heard the door slam downstairs and Sludge's muffled barking, and rose to my feet, closing the lid of the laptop as I did so.

"Sludge wouldn't stay out," called Jackson, as I went down the stairs. "She kept whimpering and dragging at the lead. She did a poo on the front lawn of those people with the smart house near the pub and we didn't have a plastic bag."

"Where's Dad?"

"He had to go and fetch the car where we'd left it. He'll be here soon."

Jackson's eyes glittered and his cheeks were flushed. I wondered if he might be feverish, and put a hand on his forehead, but he winced irritably.

"Mum?"

"Yes."

"You know you asked me to make that list?"

It took me a few seconds to remember the instructions I'd given him while I was waiting for the police.

"Yes. Did you?"

"Shall I get it? It's not very long. Really, it only says a few words. It says, have you looked at her computer?"

"I've just been looking through her messages."

"And have you looked at her diary?"

"What diary?"

"You know."

"No."

"It's in her schoolbag probably. That's where she usually keeps it."

"Her bag?" I hadn't come across that either, nor had I thought about it. "Where is it?"

"I saw her put it in the downstairs toilet yesterday when she came in."

It was there, under her old coat. While Jackson watched me, I pulled it down from the hook and opened it at once. Her art scrapbook was in there, the container with the messy remains of yesterday's packed lunch, her pencil case, two or three exercise books and a maths textbook. And, in the front zip-up pocket, a little spiralbound diary. I leafed through it, my hands trembling so that I found it difficult to lift the individual pages. At the beginning of the year she'd put in almost everything: the dates that terms began or ended, coming weekends or Sundays with Rory, visits to the dentist, appointments with friends, parties, concerts, inset days. But gradually the pages became blanker. Occasional initials were put against pages with question marks. There were doodles. Phone numbers were jotted in corners. Autumn and winter were scarcely marked except, I noticed, the occasional small cross in the top left-hand corner of a day. I turned back. There was a cross against Monday, 26 July, Friday, 20 August, then again on Thursday, 16 September, Wednesday, 13 October, Tuesday, 9 November. That was all.

"What is it? Mum, what are you looking at?"

"It's all right," I muttered to Jackson. I gazed at

the crosses, frowning, turning the pages between them. They came, I saw, approximately every month, and struck by a thought I counted the days between each cross: twenty-five, twenty-seven, twenty-seven, twenty-seven.

Charlie's periods. Of course. But then an icy trickle ran down my spine and I turned to December again. Nothing. No cross. There were—I did the sum—thirty-nine days between the last cross on 9 November and today, Saturday, 18 December. Perhaps it didn't mean anything, or perhaps it meant that Charlie had missed her period and was anxious she was pregnant. Perhaps it meant that she *was* pregnant.

I closed the diary and stared blankly at Jackson.

"What is it, Mum?" he asked again.

"Nothing," I replied.

He nodded mutely.

"There, I think your dad's coming in. Why don't you run and ask him to make you one of his famous toasted-cheese sandwiches?"

"Will you have one too?"

"I've got a phone call to make."

I ran upstairs to avoid Rory and went into my bedroom. Renata was lying in the bed. Her eyes were open and she was staring blankly at the ceiling. I snatched up the phone and rang Hammill's number. It was engaged and I couldn't leave this as a message. So I rang the police station, asked for Detective Constable Beck and was put through.

"This is Nina Landry," I began. "My daughter may be pregnant, or think she is."

"How do you—"

"In her diary," I said shortly. "Did you follow up Laura's sighting?"

"I believe she's talking to DI Hammill now."

"No other news, then?" I asked, knowing the answer.

"We're proceeding. We'll let you know as soon as we find anything. Honestly, I've got a daughter of my own and I can imagine how desperate you must—"

"Right." I slammed down the phone, closed the curtains in case Renata wanted to sleep, and left the room, shutting the door behind me.

Rory and Jackson were in the kitchen. Rory looked terrible, peaky and red-eyed. He was talking nineteen to the dozen to Jackson, feverish gibberish that fooled nobody, certainly not Jackson who was gazing at him anxiously.

"I need to talk to you," I said to Rory.

"What is it?" he asked. "Charlie?"

"Alone," I said. "Jackson, darling, can you wait in your room for a bit? It's something private."

He stared at me for a few moments, then wandered disconsolately out of the kitchen. We heard him trudging heavily up the stairs.

"I've been looking through her diary," I said.

"Well?"

"It's where she writes her arrangements, but the thing is—"

The phone rang in the living room again and I ran to it.

"Nina? This is DI Hammill."

Sudden hope blasted through me, and I could hardly stand up straight.

"Yes?"

"No news yet, I'm afraid, but we're very anxious to talk to your husband as soon as possible. Has he arrived yet?"

I called Rory, who came through and took the receiver. His face was chalky; there were beads of perspiration on his upper lip and forehead.

"Yes," he was saying. "Right. Of course." He put down the phone and turned to me. "I've got to go to the police station. They want me to make a statement." He gave a twisted little smile, barbed wire across his features. "Funny how they make a man feel guilty for being a father."

I waited. My insides were churning.

"It's just off Miller Street, right?"

"Right."

He hesitated, and I waited without speaking.

"See you, then," he said.

As soon as he closed the door, I took my mobile from its charger and dialled. I waited and a young voice answered: "Yes?"

"Jay? It's Nina."

"Have you found her yet?"

"No."

"The police called. They want to talk to me." He sounded scared. But, then, Rory was scared of the police too.

"They're talking to everyone," I said. "Everyone who knows Charlie well. I wondered if I could come and see you."

"If you like." He paused. "I want to help."

"Good. I'll come to the farm, shall I?"

"OK." Another slight pause. "Don't tell my dad what it's about, though."

"I'll fetch my car and be with you in a few minutes. Five or ten at the most."

"I'll wait by the barns. You don't need to go all the way to the house."

"All right."

First I had to sort out Jackson. Rory was at the police station and it was clear that I couldn't leave him with Renata any more. She needed looking after herself. I didn't want to take him with me, to hear about Charlie's sex life, but I didn't want to leave him alone. He was eleven years old and very frightened.

I rang Bonnie's house, in case she had come home early from her Christmas shopping, but there was only an answering-machine. I tried Sandy's parents, although I knew Jackson and Sandy had fallen out over some playground football game recently. My qualms were irrelevant. There was no answer. It was nearly Christmas. Everyone was out, shopping, collecting Christmas trees, visiting grandparents, waiting in airports for their flights to the sun.

I went to Jackson's bedroom. It was cold because I had turned off the heating. I hadn't thought we'd be needing it until January. He was standing by the window, looking out at the sea. His shoulders were hunched and when he turned to me his face was pale and stunned.

"Honey, I've got to go out and I think you should come with me. Grab your jacket, will you?"

Wordlessly, he followed me down the stairs and pushed his arms into it.

"We've got to get my car. I left it by the newsagent's."

He nodded and we left. The wind was like iron. The sky had turned white and low. As if snow might fall, I thought. I held on to Jackson's cold hand and hurried him along. Occasionally I said things like "It's all right, darling," and "We'll find her." I remembered that he hadn't had anything to eat.

In The Street I took Jackson into the bakery. There wasn't an impressive selection of food—pasties and pies that looked scarily industrial. I turned to him. "Do you want a cheese roll or a ham roll?"

"Don't mind."

They were only a pound. I bought one of each. I tried to remember when I had last eaten and couldn't. At the party? I didn't know. Back out on the street, I handed the cheese roll to Jackson, then I peeled back the polythene from the other and took a bite. The bread was doughy, damp. The ham didn't taste of anything. I struggled to chew and swallow it. It didn't matter: I just needed to get something into my body so I wouldn't fall over or faint later. I took Jackson's free hand and stepped over the road towards the car. Somewhere close there was a screech of brakes and tyres. Everything slowed down and I had time to find what was about to happen weirdly, foully comic. My daughter was missing, I was running around like a lunatic, and in the middle of it all my son and I were about to be run over. Charlie would be missing and Jackson and I would be in hospital. The idea was almost restful. Somebody else could take control.

But we weren't run over. I swung round, Jackson behind me, and saw the grey bonnet of a car that had come to a halt just inches in front of me. Steam was rising through the grille as if the car itself was angry with me. I couldn't see the driver because of the shifting reflections on the windscreen, but the vehicle was familiar. I walked round and was greeted by Rick's shocked face. He wound down the window.

"I . . . er . . . Are you all right?" he said, looking really shaken.

As if I hadn't put him through enough already today. "I'm so sorry," I said. "I'm not thinking properly. I walked out without looking. It's completely my fault. I'm so sorry."

There was a sound of a car horn behind Rick. A queue was building up. A man got out of one of the cars. His hair was cropped so closely that you could see the skin underneath. He was wearing combat trousers and a green flak jacket.

"All right! All right!" I yelled.

"Fucking bitch!" he shouted. "Get the fuck out of the way."

I was briefly tempted to continue the row. Perhaps even start a fight. It would have been something to do with the fire burning inside me. But instead I looked at my son beside me and at Rick, and I swallowed my anger. It took an effort but I did it. "Sorry," I said to the man. "We'll get out of the way."

I asked Rick if he could pull in to the kerb. I said

I needed to talk. He restarted his stalled car and parked outside the café.

"How's Karen?" I asked.

He rubbed his eyes. I couldn't tell if he was just exhausted or holding back tears. "She's fast asleep," he said. "They gave her some strong medication. She needs to rest. She was drunk at your house. I'm sorry."

"It doesn't matter."

"Yes, it does."

"Is she in the hospital?"

"Yes," he said. "They didn't want her to be moved. It'll be a couple of days at least."

"Is anyone with her?"

"Eamonn said he'd pop in. For what it's worth. Children, eh?"

"What are you doing now?" I asked.

"Nothing much," he said. "I've got a couple of fairly unimportant things to get on with. I might as well pass the time. There's not much else I can do. But what am I thinking, going on like this? Have you heard anything about Charlie?"

"She's still missing," I said.

"What? Haven't you heard anything?"

"Nothing."

"Are you sure she hasn't gone off with a friend? I'm afraid she's that age."

"That's what I thought at first. But we found her bike and her bag. She'd been delivering papers."

"Oh, my God," Rick said. He stared at me, shocked. "That's awful. Have you called the police?"

"Yes, of course. They've started interviewing people. I'm not sure they've got the proper sense of urgency."

"I'm so sorry," he said. "I've been taken up with Karen. But if there's anything at all I can do, Nina, you know you only have to ask."

A thought struck me. I glanced down at Jackson, who was gnawing his cheese roll and looking bored. He knew Rick well and was comfortable with him. "There is something," I said. "I've got to go and talk to someone who knows Charlie. It's desperately urgent. Could you take Jackson for a few minutes while I do it? I've tried other people but . . ."

"Oh . . ." said Rick. He glanced at his watch— nearly a quarter to four. I could see he was already regretting his impulsive offer. At any other time, on any other day, I would have let him off but I was merciless.

"Please, Rick. It would be the most enormous help."

"I, erm . . ."

"Give me your mobile number and I'll ring you as soon as I've seen . . . er, this person. It'll be twenty minutes, half an hour tops. You know I wouldn't ask unless it was important."

Rick gave a sigh. My car. My party. And now my son.

"All right," he said. "Come on, Jackson. Out of the cold with you."

Jackson hopped into the back seat quite cheerfully. He was probably glad to be away from me. I tapped the number of Rick's mobile into my phone and they drove away. I could see Jackson talking and making gestures and Rick looking stoical, his face blank. I got into the car but before I started it, I sat for a few moments, not thinking but settling my thoughts, trying to cool down. If there was going to be any point at all to this, I had to think clearly. Otherwise I was wasting everybody's time. A few deep breaths. Then I turned the key in the ignition. The engine hiccuped loudly and stalled. I tried again. This time the hiccup was brief.

"No," I said. "Please don't."

I turned the key again and there was a faint click. Then nothing.

I leaped out and ran to the corner to see if by any wonderful chance Rick and Jackson were still in sight. I was in time to see the car turning away.

I ran back and tried again. The car was not going to start. I picked up my mobile. Rory was still at the police station; Renata was weeping in my bed; Christian was stuck on the M25, probably for the rest of his life; Bonnie was out Christmas shopping; Rick was in his car with my son. My heart sank. Maybe I should try Joel: he'd come, unless it was Alix who answered.

Then I had another thought.

"Hi."

"Jay, it's Nina. Listen, I'm in town, just near the newsagent's, and was about to drive over to you but my car won't start. I don't suppose there's any chance of you coming here? Do you drive?"

"A motorbike," he said.

"Can you come, then?"

"Why not?" he said. "Give me a minute or so."

"Thanks."

Another wait. I sat in the wretched car and drummed my fingers on the steering-wheel. I turned the key in the lock a couple more times and heard the dead click. Then, coming down the road towards me, I saw Tom, the vicar. He was carrying a large shopping-bag and had a paper rolled up under his arm. He seemed to be talking to himself. Or maybe he was talking to God. He stopped by the car and I opened the door.

"Hello, Nina. I thought you'd be in Florida by now."

"Change of plan," I said wearily. I couldn't tell the story to another person.

"Is something up with your car?"

"Yes. When I most need it, it won't start."

"Shall I have a look?" He put his paper and shopping-bag on the passenger seat, leaned across me, without asking my permission, and pulled the lever that opened the bonnet. He tugged off his woollen gloves and bent over the engine, a look of pleasure on his face. Men and cars, I thought.

Then I heard a motorbike, which pulled up beside my car. Tom stood upright as a figure climbed off. A black helmet covered his head and face, and he lifted it off. I opened the door.

"Hello," he said.

"Do you want to sit in the car?" I said. "I've got something important to ask you. Things are looking serious. Bad."

"Bad," he repeated. "Bad with Charlie?"

"Yes."

He looked at me and then at Tom, whose head was back under the bonnet.

"Can we talk somewhere else? I feel kind of exposed. It's like a goldfish bowl in this place. Especially with him there."

"Everywhere's pretty public round here," I said.

He stared at me, then gave a sudden grin. "Why don't you hop on the back?" he said. "I'll take us somewhere private."

"On your bike?"

"Why not? Unless you're scared."

It sounded like a challenge. I looked at his thin, pale face; the green-grey eyes. This boy—or young man—was Charlie's secret life. He might know something, or everything, of what had happened. He might be an ordinary teenager or he might be violent and disturbed. I shrugged.

"Nothing scares me now, except what's happened to my daughter," I said, and climbed out of the car, slamming the door behind me. "But not too far. I don't have time." I turned to the vicar, who was trying but failing to hide his curiosity. "Tom," I said, "I don't have time to explain but I've got to go now. It's been very kind of you to try to help."

"But I've hardly begun."

"Never mind," I said. "It doesn't matter."

"I tell you what, if you leave me the car key, I'll tinker a bit more, shall I? It might be something simple."

"If you want," I said. "But you don't need to, you know."

"I like mending things."

I pulled the key off the key-ring and passed it to him, then turned back to Jay. "Let's go, then."

"There's a spare helmet in there," he said, pointing behind the seat. I took it out and put it on, adjusting the chin-strap and pulling down the visor. I swung my leg up and over and straddled the seat behind him.

"Put your feet on those bars," he said. I did so. "And put your arms round my waist." I did. "Go with the bike," he instructed me. "Don't try to counterbalance it. Relax." He turned his head. "Not how I'd imagined my first meeting with you," he said, and pulled down his visor.

One minute we were by the pavement, the next we were roaring along The Street, so fast that the road melted to a grey river beneath me and the houses blurred. As we accelerated round the corner and headed east, we seemed almost to be lying flat against the surface, like our own shadow. I could have reached out my right hand and flayed the skin off my knuckles. The muscles in my cheeks dissolved and my stomach turned to liquid. For a few seconds, I wasn't thinking of Charlie, only of dying. Then the bike straightened again; the world righted itself. Past the boatyards and the caravan site, past the beach where dinghies were turned turtle on the sand, past the beach huts. Houses petering out, the road narrowing.

I held on to Jay, leaned as the bike leaned. Charlie had done this, I thought. She had sat up here and put her arms round this young man's waist, laid her cheek against the black leather of his jacket as the world ripped by. Then she had come home to me and said nothing about it.

"This'll do," he said, and we stopped on a track that led from the coastal road down to the shoreline. Behind us lay the town, with its shops, cafés, roads, cars and people. In front was a lonely wilderness of scrubland, marshes and borrow dikes, leading to the open sea. Small waves slapped and hissed against the diminishing stretch of mud. This was a side of Sandling Island that I loved and that scared me. It felt as though Jay and I were the only people in this whole flat grey world, where you couldn't tell where water ended and sky began. The wind scoured my face as I pulled off the helmet. I swung myself down and found that my legs were trembling.

"You didn't do badly," he said, pulling off his own helmet.

"Charlie is missing," I said. "It's getting worse and worse. Worse with every minute that passes. The police are asking questions but I can't sit at home. I'm going to ask you questions that no mother should ever ask her daughter's boyfriend." He gazed at me impassively. It was difficult to be anything but impassive in that wind. I could feel my own face stiffening. "It doesn't matter what you say. I'm not going to judge you. I don't care any more. I don't care what you two got up to together. I don't care that you kept it from me. I want to find Charlie. That's all. Then everything will be forgotten."

He stared out to sea and I stared at his face, looking for something, some kind of sign. A small tremor
passed over it, like wind across water.

"I want to help find her," he said. "Of course I do.
I'm sure she'll turn up. There'll be a reason. People
don't just disappear."

Do you know? I thought. Was it you? "First off,
you have to tell me if there's anything you know that
could help me. Do you know where she is?"

"No." His eyes were steady.

"You swear it."

"If you like. I swear."

"All right, are you Charlie's boyfriend?"

"You could call it that."

"How long has it been going on?"

"About four, five months. Since the summer."

Such a long time, I thought. So many days of keeping it from me, of deceiving me, of pretending she
was somewhere else. I thought of all the little things
that Charlie confided—and she'd held this back.

"Why didn't she tell me?"

"I don't know. It was between us. We liked it secret. Things change when they're public. It felt . . ."
He stopped.

"Yes?"

"We just liked it like that. Adults think they can
tell you what to do, they think they can remember
what it's like to be young. We didn't want that."

"Was it serious?"

"Serious?"

"Yes. Were you a couple?" I put my hand on my
stomach with a gasp for I had realized I was talking

about it in the past tense. "Do you love her? Does she love you?"

"Love?"

"Oh, fuck this, Jay! Don't you understand she might be in terrible danger?"

"We don't say 'love.'"

"What do you say?"

His face flamed. "Stuff," he said. "You know."

"Drugs?" I asked.

"Not really."

"Don't piss around."

"Dope. Nothing much else. Ecstasy once but she didn't like it."

"Did she tell you anything secret, anything that might be a clue?"

He ground the toe of his biker's boot into the ground. "This is weird."

"What did she tell you?"

"She talked about her father a bit."

"Go on."

"She didn't like it, the way he doted on her so much. She said it wasn't fair on Jackson and it gave her the creeps a bit. She didn't like to discuss it with you because . . . well, you know, you're her mother, it would be too weird."

"But nothing specific?" I said.

"Like . . . ?"

"Like he was sexually abusing her," I said, loud and clear. "For instance."

He winced. "No." He paused, then said, "But she did tell me that she thought all older men were perverts."

"Why? Why did she think that?"

"I don't know. At the time, it just seemed like one of her wild statements. You know what she's like. She often said things like that."

"Were you having sex?"

He mumbled something.

"I know you were, Jay, but I need you to tell me."

"How do you know?"

"Charlie was scared she was pregnant."

It was as if I'd slapped him. "What?"

"She'd missed her period."

"No," he said.

"Didn't you use a condom?"

"We didn't . . . we weren't . . ."

"I think this might be to do with her being pregnant, or worrying that she might be pregnant. So I need to know."

"We haven't."

"Haven't what?"

"Haven't had sex," he mumbled.

"I don't believe you."

"That's up to you." He raised his chin defiantly and glared at me. There were splodges of pink on his pale cheeks. "It's true."

"You're telling me you've never had sex?"

"Not as such."

"What does that mean?"

"You know."

"Tell me."

I wanted to slap him across the face, punch him in his leather-protected stomach.

The wind whipped his hair across his face and his

eyes gleamed green. He clenched his fists and, for a moment, I thought he would hit me. "It means that whatever else we've done together—*you know* what that means—I haven't had full sex with your daughter. OK?"

"That can't be true."

He shrugged and turned to the sea. "Whatever," he said.

"Do you promise?"

"Promise? Promise, swear, cross my heart hope to die. If I was lying, I'd still promise I was telling the truth, wouldn't I? She wanted to go on the pill first."

I thought of Alix, Charlie's doctor. "So is she on the pill?"

"She didn't say."

Maybe those crosses in the diary meant something different, I thought. Perhaps I was on the wrong track. "But if you're telling me the truth, why did she think she was pregnant?"

"You'd have to ask her that. Sorry, sorry, I know. I didn't mean that. Look, I don't know. Maybe . . ."

"Maybe what?"

"I don't know."

"What aren't you telling me?"

"Fucking hell."

"Tell me. Tell me what you're thinking."

"She had a one-night stand a few weeks ago."

"Who with?"

"I don't know."

"Who do you think?"

"I mean it. I don't know. You think if you go on

asking the same bloody question over and over again, I'll eventually give you the answer. She didn't say. She just said she'd done something she regretted and hated herself for it and would I forgive her."

"And you did?"

"It was like her revenge."

"You mean you'd done the same?"

"That's really not your business, is it?"

"When did she do this?"

"A few weeks ago."

"When?" I persisted.

He thought for a moment. "Towards the end of last month. I don't know the exact date. She didn't tell me. I was away in France on my exchange. She told me when I got back."

I was making calculations in my head. The last cross in her diary had been on 9 November, so Charlie's one-night stand had been about two weeks after that. Which would make her almost a couple of weeks late with her period now.

"I see," I said.

"Any other questions?"

"What else don't I know?" I asked despairingly. "If I didn't know about you, there might be all sorts of other things I didn't know as well. I thought I knew her inside out and suddenly she's turned into this mystery. Like a stranger to me. I don't know who she is."

"She says she's close to you," said Jay. "She says you let her be who she is. Not like her dad. She was going to tell you about us when you were in Florida. That's what she said, anyway."

"I just want to find her," I said. "If you've done anything to her, I swear—"

"No."

"Where did you two meet?"

"All sorts of places. On the mainland. Sometimes at my place when no one was there, and in Dad's barns. Or the hulks, though we haven't been there for a week or so. Too cold in this weather."

"You mean those old boats near the point?"

"Yeah."

He smiled, and my skin prickled. I felt cold as ice, and scared.

"Nobody goes there," he went on, "they're too creepy. But me and Charlie like them that way."

The hulks were a collection of houseboats and barges that had seen better days. They'd originally been lived in by artists and sixties' hippies. I'd seen photographs of them when they were new in the tiny library by the bookshop. Some were small, with square cabins and round wheels at the back, although they never moved away from the shore and at low tide were stranded in the mud. Some were large, and on their decks there were dogs chained to the sides, flowers in pots, chairs and tables, even ironic garden gnomes. They were made of iron and wood, painted in primary colours, and had gangplanks leading to the broad wooden jetties. I think they even used to have their own postbox. Rick had told me that on one of the barges, the couple had made pots to sell in the café; another made nut roasts, bean salads, carrot cakes.

That was then. It had been many years since the

boats had been lived in. The hippies and artists had moved away, the paint had peeled from the rusting, blistered hulls; the gangways had collapsed as the boats tipped from their moorings towards the green-grey mud on which they stood. Years of rain and wind had blasted through the cabins. Vandals had done the rest, thrown stones through the windows, ripped off steering-wheels and torn out seats, beds and tables, painted graffiti on the sodden decks, tipped rubbish into the holds. I'd walked past them a few times with Sludge, but even on a bright summer day they gave me the shivers.

"Take me there now," I said.

"What for?" He looked at me as if I was mad.

"If they're a private hiding-place for you and Charlie, she might have gone there."

"I don't want to."

"I haven't got a car, remember. You're going to have to take me back on your bike anyway. I want you to come with me."

"You won't find anything. You're wasting your time."

"Then let's get it over with."

"It's stupid."

I pulled on the helmet and fastened the chin-strap. Still he didn't move. I stared at him. "Is there something you're not telling me?"

"Course not."

"Let's go, then."

Without another word, he put on his helmet and started the bike. I climbed on behind him and put my arms round his waist. I tried to think: where had

Charlie been, that last week of November? I couldn't remember. The land blurred past me, I smelt the briny air. There had been a party she'd gone to with Ashleigh, and I'd collected them at midnight, but she'd seemed fine, hadn't she? Hadn't she? I remembered her getting into the car in her tiny grey skirt, her long legs in their ankle boots, her shining coil of hair. I closed my eyes as the wind whipped past me.

T he last time I had walked past the hulks it had been with Christian, in early October. I remembered it clearly, a sharp autumn day. The tide had been low then and the hulks lay in a massed huddle on the mud. There'd been dozens of noisy, cheerful gulls perched on the smashed decks. Now, the tide was high and vicious little waves riffled round the hulls. The wind hummed among the ripped planks. There must have been eight or nine. One of the iron barges had been set on fire since I'd last been there, and now was a charred wreck.

"Which one?" I asked Jay, as I dismounted.

"What?" He seemed dazed; his face looked bruised in the chill air.

"Which boat did you and Charlie go to? Jay?"

At my sharp tone, he stared round as if he'd never been there before, then jerked his head. "That one there."

He was indicating one of the smaller wooden boats, which had to be reached by climbing over the larger boat nearer the shore; in its better days it had obviously been bottle-green. In the gloom I could see there were still small scabs of paint flaking from its side, and the trapdoor leading to the cabin had been ripped from its hinges. It listed slightly in the rising tide.

I dropped the helmet beside the bike. "You go first."

"You want to go inside?"

"Why do you think we're here?"

He placed his own helmet carefully on the seat of his bike. "If this is what you want."

We had to walk along a gangway to get to the first boat. The wood was slimy and often broken, and several times I thought we would slither into the shallow water that was lapping over the mudflats. I clambered on to the deck after Jay and made my way across to the other side, avoiding broken plant pots, a bent and rusted bicycle wheel, the dry carcass of a gull and an empty wine bottle. We climbed on to the wooden boat.

"Charlie?" I called, as I climbed across. "Charlie, are you there? It's me. Nina. Mum. It's Mummy."

My voice echoed, bouncing off all the grimy surfaces, winding its way down into the boat's dismal interior.

I called again, louder.

I made my way across to the cabin's splintered entrance and turned backwards to lower myself down the broken rungs of the narrow ladder that led into the cabin. The air was cold and clammy, and smelt of ammonia and tobacco. Everything inside seemed greasy, ancient, abandoned. The mattresses lying across the benches had foam spilling from their split surfaces; the ceiling was damp and soiled. A blanket lay on the floor.

"Here? You came here?"

Jay, peering in from the deck, gave a little grimace.

"It was OK," he said. "Especially in the summer. Sometimes we brought beer. Charlie even brought hot chocolate in a flask sometimes."

So that was where my flask had gone.

I pushed open the door into a foul-smelling toilet. I pulled open the cupboard doors. "Charlie?" I called again, although I knew she wasn't there. The place was rank with loneliness and neglect.

"Enough?" asked Jay.

"I want to see all the others," I said.

"You what?"

"Now we're here I want to look inside the others."

"What for?"

"For Charlie."

"She's not here."

"It'll only take a minute."

When we came back outside, the search didn't look entirely possible. The next boat along had tipped over and brought its neighbour down with it. The two were splayed over in the mud and the rising water, their gangways shattered.

"You can't get into those," said Jay.

"Charlie could have walked across the mud."

"There'd be tracks."

"The tide would have worn them away."

"There's nothing there," said Jay. "They're broken and rotten. Who would come here?"

"You came here."

"It was a place to get away to," said Jay. "It's a small island."

I walked on. The next boat was a huge barge that looked as if it had been rebuilt by a madman. A junkyard of chaotic objects—planks, tin baths, paint pots, fence panels, sheets of corrugated iron, car tyres—had been nailed and bolted to the boat's upper level. The gangplank across was rickety and vertiginous and swayed when I stepped on to it.

"It doesn't look safe," said Jay.

"You're the teenager," I said. "I should be the one saying that to you."

It was little more than a plank, with no railings, so I stretched my arms out like a tightrope walker and teetered across. Once I was on what passed for the deck I found a half-open doorway, which led into the darkness below. I saw the slow shifting glint of stagnant water beneath. There was a smell of seaweed and decay. I took a deep breath and eased myself down a few steps. I looked around and saw that there was nothing I needed to bother with. I climbed back up quickly, gasping in the cold air as if I had been under water.

"I'll have to go soon," said Jay, shifting uneasily.

"I'm almost done," I said, when I was back on land. The last of the hulks was almost respectable by comparison with its neighbours. Its hull seemed intact. I could imagine its early existence as a working vessel, transporting coal or whatever it was from the deep-water ships into the estuary. Whoever had converted it into a houseboat, a generation or two ago, had done a skilful job. The windows were smashed, the roof was falling in and the tin chimney had toppled across the deck but enough survived to suggest what had drawn people here to the far side of the island, wild, distant and isolated. With a fire in the grate and a storm raging outside, this boat would have been a cosy refuge.

As I drew closer to the gangplank, I stopped.

"Look," I said.

"What?" said Jay, coming closer.

I pointed at the path, which was churned up and muddy. "Someone's been here," I said.

Jay seemed doubtful. "Maybe," he said. "People come with their dogs."

"But look," I said, pointing at the dirty gangplank. Jay shrugged. "Someone's been here." I began to shout Charlie's name and that there was nothing to worry about, I just wanted to see her, but it was lost in the wind. Nobody apart from Jay could have heard anything.

"I'll just walk across and check it out," I said. "Then you can drop me back."

"You want me to look with you?"

I went across the gangplank and stood on the deck. I felt high and exposed in the wind, almost as if I was out at sea. I turned to Jay. His mouth was moving but I couldn't hear what he was saying. I held up a finger to convey that I would only be a minute. I turned and tried to find a way inside. It wasn't very nautical, more like a dinky wooden shack built on top of the barge. There were small windows. I couldn't tell whether they were opaque or whether it was just dark inside. I walked round the deck until I found the little door. I turned the brass handle and it opened inwards. I stepped inside and then I felt many things at the same time. It was as if I had stepped off a precipice and was falling. There was a flashing inside my head, a buzzing. Tears prickled behind my eyes. My whole body was very hot, then ice cold, then hot again. At the same time I was able to remain calm and precise. I stepped back outside and waved my hand at Jay in a fiercely urgent gesture. I shouted something, which I knew he wouldn't hear.

Because what I had seen when I stepped inside that cabin, projecting out of the shadows, was the naked foot and leg of a girl. I took several deep breaths. Not that any of it mattered now. It was all for nothing. But, still, life would continue, the world would go on, things would take their course. More deep breaths. Don't cry. Don't be sick. This was the last thing I could do for my baby, for Charlie. One more deep breath and I stepped back inside. At first I looked away.

"Charlie," I said faintly, but I knew it was hopeless. There was a white, waxy stillness to the foot and the leg that was as dead as the wood it was lying on. I swallowed and made myself turn round and look at the foot with its grubby sole. "Charlie," I said again, moving closer and feeling my eyes grow accustomed to the darkness. I made myself approach.

And then, once again, a jolt and the feeling that the floor had disappeared beneath me, and there in that hulk on the edge of Sandling Island I stood and stared at the body of a young girl. With entire calmness, I walked back out on to the deck, took my phone from my pocket and clicked the number of the police station. A voice answered. I didn't know who it was. It didn't matter.

"This is Nina," I said.

"Who?" said the voice.

"You know," I said. "Nina." For a moment I couldn't remember my second name. "Landry. Nina Landry. I'm at the hulks on the south-east of the island. I've found the body of a young girl."

The voice said something. Static in my ear.

"No," I said. "No. It's the body of a young girl but it's not my daughter. It's someone else. She has white skin and straight dark hair and she doesn't look like Charlie in any way at all except that she's about the same age. I don't recognize her. I'm going to stay here now and wait until you come."

There was a blue milk crate on the deck and I sat down on it and spoke to the God in whom I don't believe and I said sorry to him and implored him for forgiveness. Because at the moment I had looked down at that girl's face with her blank dead eyes I had felt a rush of happiness that it wasn't Charlie, as if a life had been snatched away from me and then restored. I thought of another mother somewhere. Had she been doing what I had been doing? Had she been searching for her daughter? What would she have thought if she knew that her daughter's body had been found by a woman and that that woman's first emotion had been relief and thankfulness?

As the tide rose steadily, slapping against the hull

of the boat where I sat, the light was failing. They only had to come from the station and would be here very soon, a few minutes at most. In the meantime, I had to watch over a dead girl in this twilit world. The flat, bleak landscape around me was shrouded in an indeterminate grey; all colours had faded and it was scarcely possible to make out where the sea ended and the solid ground began. I wondered what the dead girl's name was, and who had left her there. A cold, ghastly dread settled on me so that I could barely move or even breathe. For a few moments, I had somehow let myself think that because this corpse was not Charlie's, my daughter was safe, as if a life had been traded for hers. But, of course, it was unlikely she had simply died in there. Someone had killed her. I thought of her puffy face and blue lips. Someone had strangled her.

Jay was trying to light a cigarette. He had his back turned to the wind and his fingers were cupped round the flame of each match he struck. Was his hand trembling? I watched him for a few seconds, then stood up and called his name. He didn't hear: the wind wiped away my words. Eventually I left the deck and crossed the narrow gangplank towards him. I called his name sharply.

He spun round as if I'd slapped him. He tossed away another spent match and tucked the unlit cigarette behind his ear. "Are you done?"

"I've found something."

The features didn't move but his face changed: his green eyes seemed to darken, the muscles round his mouth to tighten.

"To do with Charlie?" he asked, after a beat.

"I've found a body," I said bluntly. Again, I watched his expression. His face paled. He lifted a hand to cover his mouth but stopped it half-way, so that he stood for a moment in a gesture like a frozen salute, or as if he was warding me off, stopping me coming any closer. I stood quite still and waited, not taking my eyes off his face.

"Is it Charlie?" he asked at last, in a voice that broke, so he started the question a young man and ended it still a boy.

"No."

His hand made it to his mouth. He closed his eyes and I noticed his long lashes. "But . . ." he said, and stopped. Then he sprang into activity, fumbling urgently at his jacket for his phone with quivering fingers. "We've got to call the police."

"I've called them," I said. "They'll be here any minute. Before they arrive, I want you to come and see if you know her."

"Her?"

"The girl who's in there."

"Girl? You want me to . . . ?"

"Yes."

"No."

"You might know her."

"No," he said again. "I can't do that."

"Just one quick look."

"I want to go now. I've done everything I can. This isn't right."

"It's all right. She looks as if she's sleeping, that's all," I lied.

"Why do you want me to do that? What's wrong with you?"

I held him by the forearm and tugged him towards the gangplank. "I'll go first. You follow."

"I want to go home," he said. "I don't feel good at all. I want to help find Charlie, but this is sick."

"Wait till I'm across before you get on, otherwise we'll both fall in."

I walked steadily across, arms akimbo, and at the other side turned to him.

Jay mounted the plank. His face was screwed up as if he was about to cry and his arms flapped as he fought for balance. Just before he got to me he slipped and stumbled. His foot shot out and for a few seconds he wavered in the air, arms flailing. He half fell, catching himself so that he lay along the plank, legs dangling, cheek pressed into the slimy wood. He lifted himself carefully and crouched, staring at me. His eyes looked like black holes in his mud-streaked, pale face. His black leather jacket was smeared with an unlovely grey and his biker boots were scummy.

"Here," I said briskly, reaching out to him. "Just a few more inches."

He put his thin, cold hand into mine. I yanked him towards me and he clambered on to the deck.

"She's in here," I said.

I pulled my sleeve over my hand, pushed the cabin door and went in. I heard Jay behind me, his breathing coming in great gasps. I crouched beside the girl.

"We mustn't touch her," I said, although I wanted

to. I wanted to stroke her long black hair and her waxy white cheek. I saw that there were dark red marks on her throat, like violent bruises.

There was a noise behind me, like a door creaking open after decades of disuse, and a shadow fell over her empty face. Jay was bent double in the opening to the cabin, one hand pressed into his stomach. His mouth was half open and out of it came a strange, rusty groaning.

"Just one look," I said. "Do you know her? Jay?"

He brought up his face in a sharp jerk and stared wildly.

"No," he managed, then turned away from me and ran across the deck. I heard vomiting. I took a last look at the girl, lying so still in the dimness of the cabin: her long white legs, her full breasts, her uncurled hand with the bangle on its wrist, her dark hair, her open eyes staring at me, through me, beyond me. I held my breath.

I turned away and went out into the icy air to join Jay, who was crouched by the side of the boat, holding on to its railings and staring out to sea. He shrank away as I approached him.

"Here," I said, handing him a tissue from my pocket. He took it and pressed it to his mouth. His eyes were bloodshot and his hair damp against his forehead.

"I've never seen a dead body before."

"You're quite sure you didn't know her?"

He closed his eyes. "Yes."

"Here are the police, anyway. Two cars."

"What happened to her?"

"I don't know," I said, thinking of the red marks on her throat, her blue lips.

"Can I go home now?"

"They'll want to talk to you as well. You'd better ring your parents, tell them what's happening."

"Yeah," he said, but made no move.

I stood by the gangplank and raised my hands as the cars approached, their headlights cutting into the gathering darkness. "This way," I called as DI Hammill got out, followed by Andrea Beck and, from the second car, Mahoney and a small, balding man I hadn't seen before but who was already pulling on white gloves.

They walked towards me over the scrubland in the grey winter dusk, four figures in thick jackets and stout shoes. They cast an air of grim professional seriousness, all affability and comfort gone. No one said anything, and I could hear only the wind in the bushes, the waves foaming over the mud and grit of the shore and the menacing shriek of gulls. DI Hammill walked calmly across the gangplank, his skinny body upright and unwavering; DC Beck tottered more uncertainly behind him. They both wore white plastic covers on their feet.

"Will you two wait on the shore, please?" Hammill asked. "I'll be with you shortly."

In the distance I saw another set of headlights making its way towards us. All four police officers were on the deck now. One by one, they bowed their heads and entered the cabin. I thought of the girl lying there, gazing at them sightlessly as they bent over her, and shivered violently.

I opened my mobile, and selected a number, watching the scene in front of me all the while.

"Ashleigh?"

"Nina? Have you found her?"

"No, but—"

"What can have happened?" she said, in a wail. "What do you—"

"That's what I'm trying to find out," I said.

"Did you talk to Laura?"

"Yes. Listen, I need to ask you something."

"Yes? What is it? Oh, and my mum says if there's anything she can do to help you're to tell her. She says she's sure it will turn out to be—"

"A few weeks ago, you and Charlie went to a party."

"I dunno, we often go to parties or—"

"This one was towards the end of November. Jay was away on an exchange and the two of you went together. Remember?"

"I think so. I wouldn't know about the date, though."

"Whose party was it?"

"Rosie's. Rosie and her older brother, Graham."

"Where do they live?"

"Next door but one to the pub on Sheldrake Road."

"Were you with Charlie most of the evening?"

"On and off."

"Who was she with?"

A shadow fell across me. Jay was standing beside

me, listening. I half turned away from him, but was conscious of him there.

"With?"

"Yes."

"You mean, like, a boy?"

"Yes. Tell me."

"I wasn't around her all evening."

"You were with someone yourself?" I could hear my voice: cool, crisp, bossy, brutal.

"This isn't really . . . No, I wasn't."

"Ashleigh, I swear this doesn't matter to me, not a scrap. I just want—I *need*—to know who Charlie might have been with that evening."

"I think there was someone," she mumbled. "Or maybe there was. But I don't know who. Charlie didn't say. I'd tell you if I did know, honestly. You have to believe me. But the thing is, I wasn't with her most of the time. I was a bit—you know—I'd had a bit to drink, and then it was very crowded and dark, with these strobe lights and a disco. Lots of dancing and people jostling each other and laughing and shouting things at each other. It got a bit out of hand. A bit scary. Rosie was in floods of tears and saying how her father was going to have a fit when he saw the mess. Charlie kind of disappeared on me. I don't know where she went. But she was all upset afterwards. Really upset, crying and stuff. She never cries. I'm the one who cries and she comforts me. She had to go and wash her face and try to get calm before you came to collect us."

"What did she tell you?"

DI Hammill had reappeared on the deck. He

stood quite still, with his head thrown back as if he was breathing in the briny air.

"She said she'd gone and ruined everything."

"And you can't even guess who she was with?"

"I told you, I don't know. I pestered her to tell me at first but she went all silent and scowly. I thought she'd tell me in her own time, if she wanted."

"So who'd know?"

"About what happened?"

"Yes."

"Maybe Graham. Rosie's brother. He was sniggering about it a few days later, and said something about her taste in men getting weirder, or worse or something, and Charlie turned on him. She was really wild with him. I thought she was going to hit him."

"Thanks," I said.

"What's it about?" said Ashleigh. "Why do you want to know?"

"She didn't say she was worried about anything in particular, did she?"

"I don't think so." Her voice rose in panic. "I don't know. She's my best friend. I've let her down. I should know how to find her and I don't."

"No," I said wearily. "You shouldn't feel like that."

"She'll be all right, though, won't she? Nina?"

"Yes," I said. My voice cracked, so I said it again, louder and firmer. "Yes. And you're being very helpful."

I watched as DI Hammill walked towards me, but in the gloom I couldn't make out his expression. I started to go towards him but all of a sudden my body felt as heavy as a block of granite. Every blundering step took a huge effort. I looked at the hulk and thought of the body inside, then back at Hammill, who was removing the plastic bags from his feet.

"Well?" I asked, as he stood up.

He ignored me and turned to Jay. "You're Charlotte's boyfriend?"

Jay nodded. His face was blotchy and scared. There were tears in his eyes.

"The constable there"—he nodded at Mahoney, who was now coming towards us—"will take you to the station, where you will make a statement. All right?"

Jay nodded again.

"Have you called your parents?"

He shook his head.

"Why don't you do that at once?" he said. "Tell them to come to the station and meet you there. They'll be present while you give the statement."

Then he turned towards me. "Come with me," he said, and walked towards his car.

As we approached it, we were joined by Andrea Beck, who leaned towards DI Hammill and whispered something in his ear. I heard, "Brampton Ford," and saw Hammill nod. I repeated the name to myself for later: Brampton Ford. I'd never heard it.

"What?" I said. "Who is it? Who's the girl?"

"We'll talk in the car," Beck said. "It's cold. You've had a shock."

Had I? Was I in shock? I considered myself as if I were somebody else. I thought of my behaviour. Was it affecting my ability to do what I could for Charlie? That was all I cared about.

"I'm fine," I said, but she opened the back passenger door for me. I got in and she closed it. Hammill sat beside me with Beck in the driver's seat in front.

"Have you found out anything?" I asked immediately. "Who is it? Do you know? And do you know how she died?"

There was a pause.

"What the hell were you doing there?" Hammill asked, a new, hard tone in his voice.

"What do you mean?" I asked. "There's the body of a young girl over there. What does it matter why I was there?"

Another pause. When Hammill spoke it was with the care of a man taking great pains to remain calm.

"Ms. Landry. Your daughter is missing. We're conducting an urgent search for her. Now a girl of about your daughter's age has been found. And you are the person who found her. That seems strange to me."

"But who is she?" I asked again. "Do you know who she is? Is she from round here?"

"Things are getting serious," Hammill said.

"Serious," echoed Beck. "Very serious."

"They were always serious," I said.

"We've another body and—"

"What do you mean *another* body?" I said. "Have you given up hope of finding my daughter alive? She's only just gone missing."

"I didn't mean that."

"But you feel you're looking for a body?"

"It was a slip of the tongue. What I mean is that the fact we've found another girl may be connected."

"Do you think there's any possible doubt about it?"

"Stop this," said Hammill, abruptly. "What I'm starting to wonder is whether you're telling me everything you know. Because if you're not, I need to warn you that that would be a matter we would take very seriously indeed."

"Of course I am," I said. "This is my daughter we're talking about, as well as another poor girl who is someone else's daughter. I've been the one trying to get the police involved when they weren't interested."

"We're conducting the investigation. You should be at home letting us get on with it."

"I'm the one who found this body. I'm doing what you should have done. How dare you accuse me of concealing anything?"

"But that's my point," said Hammill. "How did you come to find it? What are you doing here?"

So I told them how I had contacted Jay and what we had talked about and how we had come over here. "I think it's a place where young people come and hang out," I said. "This is a small island. There aren't all that many places to get away from people without going on to the mainland. As soon as I saw the hulks, it seemed the natural place for someone to hide. Or for someone to hide a body, as it turned out."

Beck murmured something under her breath that I didn't catch.

"I don't believe this," said Hammill. "There are colleagues I know who would lock you up for what you're doing."

"What I'm doing?" I said, struggling to keep my

temper under control. "Haven't you heard? I'm a desperate mother looking for her daughter."

"Haven't you thought you might be making things worse for her? You're talking to witnesses who should be talking to us. You're contaminating the scene. That body in there may be our best chance of finding your daughter and you walked all round it."

"Contaminating the scene?" I said, incredulous. "The only reason you've even got a crime scene here is that I found it. What I feel is that we're wasting time sitting about. My head's spinning and I'm not sure what's going on but one thing is clear. Until half an hour ago, I knew my daughter was gone and I was still hoping against all the signs that she might have just run off as some sort of adolescent rebellion. What we now know is that a girl has been killed on this island and it feels . . . Oh, God, don't you understand how it feels to be sitting here in this warm car, not even driving, just sitting and watching the tide come in, and talking like this, when all the time Charlie may be out there, in danger, waiting to be rescued?" I pointed at the large watch on Andrea Beck's wrist. "Look," I said. "It's well after four. It's almost completely dark. It's freezing cold. Charlie's been gone for hours. Hours and hours. Every minute counts now, every second. And there's a dead girl. We have to hurry. We have to find her now. Don't you see? Please."

I stopped suddenly and waited for them to respond.

DI Hammill stroked his neat grey beard and stared out of the window. His eyes narrowed as if he was looking for something in the gloom. "I'm not sure what's happening here, Ms. Landry."

"We're trying to collate our information," said Beck, twisting round in the seat and blinking at me through her thick fringe. She spoke with a self-conscious importance, as if she was reciting something she'd recently learned from a textbook. "We're trying to define the boundaries of the inquiry and yet the boundaries keep altering. You see?" She ducked her head at me and turned back in her seat.

"Collate information," I said furiously, then regretted it. I needed them more than I had ever needed anyone in my life and this wasn't the time to try to score points. "I'm sorry. Sorry, sorry, sorry. I don't know what to do with myself. I just want to help."

"I'll be frank with you, Ms. Landry," Hammill said, "because I think that's what you want from us. In cases such as this, when a girl has disappeared, we talk to friends, and we search for mysterious vans that might have driven past, and we check the records for local sex offenders. But, guided by statistical probability, what we do overwhelmingly is talk to boyfriends, and, even more important than that, we talk to the family."

"I know that," I said. "That's why you're talking to Rory."

"He's at the station," said Hammill. "He's giving a statement as we speak."

"As long as it doesn't stop you searching elsewhere," I said.

"We want a full statement from you as well," he said.

"It seems to me," I said, "that what you want is to slow things down when what is needed is to speed them up."

"You can help us by coming to the station and giving a statement."

"I've given a statement. I've given two. There's nothing to say. I've said everything. I've said all I know. There's nothing I can tell you except this. My daughter's in danger and we've got to find her, and by taking another statement from me, you're letting the clock tick by and it's stupid. It's dangerous. It's wrong. I won't let you. You've got to find Charlie. You've just got to!"

"Let's go, Andrea," said DI Hammill. The young woman turned the key and the car rumbled away.

"This is insane," I said, pulled my mobile out of my pocket and dialled. "Hello," I said, when Rick answered. "It's me, Nina."

"Any news? Jackson and I were just—"

"No," I said shortly. "Listen, I can't fetch Jackson just now. I've got to go to the police station again."

"What for?"

I was going to mention the body, then realized it would demand explanation and another telling of my story. "Another statement," I said. "I'll be quick but I won't be picking Jackson up for a bit."

"But—"

"I really am grateful," I said. "Can I speak to Jackson?"

"Mummy?" His voice was small and hopeful. "Have you got Charlie yet?"

I swallowed hard and gripped the phone. "Not yet, darling. I won't be long. Either Dad or I will come and fetch you from Rick's soon, all right?"

"Dad's got my Game Boy in his car. I left it when we—"

I cut him off in plaintive midstream. "We'll bring it."

"I want it now."

"Jackson."

"I want my Game Boy. I'm bored here and I want my Game Boy."

"This isn't the right time, Jackson. You're going to have to be patient."

"She's ruined everything."

"What do you mean?"

"Charlie. She's always wrecking things for me. She's the one you care about. Just because she's the oldest and you and Dad worry about her. And now we can't go on holiday because she's run off. She just wants attention. You don't think about me, do you?"

"Darling—"

"I want my Game Boy."

"I'll get your Game Boy," I said. "I'll come and get you soon."

"Promise?"

"Promise."

"Children," said Beck, as we drew up outside the police station.

I glared at her back, feeling the strongest impulse to punch her in the neck. I curled my fists in my lap and tried to think only of the things I would have to do as soon as I left there. The first was to track down Rosie's brother and find out who Charlie had been with at the party. I frowned, forcing myself to concentrate, blocking out the terror, erasing the image of the dead girl from my mind. One step at a time, I told myself. The light thickened outside. A flake of snow fell on my cheek, and the wind hummed in the electric cables above us.

Behind us, Mahoney was also drawing up. Jay got out of the car. He seemed to have grown thinner and younger in the past hour.

"This way," said Beck. "Ms. Landry? You're going to have to wait in here until we're ready for you."

"Wait? I'm going to have to wait here?"

"Just a few minutes. Have you got anything to read?"

"Are you insane?"

"I know you're upset but there's no need—"

"I'm not going to wait. I've got to find Charlie."

"It won't be long."

"Charlie needs me."

"Ms. Landry." Blink. "What Charlie needs at this minute—"

Just then, Rory was shown out of a small side room, a uniformed police officer at his side. If Jay had grown younger, Rory had grown older. He was grimy and creased with exhaustion. His hair stuck up in greasy peaks. He was dragging his jacket along the floor and walked with a shuffling step.

"This way, sir," said the police officer, pointing to the toilets.

"What's going on?"

"They're making me feel guilty because I'm her father. What kind of world are we living in?" he said. "You believe me, don't you, Nina?"

I looked at his angry face. I thought of the creepy messages he'd sent Charlie. I couldn't think of anything to say.

"Sir," said the officer, holding open the toilet door.

"Nina?"

"I need something from your car," I said politely. "Jackson's Game Boy. He left it in there."

"Did you even hear what I said?"

"Keys," I said.

"Our daughter's missing, they're treating me like a criminal and you're going on about Jackson's Game Boy?"

"This way, Ms. Landry," said Beck.

"Just coming," I said. "Go ahead and I'll be with you in a minute." She sighed and went into the small waiting room. I glimpsed two chairs, and a low table with a large box of tissues on it. Probably a lot of weeping went on in this station. "Give me your keys," I said, holding out my hand to Rory. "You're parked outside, right?"

"I'll get it later."

"But—"

"I'll fucking get it later," he shouted, his face crimson with rage.

He dropped his jacket on the floor and shuffled through into the toilets. I picked it up, pulled out the key, and walked out of the station. It was heaving with activity, radios crackling, phones ringing, and nobody noticed me go. If I was going to have to wait, I could at least fulfil my promise to Jackson.

I'd spotted Rory's car when we arrived, parked a few yards down the road, one wheel on the kerb. I unlocked the driver's door and peered into the familiar messy interior: crisps packets, tapes with broken cases, sweet wrappers, torn road maps, an apple core, orange peel, an empty mug on its side with coffee stains round the rim, old newspapers, a plastic bag containing, when I looked inside, a pair of mucky trainers. No Game Boy. I felt under the seats.

"Ms. Landry."

Beck had followed me out of the station. I ignored her, wriggled out of the car and unlocked the boot. There was the usual stuff—a spare tyre, a single wellington boot, a coil of rope, a couple of spanners, a hessian sack. And a flash of colour in the corner. I reached over to investigate it. For a moment I thought I would be sick. I was feverish, icy, clammy. I bent double, seeing the ground loom queasily towards me. Then the world righted itself and I was standing upright again, beside Rory's car, holding Charlie's scarf.

It was pale blue, pink and silver, with tiny sequins sewn into it. We had seen it together when we were on holiday in Italy, eighteen months ago. She'd fallen in love with it and I had bought it for her secretly, and given it to her months later, for Christmas. She wore it all the time, round her neck, tying back her hair, wrapped round her head. She'd been wearing it when she walked out of the door last night, smiling back at me over her shoulder. The last time I had seen her. Now it was here, in the boot of Rory's car.

I plucked up the hessian sack and there, underneath it, was her leather shoulder-bag. I lifted it up with trembling fingers.

"Ms. Landry," said Beck, crossly, "can you come with me, please? DI Hammill is asking for you and he's—"

I wheeled round, holding the scarf and bag, and started to run. I think I may have been shouting something, but I don't know. I saw startled faces, mouths open, as I sped up the steps, into the station, past the reception desk. I hurtled up the corridor and threw open the door of the small interview room. Rory was sitting on one side of the desk, DI Hammill on the other. As if in slow motion, I saw the cup of coffee jump out of Rory's hand and slop in wide splashes round his chair. I saw his startled face and its expression changing as I brandished the scarf. I saw him half rise, and his mouth was open to say something but I took two strides across the space that separated us and, raising my fists, banged him violently back into his seat, the bag bumping against his chest. Then I leaned towards him and shouted so loudly that it hurt my throat: "Where is she?"

I felt myself being restrained and pulled back as if I were taking part in a pub brawl. I tried to wrestle free but the grip on me was too strong. I was held tight, then forced down on to a chair. I was breathing heavily. Everything around me was like a red fog. I couldn't identify people, or make out what was being said. Gradually I heard someone speaking my name and I thought of Charlie and made myself calm down. "I'm fine," I said. "You can let me go."

"What's the meaning of this?"

It was DI Hammill, astonished and angry.

"That," I said, pointing at the scarf and bag on the desk. "I went to get my son's Game Boy from the car. That was in the boot. Charlie's scarf and her bag. She had them with her when she went to the sleep-over yesterday. It's Rory."

Hammill and Beck both looked at him. His skin had turned beyond white to an awful blue, like that of a corpse.

"Mr. Oates," said Hammill, in a quiet voice, "do this scarf and this bag belong to your daughter?"

Rory dabbed at his lips with his tongue. "I'm sorry, Nina," he said.

"You bastard," I said.

He looked back at DI Hammill.

"Yes," he said. "They're Charlie's."

"Did you get them from her today?"

"Yes."

"Where is she?"

"I'm sorry," he said. "I'm so sorry. I don't know." He put his face on the desk and started to weep, a snotty wet howling in the silence of the room.

I felt a pain growing inside my chest and spreading through my body. If there had been a heavy object within reach, I would have grabbed it and smashed it into Rory's sobbing face. Into the face of the man I had once loved, the man I had married.

"Mr. Oates," said Hammill, "I want to give you another chance. I'm not sure that you recognize the seriousness of the situation."

"I do," he said miserably, raising his face from the desk. "Oh, God, I do."

"I don't mean for your daughter," said Hammill. "That goes without saying. I mean for you. Before we get on to other matters, do you admit to seeing your daughter today?"

"Yes."

"Has she been in your car?"

"Yes."

"What the—" I began, but Hammill quickly shut me up.

"Stay out of this, Ms. Landry," he said. "Try to restrain yourself." He picked up a chair and moved it closer to the desk behind which Rory was sitting. "Time is precious, Mr. Oates. Do you have any idea where your daughter might be now?"

"No."

"Where did you see her? And when?"

Rory gave me another glance. I could feel that my face was like a mask.

"Nina is taking our children on holiday," he said. "I was in the area this morning. I drove over because I wanted to see them for a moment and say good-bye."

"You mean," I said, in a quiet, almost strangled voice, "that when we talked on the phone this morning, you were on the island."

Rory continued as if I hadn't spoken. "When I drove into the town I met Charlie. She was doing her paper round. She sat in the car and we talked for a couple of minutes. She'd been on a sleepover and she left some things with me to save her the trouble of carrying them. In fact, it didn't look safe to me, carrying her own shoulder-bag as well as the bag of newspapers. And she looked a bit rough, not her usual self. I was going to drop them at the house later."

"What time was this?" asked DI Hammill.

"I'm not sure. About quarter to ten, something like that. It wasn't for long," he added.

"And where? Exactly."

"On Lost Road. It must have been fairly near the beginning of her paper round. Her bag was still quite full."

"What was her mood?"

"She was surprised to see me, but we had a fairly normal conversation. She mentioned the holiday."

"What did she say?"

Rory paused. "She said she was looking forward to it."

"Did she say anything else?" asked Hammill. "Did she mention plans for the day?"

"No. She said she had to get on with her paper round."

"Mr. Oates," said Hammill, a hard edge to his voice now, "Why on earth didn't you tell us this before?"

I saw Rory's jawline flex. His face had a sullen, expressionless quality that I remembered from the worst of the days before he left.

"It didn't seem relevant," he said. "I didn't have any new information to give. I met Charlie before she disappeared, obviously. And people saw her after that."

"Are you insane?" I said, aghast. "This is our daughter you're talking about. Are you out of your fucking head? Are you drunk? Is that it?"

Rory glanced at me and turned back to Hammill, as if in exasperation. "No," he said evenly. "I'm not drunk."

I looked at Hammill. "You don't believe this rubbish, do you?"

Hammill frowned. His entire face furrowed. "Mr. Oates, I'm inclined to agree with your ex-wife. I cannot understand why you didn't tell us you had met your daughter."

"It didn't make any difference," Rory said, almost in a mumble.

"It *did* make a difference, though," said Beck. "One witness told us that she saw Charlie talking to a man while she was doing her paper round. We've been searching for this man. It now seems that he was you."

"You need to explain yourself," said Hammill.

Rory crossed his arms hard over his chest, as if he were shutting the rest of the world out. "I'm not sure if this is the time or the place, but Nina has probably said things about me to you. She's certainly said them to me over the phone today. She's clearly suspected me of having something to do with Charlotte running off. That's the opinion she has of me."

"So?" asked Hammill, bluntly.

"I've had some difficulties recently," said Rory. "Business difficulties mainly. And my ex-wife has used these problems as a weapon to separate me from my children."

"Rory," I said, "I can't believe that we're having this discussion while Charlie's somewhere out there, maybe dead, maybe alive. Yes, you're right, you've had terrible problems. You had some sort of breakdown, you have a serious drink problem and you behaved in a way with the children that made me think you weren't safe to be with them. Can we discuss this at a later date?"

"I was trying to explain why I hadn't told you or the police about meeting Charlie." He looked pleadingly at Hammill. "Nina's been threatening me with some sort of restraining order. It would stop me seeing Charlie and Jackson. When I came to see them this morning, I was breaking our agreement. I couldn't stop myself. I had to see my children before they went away. I wouldn't see them at Christmas. But I was worried that if Nina found out about it, she would start proceedings against me. I'm sorry, I panicked."

"This is all rubbish," I said. "Haven't you got it into your completely self-centred thick skull that something terrible has happened to Charlie? Do you expect us to believe that, with what's going on, you were still thinking about a dispute over visiting arrangements?"

"I'm sorry," he said. "I didn't think it would do any harm."

I felt darkness descending round me. "Harm?" I said. "Maybe we'll never know about that."

"Stop all this," said Hammill. "We are where we are. We have to deal with it."

"You mean you're satisfied with this cock-and-bull story?" I said furiously.

"And you're not?" said Hammill.

I leaned forward in my chair and put my face into my hands. Suddenly I felt so miserable that I didn't want to speak. I didn't even want to think. When I finally spoke, I felt as if I was trying to walk while dragging a heavy weight. "I don't know," I said. "Rory didn't say anything until I found Charlie's stuff in his car. If I hadn't found it, he still wouldn't have admitted meeting her. Why should we suddenly believe him now?"

"What are you suggesting?" shouted Rory, violently, rising out of his chair. "What are you fucking suggesting, Nina? You think I'm a murderer? A pervert? You think that?"

"I'm saying that—" But I stopped and pressed my fingers against my temple. "Hang on a minute," I said. "There's something wrong about this."

"Nina, Ms. Landry—"

"No, *listen*. This is important." I pointed a finger at Rory. "You talked to me at half past ten. I remember Karen telling Eamonn that was the time just before you rang."

"What's your point?" asked DI Hammill.

"You're telling us you saw her at about a quarter to ten and then at half past ten you rang asking if you could see her."

"Mr. Oates?" said Hammill. His face was stern, grim.

"I was upset," Rory mumbled. "Everything felt wrong. She didn't really seem to care that I'd driven all that way to see her. She was just excited about going on holiday with Nina and this new boyfriend. It made me upset. I wanted to see her for more than a few snatched minutes sitting in my car. I wanted to see her properly, and Jackson, like a family."

"What were you doing between approximately ten and half past?" asked Beck. I'd almost forgotten she was in the room with us.

"I had some beer in the car," said Rory. "I drove to the causeway and I was going to go home but then I stopped at the lay-by and walked along the marshes and had a bit of a drink. I was thinking. What? Don't look at me like that. It's true. I know what it sounds like, but it's true."

"Where's Charlie? Where is she?"

"I love her," he shouted. "She's my daughter, for fuck's sake."

"Stop this, both of you," said Hammill. "This is a mess. It's my fault for having you in the room together."

"What are you talking about?" My voice cracked. "If I hadn't found Charlie's things in Rory's car, you'd be wasting your time with him lying to you. If he's not going to admit the truth, you've got to get a move on."

"No," said Hammill. "Wait. There's a lot we need to get straight. I'm not clear about the involvement of you and that young man, the boyfriend, in the finding of the body. And it seems to me that there is a good deal that needs to be established about the involvement of you and your ex-husband. I agree that we need a full account of his movements this morning. But I also need to know more about the dispute over the children between you and Mr. Oates."

"No," I said. "That's a diversion. I've told you all you need to know about that. Of course you need to know Rory's full story. And you need to find out if she was pregnant." I saw the spasm of shock on Rory's face. "And who by. It's urgent. You don't need to speak to me. You need to get on with the search. Everything I know I've told you. Everything. I've hidden nothing. Just find Charlie. It's urgent. Please."

"Excuse me, Ms. Landry," said Hammill, "but for now I'd like you to leave me to decide what's urgent. At the moment the danger is to be distracted by a single clue, which may be irrelevant or misleading. What's important is to get the whole picture clear. So, what I propose to do is to take a full and detailed statement from Mr. Oates here." He looked at Rory sharply. "And I mean complete. I can tell you that there is a possibility of charges being brought against you. This means we will now be interviewing you under caution. It means we have grounds for believing that an offence has been committed. Therefore I have to give you certain warnings. That the interview will be tape-recorded, that you are not under arrest, that you are free to leave the interview at any time and that you may seek legal advice at any time. Do you understand?"

"Yes," said Rory.

"Do you wish legal representation?"

There was a pause. Was it possible that Rory was going to hold up the proceedings while a solicitor was rustled up from somewhere? I could see that he was considering it.

"No," Hammill said finally. "I just want to help."

He turned to me. "I want you to wait outside. We'll take your statement as soon as we have finished with Mr. Oates."

"I've been giving statements all day. I've told you, there's nothing left to say."

"However, I believe that there's a great deal more we need to know from you," he said. "Please. The quicker you co-operate, the more effective we can be."

He nodded at Beck who escorted me out and along the corridor into the office, where a WPC was talking on the phone. Beck asked me if she could get me tea or coffee. I said no automatically, then changed my mind. I needed something to put into my body, like a car taking on fuel. I tried to think which was more powerful, more like a drug.

"Coffee, please."

It was from a percolator in the corner of the office, so it came instantly. I added milk from the little plastic tub, then tore open two packets of sugar and emptied them into the cup. Beck said she would join me again in a minute, then left. I saw that a young uniformed constable was standing outside the room, presumably to keep an eye on me.

I gulped the coffee, which seared my mouth. I was grateful for the jolt that the pain gave me. It helped to clear my mind.

I had to think of what I could do, all the while holding in my mind the knowledge that what I did might be useless, a frenzy of activity in the wrong place. I wasn't sure what to make of Rory, whether he was criminally stupid or guilty of something monstrous. But now he was with the police and there was nothing more I could do, I had to assume it wasn't Rory and consider other possibilities.

I thought about the dead girl, pictured her silent face and sightless, open eyes. I remembered how Beck had whispered something into Hammill's ear as she came from the boat where the dead girl lay. Brampton Ford. What was it? A name? A place? I saw that a stub of a pencil lay on the floor in the corner. I picked it up and pulled a tissue out of the box. In large, clumsy letters, trying not to shred the tissue, I made a list:

Dead girl. Who?
Brampton Ford?
Knew Charlie? If so, how?
Pregnant? Who?
Rosie and Graham (by pub on Sheldrake Road)

I stared at the words, making up my mind, steadying myself, then pushed the tissue into my pocket. I swilled back the last of the coffee, stood up and crossed to the window. I tried to pull it open, but it was locked. I thought of the young constable standing outside the room, and of Beck returning any minute. I pulled open the door.

"Can I help you?"

"Where are the toilets?"

"Just down there, to the left."

"Thanks."

I went inside, had a pee, swilled cold water over my face and wiped it dry with paper towels. Then I walked past the desk once more, trying to appear relaxed and purposeful. No sign of Beck. I nodded and smiled at the officer on duty, who was on the phone.

"Back soon," I mouthed at him, and tapped meaninglessly at my wrist, where my watch should have been. He glanced at me, then away again. I walked out into the street, into the cold dusk, almost tripping over a cat that shot past my feet in a silent black streak. I didn't run until I turned the corner, out of sight of the station. Then I took a deep breath and sprinted as fast as I could past the school, the church, into Lady Somerset Road and then took a left and immediate right on to Sheldrake Road.

Ashleigh had said that Rosie and Graham lived next door but one to the pub that was at the other end of Sheldrake Road. I had a stitch in my side and my legs felt heavy when I arrived at the Barrow Arms, which had a huge inflated reindeer outside the front door, and a garish Christmas tree in the large bay window. The lights inside were all on and I could hear laughter through its closed doors.

Next door but one to the pub was a pink, pebble-dashed house that looked bare and exposed, as if it belonged somewhere else but had been abandoned there. The curtains were drawn and lights were on, both upstairs and down. That was a good sign.

I rang the doorbell and stood, panting, while I waited for someone to answer.

"Hello?" The fattest man I'd ever seen stood in

the doorway, looking as if he was about to burst through it. He had sad brown eyes, like Sludge's when she's being told off.

I tried to smile at him. "Sorry to bother you," I said. "Could I speak to Graham or Rosie?"

"Rosie's not here. Graham's around. Who shall I say it is?" he asked politely.

"He won't know me. I'm Nina Landry. Tell him I'm Charlie's mother, Charlie Landry Oates, and I need his help. It's urgent." Slowly he turned his bulk on the patterned carpet. I saw he was wearing no shoes, just socks, and his feet were tiny. "Really urgent," I added.

"Graham," he called up the stairs. "Graham, a lady to see you. She says it's urgent." Over his shoulder he asked me to come in and I followed him down the hallway and into a warm living room where a bar fire glowed in the corner. On every shelf, there were massed armies of tiny, brightly painted warriors and strange creatures.

"Graham and I painted them together," he said, following my gaze. I had the awful feeling that he was settling down for a conversation. "After his mother died. It was something to take his mind off things. There's three different armies there. Over two thousand of them."

"Amazing," I said. "Is Graham coming?"

"He doesn't play with them now, of course. He hardly even talks to me. They get like that as they grow up. He's on his way down. Are you all right? Can I take your jacket? Get you a cup of tea?"

"I'm all right. No tea, thanks. I'll keep my jacket

on, I won't be a moment. I just need to talk to your son."

"Has he done anything?"

"No. I need to find something out."

"Hi, you wanted to talk to me?"

I turned towards the young man. He was tall and slim, with the brown eyes of his father, who might once have resembled him before he became sad and fat.

"I'm Charlie Landry Oates's mother, Nina."

"Yes?"

"She came to a party here."

"Yeah, that one time." He cast an amused, contemptuous glance at his father. "You were away."

"A party?" said his father. "Here?"

Graham made a dismissive gesture.

"You should have told me," his father said.

"We cleared up, didn't we?"

"Yes, but—"

"Can I ask you one thing?" I interrupted. "Then I'll go."

"Right. This lady doesn't want to hear you complaining. She's come to talk to me."

"Do you want me to leave?" asked his father.

"It doesn't matter," I said.

"Yes," said Graham.

His father struggled to his feet. "Are you sure I can't get you tea?" he asked.

"Quite sure."

"I'll leave you two together, then. Let me know if—"

"Thanks."

"Right," said Graham. "That's him out of the way."

"I want to know who Charlie was with that evening."

"You mean who she got off with?"

"Yes." I gritted my teeth and stared at him. "That's what I mean."

"Why would you ask me something like that? And why would you think I'd tell you? It was a party. People were with other people. That's what happens at a party." He gave a shrug. "I don't want to get into all of this."

"Charlie's missing," I said. "She's in danger."

"Missing? I wouldn't worry too much. She's a cool one. I'm sure she can look after herself."

I thought about kneeing him hard in the groin to wipe the smile off his face. "She's been snatched. The police are involved. She's in danger and every minute counts. Whoever she was with at your party might be involved. So, tell me."

"Right, right." He raised his hands in mock surrender. "But tell her I tried to stop you."

There was something obscene about talking to this jerk about Charlie, let alone her sex life. I was far off all acceptable limits of behaviour, in a nasty fog of perversity. I locked my fingers together and squeezed them hard so they hurt. "Who?" I said.

He spoke slowly, taking pleasure in it. "If you really want to know, it was that Goth boy. The teacher's kid."

I opened my mouth but no sound came out.

"You know. The weirdo. Eamonn. The one with the ponytail and black nails."

"Eamonn and Charlie? You're sure?"

"Oh, yes." He gave a horrible suppressed snigger. "Quite sure."

I closed my eyes. I saw Eamonn's face at the party as he asked after Charlie. His expression, which I'd read as one of furtive supplication but now saw as something different. Lust? Triumph? Fear?

"Thanks," I managed.

"You asked."

"Say goodbye to your father, will you? I'll let myself out."

He watched me go, amusement on his face. Everything seems like comedy to someone.

I shut the front door before the vast, mournful father could accost me, and walked back down the street. I felt cold, damp, slightly sick. The road stretched out interminably and my feet slapped heavily along its surface. A car drove by with undipped headlights, dazzling me and splashing water from puddles over my legs.

Eamonn and Charlie. Charlie and Eamonn. He was a Goth, a clever, lonely boy flooded by dark, troubled thoughts. I'd always liked him, felt sorry for him, but now, with no difficulty at all, I could imagine him as someone who would harm my daughter. Him, Rory, Jay. My mobile rang in my pocket. I pulled it out and looked at the number. No one I knew. I guessed Hammill or Beck was wondering where I was, ordering me to report back to the station, like a schoolgirl caught truanting. I let it ring. A flashing symbol on the screen announced that the battery level was low. I saw that there were two messages and listened to them. The first was from Jackson, who must have left it before I talked to him in the police car, and the second from Christian, saying he was out of the snarl-up at last, but the traffic was still crawling along at walking pace and it would probably take him another couple of hours before he could be with me. He told me he loved me. He'd never said that before, and now it meant nothing. Words were of no use to me.

I had to find Eamonn. I didn't have his mobile number, nor did I know any of his friends. I'd have to ring Rick. The screen on my mobile went blank. I pressed the on button and nothing happened. I shook it furiously and pressed the button once more. Nothing. The battery had run out. I'd have to go there.

Sheldrake Road wasn't far from Karen and Rick's house, although as I jogged along the unlit street, gasping for breath, it felt impossibly far. I raced past Miller Street and on to the Saltings; the road ran along the shoreline. On my left there were houses with lights glowing through drawn curtains, smoke rising out of chimneys, on my right the dark, lapping water. The tide was nearly up now. I could hear little waves rattling against the shingle.

The lights were still on in Rick's house, but when I rang the doorbell and banged furiously with the knocker, no one came. I banged again, then stood back and yelled their names. My voice echoed over the water behind me. There was no response. I faced the water. I could see the lights of the mainland to my right, where the causeway was. Opposite me was the army range, empty, silent and bare.

Maybe, I thought, Eamonn was in the pub. I retraced my footsteps towards Graham and Rosie's house, and pushed open the door of the Barrow Arms, squinting in the smoky brightness. People lifted their heads to stare at me, but I ignored them and gazed around, trying to see Eamonn.

"Looking for someone special, love?" called a voice from a corner. There was a splutter of laughter around him.

"Eamonn," I said. "Eamonn Blythe."

"Never heard of him."

"The Goth."

"You've come to the wrong place."

I backed out. There was another pub in the town, near to Rory's restaurant that never was. I could try there. I knew it was hopeless. I knew Eamonn wouldn't be there, that I wasn't going to find him like this, but I didn't know what else to do and I had to do something. This time I ran all the way down Sheldrake Road to Tinker's Yard, where old boats were turned belly-up beneath rotting tarpaulins, and rusting trailers stood in a skeletal line along the fence. Past the restaurant, with its boarded-up windows and old sign flapping in the wind, and into the second pub. It was smaller and dingier than the Barrow Arms, cracked orange lights draped round the bar and an ancient dog lying in front of the jukebox. Eamonn wasn't in the front room. I went to the back, where four youths with shaved heads and tattoos on

their bare arms were playing pool in a fug of cigarette smoke, and asked if they'd seen him.

"Who?"

"Eamonn Blythe."

"Never heard of him."

"He's got long hair in a ponytail and usually
wears black clothes. You'd remember if you'd seen
him."

"The Goth? He never comes in here. He wouldn't
dare."

The boys smirked at each other and turned away.

"Thanks," I said miserably.

I stood outside in the icy darkness, thinking. If I
couldn't find Eamonn, I had to concentrate on finding
out who the dead girl was. I turned and walked along
the seafront, past the old restaurant once more, past
Tinker's Yard and the boatyard, where the massed
shapes of boats drawn up for the winter stood, and to
my front door. The house was dark, its windows like
blind eyes.

In the gloom, I fumbled the key into the lock, and
as I pulled the door open Sludge shot forward and
banged into my legs, nearly bringing me to my
knees. Her pink tongue slavered at my hands and she
jumped up, putting her paws on my chest, all smelly
fur and hot mouth and shining eyes. Had she been
fed? I couldn't remember. My memory for such
things had stopped working. Sludge's behaviour
was no clue to this. She always behaved as if she was
hungry. If food was put in front of her, she would always eat it. If any food of any description was put
on any surface that was accessible to her, and there

was no one in the room to restrain her, she would eat that too. I had lost entire meals to her. On Jackson's previous birthday she had eaten half of the cake. I might as well give her something.

As I brought her inside I saw an envelope on the mat. I picked it up and felt something heavy inside, like a large coin. I tore it open. It was my car key and there was a note with it from Tom the vicar: "Dear Nina, The terminals just needed a wipe. Buy me a drink some time. Cheers! Tom." I took that to mean my car was functional once more.

I picked up Sludge's feeding bowl and she started quivering and pirouetting, giving a strangled excited yowl. I flung some dried dog food into the bowl, scattering most on to the floor, and put it down for her. She ate it all in a few seconds. I filled the bowl with cold water and she drank that with huge laps of her long pink tongue.

I plugged my phone into the charger and a little digital plug on the screen winked at me.

I thought of seeing Eamonn that morning, wandering sleepily out while his father was trying to fix my car. Eamonn and Charlie. Eamonn and my little girl. I tried not to think about them together and so, inevitably, that was all I could think about. My daughter had been living in the house with me, talking to me, eating meals and doing her homework, and meanwhile everything important in her life had been happening elsewhere in a world I knew nothing about. Her boyfriend and her betrayal of her boyfriend, if that was what it was, and then her fears of being pregnant, and then . . . And then what?

She had been living in my house like a double agent, maintaining her cover. She had told me nothing. Was it that she didn't trust me? Or didn't respect me? Or was it that I was an adult?

I took the list from my pocket and flattened it out on the kitchen table. Brampton Ford. I opened the cupboard that contained telephone directories, maps and holiday guides. I found an old road atlas and looked it up. It was a village further down the coast but a few miles inland. So she was from nearby but not near enough to walk or cycle. I had an idea. I ran upstairs. Before entering Charlie's room, I opened the door to my own bedroom. It was dark but I couldn't hear Renata's breathing and neither, when I went to the bed, was there a submerged hump there. I turned on the light and saw she had gone. No case, no clothes, no Renata. Then I saw a scribbled note on the pillow: "I was only in the way," it read. "I'll be in touch. Rxxx."

Charlie's bedroom was like an orange from which I had extracted the juice but which I kept squeezing and squeezing to see if there was any left. But in truth the problem was the opposite. There was a Niagara Falls of juice and what I had to do was find something I could use. There was so much data, so many clues, so much information that I could lose myself in.

I sat at Charlie's laptop and went to Google. I typed "Brampton Ford." This was hopeless. There were a quarter of a million entries. It turned out that there was a Brampton Ford in Australia. It had a squash team that had been promoted to the third division of a league in New South Wales. There was a car dealership in Canada. There were also entries for every time "Ford" and "Brampton" appeared in the same entry.

Charlie had been good at searches. What would she have done? I looked at the list. I drew a circle round Brampton Ford. What would the sort of information I need consist of? Nobody knew yet that the girl was dead, but her body had to have lain there for a few days. I added the words "girl" and "missing" and pressed search again. I knew instantly that I had found what I was looking for: "Local school-girl, Olivia Mullen, 16, has been missing since . . ." I clicked on the link. It was a series of short items on a news report from the south-east of England. "Local schoolgirl, Olivia Mullen, 16, has been missing since 12 December, when she failed to return from a shopping expedition at the Coulsdon Green centre. At a press conference, her parents, Steven and Linda Mullen, made an emotional appeal for information."

Steven and Linda. Two people who had been waiting for their daughter, as I had. Had they been told yet? Two uniformed officers on their doorstep with undertakers' expressions. Some time today or tomorrow they would have a last look at her for identification purposes. When would I next see Charlie's face? Would she be lying under a sheet? I had to push thoughts like these away because they would drive me mad, but they kept forcing themselves into my mind.

Olivia Mullen. It provoked a distant, elusive memory. Olivia Mullen. Livia Mullen. Livvie Mullen. Liv

Mullen. Li Mullen. I knew that name. I went through
my memory, looking for it as if it were a book in a library, eliminating section after section. I'd never met
her. The names of her parents meant nothing to me. I
said the name aloud to myself: "Olivia Mullen. Liv
Mullen. Liv." I was sure. I had never heard her name
spoken. So I had seen it printed. No, not printed. Written. In handwriting. Where would I have seen a girl's
name written out by hand? It could only have been
here in Charlie's room. I made an effort of searching
my memory that was almost physical, that hurt, as if I
were pushing my hand into a tiny dark space for
something that was just out of reach. It was on a letter
or a postcard. I was sure of it. No problem. Charlie's
bedroom was now my special sphere of knowledge. I
was the world expert. Charlie kept her letters in the
bottom two right-hand drawers of her desk.

I pulled them all the way out, one by one, and
tipped them on to the floor in a large pile. One by
one I scanned them. Words and phrases leaped out
of the page at me, confidences, revelations, gossip,
betrayals, judgements, descriptions, denunciations.
Secrets, other worlds. Some of them, in stiff, halting
English, were from Charlie's French-exchange student. None of it mattered. I was just scanning for
names, running my forefinger down the middle of
the page, moving the letters to another pile when I
had found no mention of Li or Livia or Olivia. There
were names I knew and names I had never heard of.
How had Charlie made time for all these people?
And me as well? The pile shrank and then I was at

the end and I almost howled. I had found nothing. But I was right. I knew I was right.

I started pulling out the other drawers and tipping the contents on to the floor. I rummaged through them, looking for a letter or a card I might have missed but there was nothing. In this one lonely respect, Charlie had been organized. She might have lived in chaos but it was an organized chaos. The letters and cards she received went into those drawers and nowhere else.

Except for one other place. Charlie had spent much of the last few months working on her coursework for her art GCSE. This consisted of a bulky, Byzantine scrapbook full of drawings, text and pictures. There were images downloaded from the Internet, cut from magazines. And postcards. It was probably Charlie's most precious possession. She had expended so much time, thought and imagination on it. I sat at her desk and began to flick through it, ripping out postcards and checking the text on the back. In some cases I had to rip the whole page apart to get at a card that was part of an interlocking whole. I felt as if I was pulling pages out of an ornate medieval Bible. Suddenly I thought of what would happen if there had been a simple misunderstanding and Charlie was to walk through the door and see me destroying her coursework and that must have been the closest I came to laughing in all of that terrible day, and it wasn't very close.

And then I saw it, and knew immediately, without having to turn it over to see the writing. It was a picture, sub-Impressionist in style, of a row of beach huts, in pastel colours: blues and yellows, greens and pinks. A cross had been drawn on one in ballpoint pen and the single word "Remember?" written perkily beside it. I peeled off the card and turned it over. That was it. She wrote in a large, beautifully formed schoolgirl handwriting: "And being blown over in the wind? And the wettest wetsuit in the world. Sorry for silence. Computer down. Yeah, you're right. Gonna finish it. Don't know why I ever let it start. See soon. Luv Liv."

That was what I'd remembered. The funny salutation, like a tongue-twister from the Dr. Seuss books I used to read to Charlie and then Jackson: "Luv Liv." I stared at the words until they blurred. "Gonna finish it. Don't know why I ever let it start." What did that mean? Finish what? Finish with whom? For a moment I wondered if I was right to connect the Liv of the postcard with the Olivia I had seen lying in the abandoned hulk. Was I just like someone looking at clouds and seeing shapes that weren't anywhere except in my imagination? But I put the thought away. I felt instinctively certain that Liv was Olivia Mullen, and that Olivia Mullen was the girl I had found dead in the hulk.

Charlie had known Olivia. Olivia had disappeared; she had been killed at the hulks where Charlie used to go with Jay. Perhaps Olivia had gone there to finish "it," whatever "it" was. Whom had she met there? And now Charlie had disappeared too and . . . The thought rose in my throat, choking me. I jumped up and ran downstairs, catching my foot half-way in my hurry and twisting my ankle. Somewhere, far off in the distance called normality, I felt a sharp, searing pain. I reached the phone and dialled the number for the police station from memory. When a woman answered I cut her off half-way through and said I would like to speak to DI Hammill or DC Beck, at once, now, an emergency. To do with the dead girl, I added, to make them hurry.

It did make them hurry. In less than thirty seconds, Beck was on the phone.

"It's Nina," I said.

"Nina—Ms Landry—would you please come to the station immediately," she said, trying to inject authority into her voice. "DI Hammill is not at all pleased that you disappeared. Well, actually, I've never seen him so furious. He's usually very calm even when things are going wrong. I'd hate to be in your shoes right now. He's talking about an—"

"Never mind all of that now. I have some important information for you. Charlie was a friend of Olivia Mullen."

"Olivia Mullen? But how do you know? What makes you think—"

"I don't have time to explain. I know who the dead girl is and I know that Charlie knew her. There's a postcard from Olivia to Charlie that I've just found."

"But—"

I heard a voice and the rattle of the receiver being seized.

"Is that her? Let me take it. Give it to me now." Beck was right. DI Hammill sounded very cross indeed. "Ms. Landry, I am warning you that if you don't come to the police station this instant—and I mean this instant—there will be serious consequences."

"Shut up!" I shouted over him. "Charlie knew Olivia Mullen."

"How do you know?"

"There's a postcard from Olivia to her. I've just found it. And it has a picture of beach huts on it. That may be important."

"Ms. Landry." He was shouting too, hard and fierce. "Your behaviour is improper. It is inappropriate and it may be dangerous. You may be putting your daughter at greater risk because of it."

"Did you hear? They knew each other. This is what she said: 'And being blown over in the wind? And the wettest wetsuit in the world. Sorry for silence. Computer down. Yeah, you're right. Gonna finish it. Don't know why I ever let it start. See soon. Luv Liv.'"

"*Ms. Landry!*"

"Did you get that? She was going to end an affair or something. And she knew Charlie."

"I'm sending a police car to collect you. Do you understand? And if you're not there . . ."

I put the phone down. I shut my eyes and pressed my fingers to my temples, trying to think. Olivia and Charlie were friends. How were they friends? I didn't think I'd ever heard Charlie speak about her and I'd never seen her myself. Who would tell me? Ashleigh? I picked up the phone and dialled Ashleigh's mobile.

"Hello, Ash—"

"Did Charlie know someone called Olivia Mullen?"

"What? Olivia? I don't know. She didn't say. Maybe, but you know Charlie has all these different compartments in her life and she kind of keeps them separate, so there's school and then—"

I cut her off, and stood holding the receiver, keeping the police calls at bay. A nasty little thought sneaked into my brain. Who would know? Olivia's parents, of course. But Olivia's parents probably didn't yet know that their daughter was dead. I couldn't call them. That would be unforgivable. Yes, I could. I could do anything, however terrible, if it meant that it helped me find Charlie. I could ring up the parents of a girl whose body had just been found and ask them questions. It was a brutal thing to do, but I didn't care. I could save my guilt and my pity for later. I didn't have time for it now.

I dialled 118118 and an operator asked me what number I was looking for. "Mullen," I said. "Steven Mullen, from Brampton Ford."

There was a pause.

"I have the number here," said the operator. "Shall I put you straight through?"

"Yes," I said. My heart was thumping so loudly I felt she must be able to hear it at the other end of the line.

An automated voice came on, giving me the number, which I didn't write down, and saying that the remainder of the call would cost ninepence a minute. Then there was a ringing tone. Then there was a voice.

"Yes?" The woman sounded quavery and breathless. I knew at once it was the mother, and that she hadn't heard yet about her daughter. I knew she was sitting in the house, waiting for the phone to ring, and every time it rang she would snatch it up and say, with that same breathless anxiety, "Yes?," thinking it might be Olivia, or someone ringing about Olivia. I knew exactly the sickening dread and the choking hope she was feeling. I knew all that and still I pressed on. Did that make me a monster? Yes.

"Is that Linda Mullen?"

"Speaking."

"Mrs. Mullen, this is Detective Constable Andrea Beck," I said.

"Olivia?" The question came out in a gasp, as if someone had punched her in the stomach.

"There's no news as yet," I said. "I just wanted to ask you a question."

"Yes?" This time the voice was flat and dull.

"Do you know if she ever went to Sandling Island?"

"Sandling Island? Yes, yes, she did. I think I told that other detective she—"

"That's fine. It's just something we're checking. Can you tell me why she was there, and when? The exact dates, please?"

"She went on a five-day windsurfing course."

Charlie had done the windsurfing course. I remembered her at the end of each day, her hair streaked and bleached by sun, sand and salt, her skin gritty and golden.

"She had a wonderful time, made friends with some other teenagers there. She came back all

tanned and glowing," continued Linda Mullen. "She
wanted to go again next year." There was a tiny sob
at the end of the line. "Um, sorry—when? Hang on,
I've got my diary here, I can check the exact dates."
There was a rustling of pages. "Here: Monday the
ninth through to Friday the thirteenth of August."

"Thank you," I said.

"Why? Is there something you've found?"

"One last thing: did she ever mention a girl called
Charlie. Charlotte Landry Oates?"

"Charlie? Yes, she really liked her. There's a
postcard from . . . Hold on. There's someone ringing at the door. I won't be a minute. I'll just see
who it is."

Now she was walking across a tiled floor. I could
hear her feet clipping, her breath still coming down
the line. There was the sound of a door opening.
"Hello," she said, to whoever was there. Then her
voice changed. "What? What is it?"

I banged the phone down and pressed my forehead against the wall. There was sweat running
down my face, and I felt sick with shame.

But I had no time for that. The police would be
here at any minute. I picked up the car key and my
charging mobile, and ran out of the door, banging it
shut behind me. As I ran, my ankle throbbed and my
head throbbed and the blood in my veins banged and
the wind howled against my sore eyes, which were
straining in the gloom to see where I was going, and
the waves crashed on the shore, sucking and slapping
against the shingle. I tried to think. Ideas, fragments

of thoughts, bounced around in my head, splintered against my skull. Charlie and Olivia had met at a windsurfing course last summer. And who had taught them? Well, among other people, Joel. Bloody Joel. The man who'd held me in his arms and told me he loved me.

I ran up The Street towards my car, praying it would work. A police car passed me and I put my head down, hoping they wouldn't see me. Music and light spilled out from the pub. I reached the car, fumbled the key into the door, flung myself into the driver's seat. There was a newspaper on the front seat folded up in a roll. It must have been left by Tom the vicar because on a white space he had written, in large capital letters, "Service ME!" I think he meant the car. I put the key into the ignition and turned it. The engine coughed and rasped, then started. One day I'd buy the vicar his drink.

I plugged in my mobile, then swung the car out and accelerated into a racing-driver's start. Past Tinker's Yard, right on to Lee Close, left on The Street, then on to Flat Lane.

I screeched to a halt outside Joel's house, leaped from the car and hobbled up to the front door, where I leaned on the bell, banging with my other fist. When the door swung open, I almost fell into the hall, stumbling upright to see Alix staring at me in a kind of angry astonishment. I could see Tam's frightened face through the banisters.

"Where's Joel?" I shouted into Alix's face.

"What on earth—"

"Where's Joel?" I repeated, even louder. I saw her eyes narrow, her face pinch.

"He's at the back. He's just come in and is about to take a shower. I really don't see why—"

I barged past her, my muddy feet slapping on the floor. "Joel!" I yelled. "Joel!"

"Nina!" He came out of the utility room, still in his work clothes, although his shirt was half unbuttoned and his boots were off. "What on earth . . . ?"

"Olivia Mullen," I said, advancing on him with Alix behind me.

"What?"

"Olivia Mullen? Did you teach her windsurfing in the summer?"

"Hang on." He put one hand on my shoulder to steady me and I twitched it off. "Calm down and tell me what's going on. You haven't found Charlie?"

"I don't have time for all of that. Olivia Mullen. I think her friends called her Liv. She was knocking around with Charlie."

"I don't remember her."

"You must do."

"Nina, I'm telling you that—"

"She was there from August the ninth to the thirteenth."

He stopped and thought for a moment. "For what it's worth, I was off that week."

"You weren't," said Alix, coldly, from behind him.

"I was."

"Where were you, then?" said Alix. "Off with some woman?"

"Mum?"

Tam was standing in the doorway. Her eyes were red and her face was puffy. "Mum?"

"Don't worry," said Alix, not turning. "I'll be with you in a minute. Wait upstairs."

"I don't believe you," I said. I glared at Joel and his eyes were cold and steady on me.

"I don't want to wait upstairs."

"I don't care what you believe," he said. "It happens to be the truth. I don't know what this is all about anyway. What's this Olivia got to do with Charlie disappearing, and what makes you think that I'm in any way involved? If you're suggesting that I had anything to do with her disappearance then I'd like you to come out with it." For a moment his face was taut with anger, then his expression softened. He took a step forward so his face was now just a few inches above mine. I could see the stubble, the pinpricks of sweat on his forehead, the tiny veins in his irises, the little pulse at his temple. "Look, Nina, I know how desperate you are about Charlie. It's every parent's nightmare, and if there's any way I can help you, any way at all, I will, but you should know who your friends are." Alix gave a loud snort behind us but I paid no attention. "I'm your friend," he continued. "And you can trust me—"

"Right. Give me that," I said, pointing at the large wooden mallet that was protruding from his toolbag.

"What on earth do you want it for?"

"Never mind," I said, and bent down to pick it up. Its heaviness surprised me.

"She's gone mad," said Alix.

"Maybe. Maybe not. I need a powerful torch."

"I'm calling the police," said Alix.

"There's one in the bag," said Joel. "Here."

"This is insane."

I walked past them all and out of the front door, carrying the mallet in one hand. I was huge and strong with despair.

I climbed into my car, and as I was about to pull away, the passenger door opened.

"Nina."

"I don't have time," I said.

He got in and shut the door. "I'll come with you, then. Wherever it is you're going. I'm not leaving you like this."

I shrugged and moved off, out of the corner of my eye seeing him wince at the sudden speed.

"I don't know Olivia Mullen, whoever she is."

"That's what you say," I said.

"You have to believe me, Nina. How can I help you if you don't believe me? And how can you not believe me, after all the things we—"

"No more, Joel. I'm through with people's promises, and I'm through with trust. It doesn't matter what you say."

There was a brief silence.

"Where are we going?"

"Not far."

I turned on to the Saltings and drove past my house. A thought occurred to me. "If you weren't teaching that week, who would have taught her?"

"It's not like that," said Joel. "In the summer there are dozens of people teaching sailing, kayaking, windsurfing. Some of them belong to the yacht club. Some are just students hired for the summer. Some instructors come with their groups. Then people from the island help out as well. Lots of us, even if it's only for a day or so. Me, of course. Bill usually, but then boats are his business. Rick, though it's become a bit of an issue that Eamonn always refuses to join in. Tom occasionally, and some of the kids think it's a hoot when they find out he's the vicar. Even Alix has been known to rig a dinghy or two on weekends off. If you want to find the one who taught this girl, I wouldn't know where to start. We could go to the yacht club when it opens tomorrow morning, but it would be a long business."

"I can't wait till tomorrow morning."

Everything that was familiar now looked strange. The moon was low in the dark sky and I could see the first scattering of diluted stars above the inky, shifting water. I used to love Sandling Island at night: the silence, the slap and murmur of water, the smell of salt and mud, the chime of halliards and the forlorn cry of birds. Now it terrified me.

I rounded the corner, past the boatyard, with the skeletons of boats, and above the sandy beach. I drew to a halt and climbed out, dragging the mallet.

"Bring the torch," I called to Joel, over my shoulder.

"Nina, what are you doing? Where are we going? Wait. Let's talk about this. Nina!"

Joel was behind me, slipping on the soft sand in

his big boots. I ignored him and marched towards
the beach huts, my ankle stabbing pains up my leg.
They stood in the gloom like a row of sentinel boxes.
They weren't like the pastel pictures in Olivia's postcards. Some were smart and freshly painted, with
names above their doors—"Pitlochry" and "Avalon"
and "Nellie's Squat," like punch lines to jokes you
hadn't heard. Some were run-down, with peeling
paint and rusty locks. They were numbered, as if in
a residential street. There weren't that many—
twenty or thirty, perhaps.

I started with number one, a green hut with curtains at its windows and a white door on which there
was a knocker in the shape of a seagull. After a cursory push to make sure that the door was locked, I
lifted the wooden mallet to one side, like a cricket
bat, and swung it violently. There was a satisfying
crash, a splintering sound, and the door caved in.
When Joel spoke it was in a faint, strangled tone:
"Nina! What the hell . . ."

"Torch. Shine it inside."

Joel turned it on. I saw his face glowing eerily
in its light, then the beam turned on the interior of
number one. It was all put away neatly for winter,
everything in its proper place, not a thing awry.

"You can't—"

"I can do anything. Charlie might have been in
there."

I stepped out, picked up the mallet again, and
walked the few steps to number two, which had seen
better days. It was a faded red, and someone had
patched up its holes with rusting corrugated iron. I

laid the torch on the ground, its beam pointing at the door, swung the mallet again. This time, I aimed wrong and missed, spinning with it, and feeling the force of the blow wrench my shoulder almost from its socket. The mallet glanced off the side of the door, leaving an ugly welt in the wood.

"Are you planning to break into all these huts?"

"That's the general idea."

"There's no point in me talking about things like criminal damage or breaking and entering?"

"No."

"Here," said Joel. "Give it to me."

"Get off."

"Nina, give the mallet to me."

"No."

He put his hand on the handle, and for a brief moment, we struggled. I saw him in the torch light, his face a luminous whitish-green and his mouth and eyes black holes. Then he wrenched it from my grip.

"I need to see," I said.

"Stand back."

He lifted the mallet and with one efficient blow on the lock, sent the door swinging open.

"It's about hitting it at the right point," he said, with a note of pride in his voice.

I picked up the torch and peered inside. It was a mess—old towels, plastic bottles and crisps packets on the floor, baggy swimming trunks and a stained T-shirt flung across a chair—but nothing sinister. What was I expecting? Charlie tied and gagged, waiting for me there?

"Number three?" asked Joel. I nodded, and he chopped into that door. There was a faint smile on his face as the wood splintered. "Don't tell Alix," he said. "I don't think she'd be very understanding."

I didn't reply. I had no words left for anything except the task in hand. I couldn't say "please" or "thank you" or "sorry." I could only pickup the torch and shine it into each unfamiliar interior, stare in on the intimate details of some stranger's life, turn away again.

Joel got into a rhythm, smashing a door and moving on. I followed. The water licked the beach; the torch threw long, quivering shadows against the rippled surface of the sand and the sea. The moon hung its sickly light above us. The ripped doors of the huts banged uselessly in the wind. A dog barked somewhere. The world was as unreal as a nightmare.

"That's all," said Joel at last.

"Yes," I said blankly.

"Are we done?"

At that moment I thought, Yes, I'm done. The idea of the beach huts had seemed like an inspiration, a brilliant deduction, which would end with Charlie back in my arms. Now I realized it had simply been a last act of useless despair and nothing had come of it. "I think so," I said.

"I'm sorry, Nina," he said. "The police are, you know, making their inquiries. But if we're done here . . ."

"Yes, Joel, I'll drop you back."

We got into the car and I started to drive. We didn't speak for a couple of minutes.

"I won't say anything about all the damage to the huts," said Joel finally.

"I will," I said. "I'll be seeing the police in a minute. I'll tell them about it."

"Don't," he said. "They'll assume it was the usual vandals. It'll all come off insurance anyway."

"Joel," I said, "I don't care."

There was more silence. Silence and darkness outside, and beyond that the sea. All hope had gone, really, and I felt now I needed activity to stop myself thinking about the darkness outside and the darkness inside and the horror of what the rest of my life would be. I saw my mobile phone blinking up at me as it charged.

"Could you phone Rick for me?" I said.

"Sure."

"The number's on the phone," I said.

"I know it anyway," said Joel, punching it in. He put the phone to his ear. "Hi, Rick, it's Joel. I'm with Nina . . . No, nothing yet . . . I know . . . Yes. Any word about Karen? . . . Right. Well, let me know if you hear anything." He looked at me. "What do you want to tell him?"

"Tell him I'll be along in a few minutes to pick Jackson up." I remembered something else. Did it matter any more? Well, what else did I have to do? "Ask him for Eamonn's mobile number. There's a pen in the glove compartment."

Joel wrote the number on the rolled-up newspaper. The rest of the short journey took place in silence. I pulled up outside his house.

"I hope things are all right with Alix," I said.

"Not too good," he said. "As you saw."

"I've probably made it worse."

"I'm not sure that's possible, just at the moment." He opened the passenger door and started to get out, then paused. "Nina, I'm not sure if I've ever properly told you how much—"

"Joel," I said, stopping him saying what I knew he was going to say. "This in so many ways is not the time for it. I've got to go."

He got out, shut the door and walked slowly up the path to his house. I put the little light on above the rear-view mirror so that I could read Eamonn's phone number and dial it. It was answered after several rings.

"Eamonn? It's Nina. Where are you?"

He didn't seem sure. I heard him ask someone the address. I heard the someone say it slowly and clearly, as if to a deaf person. It was Grendell Road, just round the corner on the way out of town. "Don't worry," I said. "I heard. I'll be there in a minute or two. Meet me outside."

There are streets on Sandling Island that could be in the suburbs of any English town. Built just before the war, covered with pebbledash, bright new conservatories and paved driveways, sheltered from the wind by rows of leylandii. You would never have known you were out on an island in the North Sea, except for the occasional boat parked on a trailer in a front garden. I was outside number fourteen less than a minute after I had talked to Eamonn, and when I arrived I could see that the front door was ajar. As I shut the car door I could see the outline of a person standing to the right of the porch. There was the glow of a cigarette. I pushed open the gate and walked up the gravel path. "Eamonn?" I said.

"Yeah."

He stepped out of the shadow into the light of the lantern hanging from the front porch. From inside I could hear voices and music that I could feel under my feet. As I approached Eamonn, I realized I hadn't thought of what I wanted from him, of what I needed to know. He took a last drag of his cigarette and tossed it aside. His eyes looked different from when I had seen him last, the pupils dilated.

"Are you stoned?" I said.

He gave a shrug. "I've had some weed," he said. "Are you going to tell my dad?"

I brought up my right hand and slapped him hard, then again with the left. I felt so very, very angry. About his silence, his evasions, but also his being here, with music and friends and dope on this night of all nights, for laying his hands on my daughter, for loving her but not being out on the marshes howling her name, for letting life go on while she was in danger, for being young and thoughtless, for being safe and alive. He hardly reacted, just breathed deeply, his eyes filling with water.

"You fucking cretin," I said. "I don't care about your dad. Why the hell didn't you tell me about you and Charlie?"

"I don't know what you mean."

"Stop this," I said. "I know. I know that you and Charlie had sex. Why didn't you tell me?"

"How could I have told you?" he said.

"For Chrissake, Charlie's missing, Eamonn. Missing. Gone. That's the only thing that matters. I needed to know. And hours ago, not now."

"It's not got anything to do with Charlie going," he said. "Why should I have told you? I promised Charlie it would always be a secret between us and that I'd never tell anyone. She'd never forgive me if she knew I'd told you."

"Charlie's in danger. It doesn't matter what you promised her then. There aren't rules like that any more."

"It was just something that happened," he muttered, his face screwed up. "It happened, and then she was sorry it happened and I . . . I didn't mention it because it wasn't relevant to anything."

"Relevant?" I said, my voice raised, shielded from curious neighbours by the din inside. "Who are you to judge that? The police will be talking to you soon. I'd guess they'll be suspicious of a boy who had recently slept with the missing girl and said nothing about it."

"I'm sorry," he said, shuffling from one foot to another. "You know how much I like Charlie. I love her, if you want to know. I loved her as soon as I set eyes on her. She's different. But she doesn't love me. She thinks I'm a weirdo. She's sorry for me."

He turned abruptly and kicked the wall of the house several times; little chips of plaster flew off his massive black boot. When he turned back to me tears were rolling down his face.

"You'll need to pull yourself together before you're interviewed. But before that, I want to ask you a couple of questions."

"Yeah?"

"Do you know where Charlie is?"

"No."

"Who knew about you and Charlie?"

"Nobody," he said. "It was a secret."

"That's not true, for a start," I said. "There were other people at the party. They knew."

"They didn't really know," said Eamonn. "And I didn't talk about it. Maybe there were rumours."

"Did Jay know?"

"I don't think so. Unless Charlie told him. She might have. She's a very honest person."

"If she's so honest, why did she sleep with you?"

There was a pause. Eamonn looked as if he was really thinking about it. "Like I said, I think she felt sorry for me," he said. "I knew that even at the time. And she was a bit drunk."

"What did that make you feel?" I said. "Did it make you angry with her?"

"No, not angry. I suppose I was grateful. That's a bit pathetic, isn't it? Maybe I was a bit angry when she told me it had been a mistake. But it was what I expected in a way. It seemed too good to be true."

"Did your parents know?"

"My dad found out."

I felt a terrible plummeting sense of misery that was almost physical, as if my stomach had been pummelled. Did everyone know more about my daughter than I did? Rick should have told me. He owed me that. That was what I needed. Honesty, not someone mending the rattle in my car.

"What did he say?"

"He said what he always says, which is basically that I'm a piece of shit and that I'm not worth anything. Which is probably about right."

That was presumably my cue to say something reassuring and nurturing but I didn't have time for any of that.

"Do you know a girl called Olivia Mullen? Her friends call her Liv."

"Who's she?"

"I think Charlie got to know her over the summer. They learned to windsurf together."

"I didn't know anything of that bit of her life," Eamonn said, with a faint smile. "I don't get to the beach much, as you can see. That's another of my dad's gripes with me. Why can't I do outdoor things like other teenagers? Like he does?"

"One more thing," I said, watching his face. "Did you take precautions that night?"

His face flamed and he turned away from my gaze.

"Eamonn?"

He mumbled something.

"Does that mean you didn't?"

"It wasn't something either of us was expecting," he muttered.

"So you didn't?"

"No."

"Did Charlie say anything afterwards? I don't mean immediately, I mean recently."

"Like what?"

"Like being worried."

"Worried about what? What are you getting at?" Suddenly a gleam appeared in his stoned eyes, horror or even a mad pride. "You mean she thought that maybe . . ."

"Did she say anything?"

"No," he said. He seemed simultaneously dazed and agitated. "No. I swear."

I couldn't think of anything more to ask. I had to trust him, this sad, strange boy. "All right," I said. "You'd better get yourself some coffee or whatever you need to clear your head because I think you're going to have a difficult couple of days. I'm driving to your house now to get Jackson. Do you want a lift?"

"No," he said. "I don't."

"If you remember anything else, call me on my mobile. You've got my number now."

"All right. Nina?"

"Yes."

"The police haven't found anything?"

"No," I said, as I walked away. "They've found nothing at all."

As I turned round in Grendell Road and drove back on to The Street I felt like a shell of a person. I would be able to drive and talk and do things but inside there was nothing. All there was to do now was to collect Jackson and then go back to the police station to face the music. Wasting police time. Criminal damage. There was probably plenty more. As I turned towards Rick and Karen's house I could see the lights on the mainland. Everywhere there were homes for which this had been just another day. But Karen was in hospital and I was . . . Well, where was I? I turned right along the seafront and pulled up outside their house. The lights were on now. I knocked at the door and heard voices inside. Rick opened the door and I saw Jackson behind him. I thought, What would a normal person with real, human emotions say at a moment like this? They would express regret and gratitude.

"I'm so sorry," I said unconvincingly. "I'm really grateful to you for looking after Jackson. Especially after everything that's happened to you with Karen."

"That's no problem, Nina. Jackson and I have had a rare old time, haven't we, big guy?"

Jackson didn't answer. He was leaning on me, clutching my hand, rubbing himself against me, something he would do only if he was very, very tired. It almost made me feel human.

"I'm sorry," I said. "I came earlier but you were out."

"We went to do some shopping," he said. "Your son's good company." His face shifted to that look of useless concern I had become used to. "Any word of Charlie?"

I shook my head. "I heard about her and your son," I said.

There was a long pause. I tried to make out the expressions that flickered across his face: surprise, contempt, anger. For a moment, he looked like a stranger.

"Rick? You should have told me at least."

He rubbed his face and when he turned to me again it was simply tired. "Maybe you're right, Nina. God knows, I thought about it at the time because I was worried and, of course, I thought about it again today and wondered if it was relevant in any way. I honestly don't think it is. The boy's a disaster zone, Nina. He always has been. I was furious with him at the time. But even then . . . It was just a mess, a typical bloody teenage mess. I thought Charlie might have told you. Did you have no idea?"

"No. But I'm discovering that there was a lot she didn't tell me."

"A girl of secrets?"

"Yes," I said. "That's it."

"I'm sorry. So sorry about everything." He put a hand on my shoulder and squeezed it. Jackson tugged at my hand, trying to pull me away.

"I know," I said. "And I don't mean to blame you. I've spent the day shouting at people."

"That's all right," said Rick. "You know I'll do anything I can to help you. Anything at all."

"I'd ask you if there was anything I could think of," I said wearily, "but there's nothing left. You've done too much already. I'll give you some rest. Come on, Jackson. We'll go home. Thanks, Rick."

"She'll turn up," Rick said. "I'm sure of it."

"I guess so," I said. "You've never come across an Olivia Mullen, have you? Or Liv Mullen? Charlie got to know her over the summer."

Rick looked thoughtful and shook his head. "It doesn't ring a bell," he said. "But there are so many people who come to the beach in the summer. It's hard to keep track. Who is she?"

"That's what I'm trying to find out. Joel said the same about her. Nobody seems to have met her except Charlie. Anyway, thanks for everything."

"That's all right, my love," said Rick. "Go home and get a good night's sleep. You look as if you need it. Things will be all right, Nina."

I thought that for the first time in that frenzied day, with his wife, the injury and the visit to the hospital, he seemed calm, composed. Perhaps it was a relief to have Karen away for a night. He closed the door and I walked to the car with Jackson, my arm round him. I held him as close as I could, feeling his warm, solid body against mine. I opened the front passenger door for him. He took the newspaper that was lying there and opened it on his lap. I switched on the car and drove away from the kerb. "What did you do with Rick?" I asked.

"Played on the computer."

"And then you went out?"

"Yeah."

I imagined Rick taking Jackson for a treat, like the uncle my son didn't have. "Did he buy you anything nice?"

"No, nothing. Just a booklet he needed. He was looking for it in all his drawers and then he said we might as well buy another."

"Oh, right," I said. "We're home."

I opened the door and the light inside the car came on. Jackson looked down at the paper on his lap. "What's this?" he said.

"The local paper," I said. "The vicar left it. He fixed the car. First Rick tried to fix it when there was nothing wrong with it, and then the vicar fixed it when it wouldn't start. People have been trying to fix things all day."

"I mean why's her picture in the paper?" asked Jackson.

"Who's her?"

"That."

He held up the paper. On the front page there was a photograph of a girl, full face, smiling at the camera. She was wearing a hooped T-shirt. The picture was taken in bright sunshine and she was blinking at the camera, dazzled by the light. She had dark brown hair and looked happy and young. The headline read, "Missing Girl, 16," and in smaller letters, "Police Hunt." I looked at the caption to the photograph and saw what I expected: "16-year-old schoolgirl, Olivia Mullen, missing since last week."

I put my hand on Jackson's. "It's very sad," I said. "Her body was found here today."

"She's the girl who took the photo."

"What photo?"

"The one of me and Charlie. The one she sent in the post."

The one I'd given to the police. My head was spinning. My thoughts were like mud. I leaned towards him in the half-darkness, and gripped his arm.

"You were saying who was she, and I didn't know, but it was her."

"Liv," I said.

"Yeah, that's it. Now I remember. She was nice.

Giggly." Suddenly he jerked away from me. "What d'you mean, her body?"

"She was with you and Charlie last week?"

"Is she dead?"

Somewhere deep in the recesses of my brain, I knew that things were piling up that I would have to deal with on another day: careless words, cruel ones, people insulted and hurt, secrets exposed, wounds reopened, trust abused; above all, Jackson, my little boy, who had stumbled unaided through this terrible day. One day, not now. Not yet.

"Darling Jackson," I said, "she'd dead, yes, but I've got to find Charlie . . ."

"What's Liv got to do with Charlie going?"

"I've got to think," I said. "Don't say anything. Wait."

I turned on the car light and scanned the story. Olivia had disappeared last Sunday. She had told her parents that she was going shopping with a friend, and had seemed cheerful, but they had neither seen nor heard from her since.

Did this change anything? I tried to clear my brain of everything but the necessary information. I had the feeling that I knew all I needed to know but hadn't been able to make it add up, and the effort now to connect the pieces felt physical. I could almost feel my brain humming, fizzing, overheating.

Outside, a young couple walked past, leaning against each other and laughing. They were both smoking cigarettes. I stared at them blindly for a couple of seconds, then leaped out.

"Excuse me, can I nick a cigarette from you?"

"You what?" The youth goggled at me and the girl he was wrapped round snickered. For a flash, I saw what he was seeing: a middle-aged woman with wild hair, red eyes, dirty hands and shabby, rumpled, mucky clothes, begging for a smoke.

"I'm desperate," I said.

Wordlessly, he handed me one. I took it and leaned forward while he struck a match, cupped his gloved hands round the frail flame, and put it to my cigarette. I sucked until the end flowered and I felt the acrid sting in my lungs. "Thanks."

I stood by the car with my back to the house, aware of Jackson still huddled inside, tired, hungry, wretched and scared. I gazed out at the sea, almost invisible in the dark, the frosty ground glinting beneath me, and smoked the cigarette.

Olivia Mullen had come to see Charlie on the morning of Sunday, 12 December. I knew that from the date printout on the photograph. I even knew the time: 11:07. According to the paper, that was the day she had gone missing. So she had visited my daughter and then she had disappeared. And she had said she was going to "finish it."

Then—I took a huge drag at the cigarette and, for a moment, felt dizzy and sick—a story about Olivia's disappearance had been published this morning in the paper that Charlie was delivering, and Charlie had also disappeared. The two linked facts whirled in my brain: Olivia went missing after she'd visited Charlie. Charlie went missing when a story about her friend's disappearance was published.

What else did I know? I knew Charlie had been bullied and yesterday night had had her drinks spiked by her so-called friends.

I knew that she had a boyfriend, but had kept it secret for months, creeping out to assignations with him on the hulks.

I knew she'd had a fling with Eamonn and had feared, or maybe known, that she was pregnant.

I knew that Eamonn had told his father.

I knew that someone had come into my house while the abortive party had been going on and taken things that belonged to Charlie, but that it couldn't have been Charlie. Why had they? This was after the bicycle had been abandoned half-way through the paper round. Could it have been as a decoy? To make it look as if Charlie had run away when she'd done no such thing? Whoever had done it had only done it for show. They had only taken things that were visible, things whose absence would be noticed.

I knew that Rory had been there this morning, secretly, and had met Charlie on her newspaper round, that he'd lied about it to me and then to the police, and had only come clean when I'd discovered Charlie's things in the back of his car.

I knew that Olivia and Charlie had met in the summer on a course that Joel had taught on. But so had dozens of others. There'd been hundreds of them down by the beach, sailing and windsurfing.

"Hang on," I said, under my breath, dropping the cigarette on to the ground where it glowed up at me, a winking red eye. "Wait."

Something had crept into my brain, a tiny wisp, like fog. What? I stared at the darkly glinting sea and tried to catch it. Yes: something about so many people coming to the beach that it was hard to keep track. Who'd said that? Who'd just said that?

"I never said the beach," I whispered aloud. "I never said Liv was connected to the beach."

Think. Think. Joel had said that many people from the island taught kayaking and sailing in the summer: himself, Alix, Rick, Bill, Tom . . . I remembered Rick's calm look, the sudden sense of composed purpose. Why would Rick be calm? What was his purpose?

The waves licked at the shingle a few feet away from where I stood; a soft shucking sound. They gave me my answer: calm because the tide was rising to the full flood and my time to find Charlie had all but run out. I opened the car door and leaned in. "Jackson."

"Mummy? Can I—"

"What did Rick get when you went out with him?"

"What?"

"Tell me what he got. You said a booklet."

I knew what he was going to say and he said it. "For the tides. When it's high and low."

I tore open the car's front locker and pulled out a pile of maps, service records and, yes, a tide table. I opened it and followed with a finger the tides for Saturday, 18 December. Low tide was at 10:40 a.m.; high tide was at 4:22 a.m. and 5:13 p.m. Beside the day's times was a dotted black line, signifying that today's was a relatively high one. I glanced at the screen of my mobile: 16:56.

Rick had left Charlie just before low tide, and had spent the whole day—with Karen at the hospital, with Jackson, of all people—being hampered from getting back to her. But now, when the tide was up and the waves were lapping on the shore, he had relaxed. There was only fifteen minutes before it was at its highest. And Rick had been calm, knowing that.

I pulled out my mobile and punched in the number of the police station. A familiar voice answered. "This is—" I began, but then, with a start, I disconnected.

Because now I was thinking with complete clarity. I knew what would happen. The detectives would bring Rick in and he would spend hours giving a statement, admitting nothing. And all the while the sea would be doing his work and everything would be lost. There were few certainties, but I was nearly sure that to call the police would be finally to lose any chance of finding Charlie.

"No," I said.

I turned to Jackson. I took a breath and made my voice slow, calm, reassuring. "A change of plan, honey. You're going to have to wait for me in the house."

"No," he said, in a wail.

"It's important and I'm very proud of you, my darling."

"No!" he shouted, his voice high with hysteria. "I

won't. I'll run away. I'll follow you. You can't leave
me again. It's not fair."

For a desperate stupid moment, I thought of taking him with me. He could hide on the back seat. He
could stay quiet. He might fall asleep. I was considering it, even though at that moment I had no time.
Then, somewhere out of my reverie, I saw two figures walking down the road, an adult and a child.
The adult was laden with shopping-bags, shuffling
towards me. I saw that they had come from the bus
stop. And then I recognized them: Bonnie and Ryan.

"Bonnie," I called, opening the door.

She recognized me and smiled. "We're all done,"
she said. "It took us five hours and we hardly had
time to eat but we've got presents for everyone,
haven't we, Ryan? In fact we were so busy examin-
ing them we missed our stop." Then her expression
changed. "But weren't you supposed to be on your
way to Florida by now? Nina, you look terrible."

"No time," I said. "An emergency. The biggest
emergency. You've got to take Jackson again. I'm so
sorry. Charlie's missing."

"Missing?"

"No time. Take Jackson. I'll phone. Jackson, out.
Quick."

"But—" said Jackson.

"Great!" said Ryan.

"Right," said Bonnie immediately, dragging Jackson out by his forearms. Then she looked at me.
"Go."

I sped away as she slammed the door, driving
back from the direction I'd just come. When I was a

few yards from Rick's house, I drew to a halt. I
switched off my headlights but kept the engine running.

And I waited, praying that I wasn't too late, praying that I hadn't got it wrong, praying that I had and
that in the nightmare of fear I had simply concocted
a Gothic tale that had no roots in the truth. This was
my gamble, my one last throw of the dice. I was risking the life of my daughter on the chance I was right.
I knew now that Rick had taken Charlie. I believed
that he had hidden her somewhere that would be
covered by the tide, which was now almost at its
height. And I was staking everything on the hope
that he was still at his house and that he would now
go to her and I would be able to follow and stop him.
Such a frail vessel in which to place all my faith. I
knew, oh, I knew, how very likely I was to be wrong.
And if I was wrong, I would have the whole of the
rest of my life to dwell upon these moments, to re-
play them and to know what I should have done if I
could have looked down upon the story from a distance. But it was all I had. I was trapped in the foggy
darkness, groping after the truth and seeing only
tiny fragments of it.

I don't know how many minutes I sat there. Maybe
very few. There was a movement, the front door
opened and he emerged. I clenched the steering-
wheel with both fists. He carried a sack over his
shoulder that looked, as far as I could tell in the
darkness, like the nylon bag that sailors use. He
walked over to his car, slung the bag into the back,
and started the engine. I waited as he drew off. I let

him disappear round the bend, his tail-lights red. I memorized his numberplate and the back of his old grey Volvo in case I lost him, although there was no one on the roads this winter evening. They were all inside, in the glowing warmth, with their Christmas trees, their televisions and their log fires. Sheltering from the storm.

The road turned right and I could see Rick ahead. I followed at a distance, praying he wouldn't notice my car in his rear-view mirror. We crossed The Street, then took the right turn that led to the barrow, where he turned left, on to Lost Road. Everything was dark, except the red lights in front of me. I slowed the car and turned off the headlights. Now I could barely make out the road in front of me and several times the car bumped against the verge, once tipping sharply sideways. I shuddered at the thought of sliding off the road into a ditch. But if Rick saw me, broke off and returned home, that would be the end.

I leaned forward, concentrating on the road just ahead but making sure that I could still see the pair of red lights. My fingers were numb with cold, but there was sweat on my forehead and between my breasts. I could hear my breath coming in short, ragged gasps. Now on my right there was farmland and I could occasionally make out, between the trees built as a windbreak, the lights from Birche Farm. On my left there were the empty stretches of marshland. In the distance the sea came back into sight, rising up like a wall of darkness under the dark sky. The moon cast a wavering yellow path over its waters.

This was where Alix and I had been just a few hours ago. The road veered to the left, past a couple of houses. The red tail-lights followed it, going gradually down a shallow slope, but now, against all my instincts, I stopped. I couldn't risk Rick seeing me. He reached the coastal road and the car stopped at the junction. To the right was Charlie's newspaper route, which dwindled to a track, then a boggy path that led to the treacherous marshes and borrow dikes. To the left, the road ran along the low, subsiding cliffs, then turned inland again, away from the cliffs, the dikes, the land that slid and melted into silted mud and salty water, and back towards the causeway.

I watched, leaning over the wheel, ready to move forward. There were things I felt, but at a great remove—the sharp pain of my swelling ankle; the numb cold of my fingers and toes; the soreness behind my eyes; the nausea in my throat; the rough chafe of my jacket against my neck; the hollowness in my stomach; the pressure of my bladder; the bang in my skull. My skin felt too thin and frail to contain the way it hurt to breathe, the way it hurt to think, the way it hurt to be alive and not moving, not racing like a giant with huge avenging strides, like a dragon with monstrously beating wings, to where Rick sat and considered what to do with my daughter.

"Hold on, Charlie, my darling. I'm coming. I'm coming to get you. Just hold on." I don't know if I spoke out loud or not. Her name throbbed in my blood.

The two tail-lights disappeared and instead I could see the glow of headlights in the mist ahead of the car. Rick had turned left. My eyes were accustomed to the dark now and I could see the dim shape, hardly more than a shadow, of the road ahead of me. I reached the junction, turned left and saw once more the red tail-lights. It was impossible to judge the distance and for a moment I had the illusion that the two red lights were floating in front of me as if on a screen. But I was on the east side of the island now, heading north: there were still some streaks of light behind the clouds. Soon it would be entirely dark.

Where was Rick heading? We were on the most deserted, remote part of the island. I barely knew it and I tried to remember the layout of the roads here. The direction Rick was driving along the coast would eventually lead to the causeway to the mainland but I was almost sure that the road didn't reach that far. It petered out into a track and then into impassable marshland where the sea wall had collapsed.

The red lights had vanished. I stopped the car, blinked, rubbed my eyes and stared into the darkness. There was nothing now but grey behind the clouds, and along the horizon, lights from houses on the mainland. I made myself consider the possibilities. The lights could have been hidden by a dip in the road. He might have turned off again. He might have stopped and switched off his lights. Was it possible that he had spotted my car and was waiting for me? What was I to do? Waiting for the lights to reappear was the safest option, but also the most potentially disastrous. If the lights didn't reappear, I might have lost Rick completely. No. I had to continue and take the risk. Was there a chance he would hear the car, even if he couldn't see it in the darkness? I rolled down the window. The wind off the estuary blew wetly into my face. I felt sure he wouldn't hear the car unless it collided with him.

I started to move forward slowly at little more than walking pace. I stared into the darkness so hard that my eyes ached with the effort. My frustration was almost unbearable. I wanted to switch on the headlights and accelerate with as much power as I could but I was sure that if I did so I would lose any chance of finding Charlie for ever.

The silvery sheen of Rick's car loomed out of the darkness and, even at that crawling speed, I nearly ran into it. I braked and felt the scrape of gravel under my tyres. Had Rick heard anything? I switched off the engine and sat still. I looked round, expecting his face to appear at the window. There was no sign of any movement. Outside was just blackness. I picked up my mobile and found the police-station number. When it was answered I didn't ask to be put through to anyone. That would take too long. I just said, in a voice as calm as I could manage so that they wouldn't think I had flipped into a florid state of hysteria, "This is Nina Landry. I have found my daughter but she is in great danger. Come immediately to the end of Lost Road. Turn left where it meets the coastal road and drive as far as you can. Where the road ends, you'll find two cars. We're

there. Come at once. Have you got that? End of Lost
Road, turn north towards the causeway. It is urgent.
Urgent. Life and death. Send an ambulance."

I ended the call. Was there anything in the car I
could use? I remembered a possibility. I opened the
glove compartment and was almost blinded by the
light that came on. Inside there was a roadmap, the car
user's manual and a small torch. I tried it, pointing
down at my feet so that nothing could be seen outside the car. A thin beam illuminated my trainers.
Thank God, thank God, thank God. I slipped it into
my pocket.

Trying to avoid making even the smallest noise, I
opened the car door. Again a light came on inside the
car. I stepped out and shut the door. The light stayed
on. I cursed silently. He might not hear anything but
that light would be visible for miles. I took a deep
breath, opened the door an inch, then slammed it. The
light vanished. I was in darkness again but damage
had been done. My eyeballs seemed to be swarming
with fluorescent micro-organisms.

I tiptoed round Rick's car. Empty. He had gone. I
tried to think of anything else from my car I could
use. I edged my way back to the boot and opened it.
Another light came on, but hidden under the lid. I almost laughed, almost cried, to see the luggage I had
packed for the airport, long ago, many years ago,
when we had been going on holiday. Something
heavy, something solid. To one side there was the
long black plastic bag containing the car jack. I had
never opened it. I pulled at the drawstring and tugged

out a long steel handle. That would do. I pushed down the lid and looked around.

I didn't even know in what direction Rick had gone. Think, Nina, think. He had moved across the road and parked on the right-hand side. Surely he had gone in that direction over the grass, the marshland and the mudflats that led to the water and the mouth of the estuary. This was the worst of signs. I had been hoping, against the evidence of the tide booklet he'd bought, that he would lead me away from the water to a barn, a shed or an outhouse. I didn't know this landscape well but I had walked with Sludge on blustery windy days and I knew there were no buildings there, scarcely even a bush to shelter behind. Nowhere for a living person to be imprisoned. I knew that I mustn't think about that. I must do what I could.

But which direction had he taken? Rory had always laughed at me as a woman who could lose her way in her front room. I couldn't afford a mistake now. I started into the darkness. My world had been reduced to darkness. I would have felt as if I were floating in outer space, had it not been for the soggy grass soaking through my shoes and the wind off the sea that I could feel against my skin. The flicker of light, when it came, was so brief and faint that I thought it might be another trace of the light in my car still scarring my eyes. But no, there it was, a sick, wavering firefly, sometimes obscured, by grasses or ferns, sometimes disappearing altogether but always returning. It was real.

I held the torch below my knees, pointing it at the

ground. Around me was rough grass but I was on a narrow path. Bent forward I walked as quickly as I could. I couldn't see any of my surroundings but I could feel the path carrying me towards the light. My posture was agonizing but I had no choice. I had to keep the torch lit. Driving on the road, the Tarmac beneath my tyres, was one thing, walking on this narrow excuse for a path, snaking through the marshes and mudflats, was quite another. One wrong step to either side and I could be falling down a bank and lost. But for Rick to catch a glimpse of the light was unthinkable. So I scuttled onwards like a crab.

After a few minutes I switched off my torch, stood up and had to stop myself gasping because I was almost on top of him. The torch he had been carrying was now on the ground and he was squatting to one side doing something I couldn't make out. I crouched down, hoping that the scrub around me would provide some concealment.

He had apparently placed the torch so that it threw a pool of light towards him. I wondered where we were. I could hear the sea close by. I put the handle into the same hand as the torch and felt the ground. It was gravelly, even sandy. And wet. We were right by the water. I could feel the high tide round my feet. And what was this, just beyond us in the rising waters? It was hard to see through the pool of light to anything on the other side but I squinted and saw the dimmest, most shadowy of shapes against the cloudy sky. What could it be? It was solid with straight lines. But there were no buildings out there on the sand and mud. Rick owned a boat. Could he have moored it there? Was that where he had stowed Charlie?

Even in my frenzied state, I couldn't make that work in my mind. The boat couldn't have been moored in a place where the water was just a few inches deep at high tide. I wasn't a sailor but even I knew that. But something was there, looming solid in the darkness.

I rummaged through my memory. I made myself look back to those awful winter days after Rory had left, wandering the remote paths of Sandling Island with Sludge, those walks in the stinging northerly gales when I hadn't known whether the tears were of grief and anger or just the wind. I thought and remembered and suddenly I knew. Then I could see it clearly. It was one of the pillboxes left over from the island's defences during the war. With that I realized everything and saw with utter clarity what I must do and that I must do it immediately. As it was, there was almost no hope but otherwise there was no hope at all. I took the steel handle back into my right hand and held it firmly. The important thing now was not to think. I needed to feel and act. I stood and took a few steps forward, all that was necessary to close the gap between us. As I approached him I brought my right arm back. From his crouching position Rick looked round as I swung the metal bar into his head, catching him above his left eye. He gave no sound. There was just the ringing, crunch of the metal bar on his skull and he folded up on the ground. I wanted to continue, to beat his skull to mush but there was no time for anything.

I turned away from him, dropping the bar on to the ground, and shone my torch out over the water. Its frail light skewed on the small inky waves and then, as I raised it higher, picked out the massed shape of the pillbox. I ran towards it, splashing through the icy water that rose rapidly to my knees and then thighs, slowing me down. I gasped at the shocking cold, which almost took my breath away. My jeans clung to me, my feet sank into the muddy sand, salty water stung my face and made my eyes weep. "Charlie!" I shouted, as loudly as I could, wading forward, surging through the breakers, cursing the thickness of my sodden jacket, which held me back. "I'm here. Wait. Darling—darling, just wait." For I had the sense that every second, every fraction of a second, might count now. Like atoms being split, the world could fracture at any moment.

My voice rolled out over the sea and broke somewhere in the distance. There was no answer. Silence lay all around. I flung myself the last few yards, holding the torch high above me so it didn't get wet, staring through the darkness for the opening, which I could hardly make out. Black on black. Depth on depth. I reached out my free hand and found the wall at last, rough and gritty under my fingers. I followed it with the torch's beam until I found the opening, and fought through the rapidly rising waters to stand at the entrance at last. The pillbox, which had once stood on the cliffs and now lay in a wreck at their base, was tipped askew, so that its small doorway was tilted slightly upwards. This meant that the tide, which had been temporarily held back by its walls, was gushing in rapidly.

I shone my torch, my dim puddle of light, into the interior. And there was nothing. Nothing but water, rolling at the door and calmer further in.

"Charlie!" I called, in a voice that cracked apart. "Charlie!"

And then the torchlight touched on a shadow, a blur the shape of a water-lily. I leaned in to shine my torch directly on it. I heard my breath catch in my throat, for what the frail beam of light picked out was a pale patch barely breaking the surface of the incoming water. A tiny island of flesh in the flood, like the belly of an upturned fish. A mouth open like a gill, pursed for oxygen.

For a moment, I couldn't move. Then, with painful slowness and care, I inserted myself into the pillbox's small opening, feeling my jacket rip, feeling rough stone against my hands and face, blood and salt in my mouth. The sea came up above my waist and then, as I moved forward, up to my neck. But I didn't dare make any rough movement, for fear of splashing water into that tiny, pitiful mouth. I was terrified that my bulk would make the level rise enough to submerge it entirely. With tiny steps, I shuffled towards my daughter, one hand still holding the torch high, the other reaching out to touch her dear drowning body.

And at last my fingers found her—the stretched stem of her neck and the seaweed tangle of hair. "It's all right, dear heart," I whispered.

Her eyes stared at me blindly. Her lips gasped at the remaining air. Water bubbled at her upturned chin.

"I'll get you out."

I needed to put the torch down. I stared frantically around the clammy space until I saw a shallow nook, where the stone had crumbled. I crammed the torch into it, its light now shining horizontally, so that I could no longer see Charlie at all. I put my arms round her waist, under the water, and pulled. She rose an inch or so, heavy and unresponsive as a corpse, then jerked to a stop. She was tied down, but I couldn't tell with what, or to where.

"Wait," I hissed.

I sank beneath the surface of the water, my jacket opening. I opened my eyes but could see nothing except the brackish swirl of the sea. I groped with my hands and found her legs. Her ankles were tied with something rough, thick and strong. A rope. I tugged at it hopelessly. My lungs were aching now. I followed the rope to where it stopped, knotted to something heavy and cold. I tore at the thick knot with my fingers, trying to wriggle it free, but I knew I couldn't untie it. Not without seeing it, not under water, not in time. There was no time. I had seconds—Charlie had seconds.

I rose again, gasping and spluttering. I pulled off my bulky, sodden jacket, bundled it up into a thick parcel and plunged down once more. I blew air out of my lungs so I could stay submerged while I put my hands round Charlie's calves and pushed her up until the rope went tight. I forced the folded jacket under her dangling, booted feet, pushing it into a shape that would accommodate her weight, not tip her off if she shifted. Now at least I'd gained a minute or so.

Once more I surfaced. I reached for the torch and shone it into my own face.

"Wait," I said. "Don't move. Stand tall. Breathe. I'll be back in a few seconds. I swear to you that I'm going to save you."

Her eyes widened. Out of her mouth came a long, bubbling mew. It wasn't a human sound.

I turned away from my daughter and pulled myself out of the hole. I waded through the waves and the ripping wind. Past Rick, whose splayed body was now lapped at by the waves, and to my car. As I ran, my eyes scanned the land for headlights. Surely the police would arrive soon. But the road was dark.

I threw open the boot and the light came on, dazzling me. Leaning across, I unzipped the nylon sports bag and drew out Christian's Christmas present, wrapped in silver paper with stars on it. I put my torch into my mouth because I needed both hands now, then turned back to the sea and ran, tearing off the paper as I went, fumbling at the thick plastic folder inside. A snorkel. And the mask it was attached to. I yanked the breathing tube free of the packaging, dropping the rest into the mud. I took the torch from my mouth, held it in my free hand, brandishing the tube in the other, and launched myself through the tide towards Charlie, both arms raised, the water parting in a trough before me.

Into the small opening. The torch was dying. Its

beam flickered. But it found the half-open lips of my child. With one hand, I inserted the snorkel between them, making sure the mouthpiece fitted securely. Her skin felt cold and rubbery, unreal. I pushed the mask over her face and pulled the strap round the back of her head.

"Hold on to it with your teeth, Charlie," I said, my voice loud and steady. "Grip it and breathe. If the water comes above your face, don't panic, do you hear? You can still breathe. You're going to be fine. Now I'm going to get something to cut you free."

Easy to say, but I needed something strong to hack through that thick wet rope and I had no knife, no scissors, no blade. But then I thought of someone who might have something. I left Charlie alone once more, in that terrible flooded darkness, and waded to the shore.

Rick's body was half in the water now, half out. His sail-bag was still roped over his shoulder and I had to half roll him over to pull it free. His body was cumbrously heavy and limp, and my hands came away sticky with his blood. But I had the bag. It had a drawstring top, pulled tight shut, and I had to jiggle it open with my numb, clumsy fingers. Inside I found a towel, a change of clothes and a clutter of odd bits and pieces, most of which seemed to be to do with his boat—a couple of cleats, a few lengths of thin nylon rope, a small plastic bailer, a spanner, a pair of rowlocks, pliers—perhaps I could use those to ease the knot free. Secateurs: they might do. And what was this? I pulled it out and held it up to the last rays of the torch: an army knife.

I took the pliers, the knife and the secateurs and returned to the pillbox. The last of the light in the west had gone and it was quite dark. But as I reached the shelter, the moon emerged from behind a cloud and cast a faint, silvery light over the surging water. For a moment, I could see everything around me: the icy expanse of sea, the high, cold sky, the crumbling banks of mud and sand and, like a smudge, the ruined shelter breaking through the rising tide. It must be almost full now. The sand and pebbles beneath my feet were sucked by the undertow, the shallow breaking waves had curled lips, and it was harder to make my way. My jeans clung to my legs, my shoes were like bricks but they were laced up— I had no time to undo them and kick them off.

I pulled myself through the pillbox's entrance and found myself floundering for a foothold. Water rose up and engulfed me; I was almost out of my depth and had to stand on tiptoe at the higher edge to breathe properly. I managed to hold the torch above my head still, and shone its wavering light around the deathly space. Nothing. Charlie had gone. A howl rose in my throat but I pushed it down, staring at the place she had been. And there I saw a small tube rising above the water, just a few inches long. My daughter was underneath it, down in the water. Was she breathing?

My torch gave a last few yellow flickers and went out. I let it drop with a muted splash. For a moment, the moon shone a trickle of light after me, but then I was in darkness. I pushed the pliers into my jeans' tight wet pocket, gripped the secateurs between my teeth and blindly opened the knife's largest blade. One deep breath and I sank under the water, free hand stretched out. I found Charlie's body. Her arms tied and bound behind her back. Her waist under the sodden leather bomber jacket, her thighs, her legs, her ankles. I had to make sure I didn't dislodge her from my folded jacket. I felt for the rope and clutched it with my left hand. Now I was facing downwards, like a diver, while the rest of my body floated up. I started sawing at the rope with the knife. I needed to breathe but I couldn't stop. The rope was soaked and thick, the knife was small and blunt. My lungs were shrivelling, scorching with pain. Soon I would breathe, draw in great gulps of salty water. A spasm jolted my body and I let go of the rope and rose up into the air retching and gasping, nearly losing the secateurs. But I took them in my hand, opened them at the ready, and put the knife into my mouth.

Down again. The rope. My fingers found the groove where I'd been cutting. I snipped at it with the secateurs, sometimes missing and snapping them closed on water. I let the ache build in my lungs again, filling each cubic millimetre with solid pain. I imagined the threads breaking, one by one, could feel the gradual give in the rope. Just a few more cuts, surely, but it took so long, so agonizingly long, and I had no time and no breath and my body was about to explode with the pain. All the while, as I dived down, attached to the rope, Charlie hung above me, swaying with the waves.

When I thought I could bear it no longer, the rope

gave a tremor and snapped. My body floated upwards, no longer anchored. I heaved against Charlie
as I rose to the surface, pushing her head into the air,
grappling with her passive weight. She lolled against
me, and I couldn't hold her properly because I was
now out of my depth. Her head tipped back in the
water as I thrashed by her side. Violently gulping in
air myself, I put my hands on either side of her
head, over her ears, and lay on my back, towing
her the short distance towards the entrance. Once, I
thought she twitched, a tiny shudder like a reflex,
but otherwise she was unresponsive. Her legs bumped
against mine under the water.

At the doorway, I tried to haul myself backwards,
one arm wrapped round her torso, tugging her slack,
slipping heaviness upwards while her upper body
leaned away from me, as if she wanted to slide back
into the shelter. I couldn't get a proper grip on her
clothes or her clammy skin. Her fingers were like
pieces of slimy driftwood; her limbs twisted in impossible ways. Several times I almost let her go, back
into the flooding darkness. Once I had to clutch a
handful of her hair to keep her head above the water.
The concrete scraped at my face and I felt blood in a
warm gush down my cheek and neck. I tumbled over
the submerged threshold, back into open sea, feet
sinking deep into the mud, and dragged her after
me. The moon shone down on us, its rippled trail
widening over the water. The waves washed at my
neck, and Charlie's body drifted heavily behind me
like a net of dead fish. I hooked my hands under her

armpits. I couldn't see her properly, just the shape of her body and the ghostly blur of her face. Her eyes were closed now.

"You're OK, you're OK, you're OK," I was shouting, as I towed her to the shore, hauling her past Rick and dragging her by her arms on to the dry sand and the rocks beyond, where we collapsed in a heap, wrapped up together so I could feel the clammy chill of her skin. I struggled to my knees. In the moonlight, her face was grey, her lips the same colour as her skin. Her mouth was gaping open, but slack, her flesh cold as the sand she lay on.

I gathered Charlie's body to me, pressing my face into her neck and holding her head to my ear to feel or hear her breath. All I could hear was the steady, rumbling wash of the sea behind me, and the fretful moan of the wind. I pinched her nostrils between my thumb and forefinger and put my mouth to hers. I blew once, twice. I tried to remember what I knew of first aid. I pumped down on her chest several times, then breathed air into her mouth once more. Again, then again.

"Don't go, my lovely," I said. "Stay with us now." I called her by her name and crooned nonsense to her as if she were a baby again.

Suddenly, a tiny bubble of air and a gurgle came from her colourless lips. Then a helpless choking sound. I hauled her into a sitting position. With her arms tied behind her, she looked like a prisoner before execution. Her head lolling forward, she vomited into my lap. I held her against me and pressed my lips to her forehead. A terrible, agonizing hope opened its wings inside me, stopping my breath and knocking my heart against my ribs. I felt her body tremble against mine. I wrapped my arms round her as tightly as I could, rubbing her back, trying to press my living warmth into her. If only there were blankets in the car, or clothes.

I remembered Rick's bag. I laid Charlie on the ground, sprinted down the sand and grabbed it, stumbling back to where she lay. I shook out the contents of the bag and found a small metal spanner, which I twisted into the knot that bound her arms. I wriggled it free and unwound the rope, feeling with my fingers the deep welts it had left on her wrists. I tugged off her jacket, snatched up the large towel and the sweatshirt, and wrapped them round her, then folded her up in the nylon bag. I took the bulky, layered weight of her in my arms again and cradled her to me while I tried to lift her up.

"Come on, Charlie," I gasped, into the coarse salt coils of her hair. "You're safe, my bravest darling." I slung one of her limp arms round my shoulder. "I've got you now, the ambulance is on its way and I'm going to carry you to the car."

Charlie's eyes opened and she looked at me. Then she looked past me. Her mouth opened but no sound came. I saw a widening of her eyes and felt an explosion of pain so great and so sudden that it wasn't just a feeling: I could see the pain, flashing white and then in bursts of blue and red, and I could hear it too, ringing in my ears. I didn't feel my body collapse and hit the ground. I saw the ground move up and then it was against me, the slimy mud against my cheeks, in my mouth. The name came into my mind: Rick.

I rolled over and felt the pain in my left leg, spurting and flowing down to the foot, up through my thigh and into my body. As I turned, I saw Rick. He was on his knees. Even in the darkness I could see that his face was covered with filth and blood. Things were happening quickly yet I seemed to have a great deal of time to think. I realized that he had crawled towards me from behind and that I hadn't seen him. He had struck my right knee with something, which had made me collapse, and now he was raising it to strike me again, on my head this time. I realized I had dropped Charlie and I thought, All this has been for nothing. I had called the police and the police would get here and they would find Rick but it would be too late. But at least I had found Charlie, if only for a moment. She was not alone any more. While I was thinking all that, I raised my right arm to ward off the blow and there was another explosion of light and sound. I cried out again, but I snatched with my left hand and gripped the metal bar he was wielding.

Even though he was injured, Rick was far bigger and stronger than me. But I thought of Charlie and I held the bar and knew that I would never release it until I was dead, and then he would have to prise my fingers from it. My right arm was hot with pain but I clawed at his face with my right hand. I felt flesh under my nails and scratched deep. I heard a scream from somewhere close. I had been pulling the metal bar but then, suddenly, instead of trying to wrench it free he pushed it down on me, on my neck, and I began to choke. I pushed and twisted with all my last strength, I scratched at his face but he was staring down at me. I tried to speak, I tried to tell him that it was all over, that the police were on their way, but the metal was hard against my windpipe. I could see him shaking his head at me, as if in reproof, and he was saying something but I was no longer able to hear or see. I was losing consciousness and then I heard a sound, felt it as much as heard it, of something heavy hitting the earth, and his weight on me was gone.

It was several seconds before I could see. There was a shape in front of my eyes, which gradually acquired form and detail, and I could make it out as Charlie. She was barely recognizable as the daughter I had last seen on the previous day. Her skin was as pale as that of a corpse. She was drenched, her hair and clothes plastered flat against her. She was holding a piece of concrete from the disintegrating pillbox. She let it drop and stood there, looking through me with dead eyes. She swayed like a tree that was about to fall. I glanced around. There was no sign of Rick.

I cried out my daughter's name and got to my feet. I knew there was pain and damage in my arm and leg but it felt like a distant memory. I held her close in my arms; we were both trembling violently, with cold and fear. I looked into her eyes. "Charlie," I said loudly. "Can you hear me?"

She didn't answer. Her eyes were rolling as if she was drugged or desperate for sleep. I remembered Rick. Where had he gone? Was there a chance he could come for us again, out of the darkness?

Then I saw him. The force of Charlie's blow had knocked him off the bank where the remains of the pillbox stood. He had slipped down into the water and the mud. I could see the shape of his body in the water, pushed this way and that by the tide, which was now at its height. Slack tide—and before long it would ebb once more. He was lying on his back with one of his legs deep in the soft, gluey mud. I thought he was unconscious, but then his eyes flickered open and he looked up at me. He lifted his bashed, bloody head as far as he could. Occasional waves swept over him, making him choke with a horrible gurgling sound, but he couldn't move. I stared down at him. I needed to hate him for what he had done. He had killed Olivia Mullen. And he had been intending to kill Charlie, or to stand by and allow the sea to drown her. I had spent the day hating the anonymous man who had snatched Charlie, and now I knew Rick was that man.

My first thought was to stand there and watch him die, but the idea made me cold and nauseous. I laid Charlie gently on the ground, and stood up, whimpering with pain. The world rocked around me and small lights were exploding inside my skull. I shuffled, half slipping, down the bank to a few paces from where he lay. I took a tentative step on to the mud to see if it would hold my weight. But my leg sank straight to the knee and above. It was only by grabbing on to a rough bush that I could drag myself free. The pain in the other leg made me howl. I couldn't reach him.

He made another choking, gurgling sound. I didn't know if he was asking for my help, or if it was just the sound of a man who had lost all hope. With my numb, fumbling fingers, I undid my belt and pulled it free from the loops of my jeans. "Catch hold of this and pull," I said. I held the buckle and tossed the leather belt across the gap separating us. He lifted a hand feebly but missed. I tried again and this time he had it. "Get a good grip," I said. "Come on."

He wrapped the leather round his hand, pulling me a bit closer to him. I hauled as hard as I could and felt a gradual shifting of his weight towards me. A small part of me was aghast as I tried to save the life of the man who had tried to kill my daughter.

All of a sudden, his weight shifted back again. I felt it in the tightening of the belt, I heard it in the sucking sound beneath us. The tide was going out at last, drawing the shingle, grit and debris of the muddy shore with it. And drawing Rick away too. His body was drifting from me.

"Hold on," I gasped, as I strained to drag him towards me. "The police will be here in a moment."

Now Rick's weight was pulling me. I could feel myself slipping, and I knew that if I held on for much longer, I would join him in the sticky mud. For one moment, we stared at each other, the belt tight between us.

And then I let go. The belt curled towards him and he slid back, drawn by the steady tug of the tide. The waves washed over his face until I could no longer make it out. The moon glimmered down on to empty waters.

I looked round. Charlie was slumped on the ground. I hobbled over to her, crouched, and cradled her. Her eyes were shut again. Her flesh was damp and cold. I hauled her into my arms, and struggled to my feet, screaming with pain. My leg would barely hold me now but I needed to get her into the warmth of the car. I gripped her round the chest and tried to pull her, walking backwards and heaving her weight after me. I felt freezing, dizzy and sick, and was shuffling back an inch at a time. I collapsed on to the ground, Charlie on me, her hair in my mouth, and her body slack and heavy. I slithered out from under her and picked her up again, holding her, lolling, against me. I put two fingers against her neck, where a pulse should have been, but they were too numb to feel anything. As I sat there, the sea sucking back from its full flood and the wind coming raw from the east, I could feel my last reserves of strength ebbing away. My limbs would no longer obey me. I felt both as frail as a broken shell and enormously heavy. I just wanted to curl up on the cold ground with my daughter and close my eyes at last.

"No, you don't, Nina," I snarled, snapping open my eyelids. My voice was hoarse and feeble. I didn't recognize it. "Don't stop now."

Once more, I grasped Charlie and pulled her into a sitting position just in front of me, between my open legs. I started bumping us both towards the car, which was so near, yet so infinitely far away. If I could get there, into the warmth . . . For a few minutes, the world shrank to the effort of moving in tiny jerks up the slope. I knew I couldn't do it and yet I knew I must. Everything in me howled in protest, and it was as if my body was breaking up.

I saw it first as a path of light that shone past the pair of us and on to the black water, as if there was a second moon in the sky. I stopped and turned my head. Over the horizon, a yellow beam fanned out, then narrowed again as the car came over the hill. Another set of headlights followed, then a third. Blue lights flashed, and the distant wail of a siren cut through the sound of the wind in the marshes.

I put my chin on top of Charlie's head and rocked her. "They're here to save us," I said. I cleared her matted hair off her face and tucked it behind her ears, then picked up her cold hands and rubbed them between my own. The lights were nearly on us now; the siren was a shriek that stopped abruptly. I heard brakes, doors opening, voices shouting orders. Silent, empty space filled up with noise and bustle. I wiped away the thick smear of mud from her cheek. "Sweetheart," I said, "please don't go."

They came over the hill like an army, silhouetted figures behind the torches that shone down fiercely on us, pinning us in a dazzling brightness. I put a hand over Charlie's eyes to protect them, even though she lay unmoving in my lap, and I looked out on to the landscape of our blind struggle. Under the crumbling cliffs, where stunted trees leaned out with exposed roots waving helplessly in the air, the waters were receding at last, sucking at the thick, bubbling mud, lapping at driftwood, rubbish and sharp stones. The ruined pillbox stood like a gaping mouth, eddies of waves around its entrance. Tomorrow, the winter light would return all of this to a landscape I knew: the placid blue-green sea, the shingle and sand where wading birds would lift their long legs in the shallows. I stared at the sea, and saw nothing but its heaving, glinting surface. I thought of his face, the waves washing over it, but there was no sign of Rick. The tide had taken him.

Then they were with us, between us, lights shining, stretchers lowered, blankets unrolled, voices talking into radios, a sense of controlled speed, of managed urgency. There were calm voices in my ear, warm hands on my freezing limbs, something soft wrapped round me. Someone called me by my name. My eyes were burning. My arms were empty. I called out for my daughter.

"Just relax now," someone said. I saw a face looming towards me. "Don't try to talk."

I called for Charlie again.

I was on a stretcher. The blanket scratched my chin. I was being carried over the rough ground, and I lay on my back, feeling as if I was a bit of detritus tugged by the tide. I wanted to close my eyes, but couldn't. The lids peeled back in my aching face and I stared up at the white moon sailing serenely on.

"Rick," I whimpered.

"Nina." I squinted into the face leaning over me. "It's me, Nina, Andrea. Now listen, everything's—"

"Rick!" I said again, raising my voice against the throb of pain in my knee, leg, head, heart. "In the water. Help."

In the clamour of pain, in the agony of not knowing if Charlie was alive or dead, I had to try to save the man who'd nearly killed us both: it was like hanging on to the last shreds of my humanity.

"Now, Nina, once you're in the ambu—"

"What's this?" A sharper voice cutting through the hubbub: DI Hammill. I put a hand out and clutched his arm.

"He's out there, drowning," I said.

I was aware of orders being shouted, people running. I saw more lights come over the horizon. Shafts of light and long shadows slid over me. At the centre of all the frenetic activity, I saw Charlie's still figure being slid on the stretcher through the open doors of the ambulance. Her white, peaceful face. She looked so small and vulnerable. Someone pushed me down on to my stretcher.

"It's my daughter," I said. "I need to see her."

"You'll see her," said the voice. "We need to check you over. You'll be with her. But if you keep shifting around we'll drop you."

I lay back and suddenly I saw the stars. The Plough. The Great Bear. And the other one. The little one. The Little Bear. I was feeling woozy, drifting off to sleep, when I heard shouts of "Shut the door" and "Watch out." The sky had gone and my eyes were dazzled by bright lights. It was suddenly warmer. I saw green uniforms moving around me. The stretcher was put down. A young woman appeared close to me.

"How are you feeling, Nina?" she asked, just a little too slowly and loudly.

"How's Charlie? What are they doing to her?"

"She's here," said the woman. "She's being looked after. Nina, we're going to have to check you over, all right?"

"I'm fine," I said. "I just need to see my

daughter—" I broke off and howled because the woman had run her hands down my leg. I heard different voices shouting, but it was difficult to penetrate the fog of fear and pain that surrounded me.

"We've got to move. Now."

"Is everybody in?"

"Can we come?"

"They're being treated."

"It's urgent."

"Just don't get in the fucking way."

Doors were slammed. There was a jolt, and pain shot through me. I realized I was in the ambulance and that we were driving away.

"Charlie," I cried. "Where is she?"

The woman's face came close to mine. A nice face, short, dyed-red hair, green overalls. "I'm Claire," she said, talking to me, still in the overloud voice that's used for the very young or the very old or the very badly hurt. "We need to check you out, all right?"

"Where's Charlie?" I said. "What's happening?"

I made myself twist round and saw two other figures in green overalls bent over the stretcher across from me. "Is she dead?" I whispered.

"We need to think about you first," said Claire. She laid a hand on my shoulder, but I jerked away from her.

"No. Nothing until you tell me. How is she? Is she going to be all right? Is she dead?"

"Nina." She came closer to me so that I could see her brown eyes. "Your daughter has got very cold. Her core temperature has fallen drastically. We've got to get it up. We're doing all we can."

The sympathy in her eyes struck terror into me. "Get Rory," I said. "At once. Get her father."

There were shouts from around Charlie's bedding. "I can't get a BP reading."

The interior of the ambulance was taking shape, coming into focus. I could see Beck by the rear doors, swaying with the movements of the ambulance. She looked anxious, helpless. I couldn't make out anything of Charlie. An oxygen mask covered her face. Her body was obscured by the medics.

"What's happening?" I shouted. "Someone's got to tell me."

The figures were crouched over her, but they didn't seem to be doing much. One turned towards me. Young man, sandy hair, pale skin. "Your daughter is severely hypothermic," he said. "We're warming her up."

"She was moving around," I said desperately. "She saved me. You've got to save her."

"We're doing all we can."

"Can't you inject something?"

"Drugs are ineffective when she's this cold, even dangerous. We've got heat packs. She just needs to get warm."

I struggled to get off the stretcher. "Let me help," I said. "I'll—"

But he held me and I collapsed back, gasping.

"Save your strength," he said. "You'll need it for both of you. Now, let Claire deal with you."

"No! She can't die! You can't let her die!"

"We'll do everything possible," he said gently. "You need to look after yourself now."

"No," I said. "No. I need to see Charlie."

But someone put a hand against my chest and I lay back. I heard a tearing sound and felt something burning along my leg: my clothes were being cut off. I was lifted and twisted. I felt like I was being peeled and left pink, naked and raw. Pain flowed through me like a deep, fast river. "I'm all right," I whispered. "But please can I . . ."

Suddenly the motion of the ambulance ceased.

"What's happening? Are we there?"

"The causeway's still covered by the tide. We're just checking if we can get through."

"Can we talk to her?" said Beck.

"She needs rest," said Claire. "And we need to do some checks. She may be in shock."

"It's very important."

Claire turned to me.

"Can you manage a few questions?"

"No! I want to see Charlie! What's happening to her? Why won't anyone tell me?"

Claire moved across to the huddle around my daughter. There was some murmuring and then she was back, crouching by my side. "They're monitoring her temperature. They're warming her. We just have to wait."

"How serious is it? I have to know. Please tell me."

She looked uncertain. Her eyes flickered as if she wanted to avoid my gaze. "They're doing their best."

"Is she going to die?"

But she didn't answer.

The ambulance started up once more. I thought of going through so much, of pulling my daughter from the icy water, then losing her. I saw the two police officer's faces close to me. They were like figures from long, long ago. Barely recognizable.

"Call Rory," I said once more. "Immediately."

"He's being driven straight to the hospital."

So the alienated parents were coming together at last, at their daughter's sickbed. Or deathbed.

"Can you talk?" said Beck.

Her face was coming in and out of focus and the pain in my head seemed to be breaking up into lots of small fragments. "What for? It's all done. It's all over."

"Did he get away?" said Beck.

"What?"

"The man who took your daughter."

"He's in the water," I said. "I tried to get him out. Couldn't. I had to save Charlie."

"The water?" said Beck. "When we left, the officers were trying to retrieve Mr. Blythe's body. But what about the perpetrator?"

"What?"

"Did he fall in the water as well?"

I felt as if the whole world was going fuzzy around me.

"Rick did it," I said. "There was nobody else."

"Rick Blythe?"

"Of course," I said. "What have I been saying? What did I say on the phone?"

"Are you sure?" said Beck. "But I thought it was

Mr. Blythe you were with when Charlie went missing."

I looked at her, heard the words she was saying, but at the side of my vision I could see one of the figures standing back from Charlie and saying something to his colleague. What was he saying? What was happening?

"Nina?"

"What are they doing to Charlie?" My voice came out in a terrible screech.

Claire pushed her way past Beck, sat next to me and took my hand. "Nina," she said, looking into my eyes.

The world tipped and roared; my blood cascaded down my veins; my heart pounded in my chest. Then everything became ominously quiet and clear. I knew what she was going to say and I waited for the words I'd been dreading ever since Charlie had disappeared. "Yes?"

"We're nearly there. Try to remain calm."

"Is she going to be all right?"

"We're doing all we can. She's a resilient young woman."

"I should have known where she was."

"Try to stay calm."

"I should have known. If only I'd got to her earlier. I came too late."

I put my hands over my face and in my own private darkness I let myself think of Charlie's face tipped up like a submerged water-lily in the churning black waters, and of the way her body felt when I'd tugged it up the beach: slack, cold and dead. I could scarcely bear to think of the terror through which she had passed today, or bring myself to imagine what she had experienced as she waited to be rescued, watching the light fail and the waters rise. I just wanted her to know I was still here, beside her, and that she wasn't alone any more.

I felt the bumping and creaking of the ambulance as it swung through the curves. There was a hand on my forehead and dimly, distantly, I heard voices but it seemed impossible to make out the meaning of the words. I thought I made out the words "losing her." But everything was jumbled and I was sinking into the darkness behind my eyes. The voices got shriller, and then my body was being manipulated, except that it felt like someone else's body and I was only its temporary tenant. I could feel the ambulance slowing and making a turn. The surface of the road was rougher, then smoother. I could see lights outside and hear sounds. The doors were pushed open and there was a rush of cold air. There were people outside with trolleys, two of them. Life had slowed down in the ambulance. It was all about maintenance and waiting. Now things were happening quickly, with noise and bustle and surprising roughness. As Charlie was bundled out on her stretcher, I wanted to shout that they must be careful with her. They mustn't drop her. She was fragile.

"I want to go with her," I said weakly.

"You'll see her," said the sandy-haired man, covering me with several blankets. "But she needs attention. And so do you."

As I was lifted out, I looked for Charlie but she

was already gone. I was wheeled past several police officers through flapping doors and into a curtained-off cubicle where a nurse followed me with a clipboard and immediately started to ask questions. It was so bureaucratic and pedantic it almost made me scream. She wanted my name and address and date of birth.

"I'm not ill," I said, though the words came out in a slur and I'm not sure she understood them. "Just tired, cold. Is Rory here?"

She asked if I was allergic to anything, if I was on any medication, if I had eaten in the last four hours.

"I don't want to be operated on," I said. "I withhold my permission."

"Ms. Landry," she said, very sternly, "your daughter is being looked after. It does nobody any good if you don't let us look after you as well. For a start, I need to take your temperature and monitor your—"

"I need the toilet," I said. "Now."

"Someone can bring you a bedpan."

"No, thank you. I can manage quite well on my own."

"I don't think that's a very good idea," she said, with such forbidding grimness that on any other day I would probably have obeyed her. But I needed to see Charlie. They'd said she was resilient, but I'd seen her white face and her closed eyes and I remembered what her body had felt like as it lay heavy and slack in my arms. How could I rest until I knew that she was all right; why should I get better if she wasn't going to?

So I levered myself into a sitting position, the

bright lights burning into my sockets, my head woozy and aching, swung my feet to the floor, then gathered the blanket that covered my near-naked body and stood up. Astonishing pain shot up my injured leg and my knee throbbed, sending sharp pulses through my whole body. My head spun so disastrously that I had to lean over, holding on to the edge of the trolley for support while the ground tipped and the walls fell towards me. I thought I would be sick, and for a few moments I simply stood there, gasping and looking down at my bare, filthy feet on the shabby lino, my leg caked with mud. I saw that my hand clutching the trolley was streaked with grey, that a nail had been ripped off and that the knuckles were raw and bleeding.

"Where is it?" I said, when I could speak.

"Just down the corridor on the left. Shall I help you?"

"No. I can manage. I'm fine."

I clutched the blanket round me and shuffled towards the ladies.' Beck was standing by the desk, speaking to a doctor, nodding energetically, and beyond her, near the door, were two uniformed policemen. I turned away and limped into the toilet, locking the door behind me. For a moment, I let myself lean against the wall and shut my eyes, breathing in the disinfected air. The world felt infinitely strange and unreal. My day lay behind me as a trail of ruin and this was where Charlie and I had been washed up.

I let the blanket slither to the floor and lowered myself painfully on to the lavatory. Then, using my hands to pull myself up, I got to my feet and moved across to the basin. I lifted my face and, in the square mirror, met my reflection. I almost shrieked in terror at the stranger staring back at me. She wasn't me. She had wild snakes of damp black hair, bloodshot eyes, a violet bruise flowering across her muddy cheek and swelling her nose. A smear of blood ran from the corner of her mouth and her lips were puffy. She looked old.

Charlie mustn't see me like this. I turned on the tap and, when the water was running warm, pulled a paper towel from the dispenser and soaked it, then gingerly wiped away some of the mud and blood. I cupped my hands and splashed water over my face. I bent down and twisted it sideways so that water ran over my hair, which was thickly encrusted with sand and grit. When I stood upright again, I didn't look much better, but there was nothing more I could do except squeeze the water out of my hair and push it behind my ears.

I wrapped myself once more in my blanket, then eased open the door. There was no sign of my stern nurse, so I stepped out and looked around. There was a flurry of movement at the far end of the corridor— a young man in white overalls coming out, a nurse pushing a trolley going in—and I guessed that was where Charlie lay.

It seemed to take me a long, hard time to get there. As I made my way down the echoing space, I thought that this was the final stage of my journey. I had spent the day tearing around the island searching for my daughter, striding along beaches and over fields, wading in ditches, clambering into sinking wrecks of boats, scrabbling through her precious possessions, interrogating her friends and lovers, smashing up beach huts and struggling in the cold darkness. And now, at last, I was here, creeping slowly through a hospital towards the bed where Charlie lay. Just a few more steps now, and then there would be nowhere left to go and nothing left to do.

As I reached the door, it opened, and DI Hammill came out. I saw the startled expression on his face as I reeled past him like a drunken boxer, my blanket trailing behind me and my breath coming in cracked, high-pitched gasps. He reached out to stop me, then halted and let me pass. I saw his face, and I saw the figures in white coats standing beside Charlie's bed, but as in a dream. For my eyes were on Charlie, lying in the metal bed surrounded by machines, with the white sheet and the several thick blankets pulled up over her body, the needle taped to her thin arm and her face so pale and small on the pillow.

I staggered across the gap that divided us and sank to my knees beside her. I took her cold hand in mine and held it to my cheek. "Charlie?" I said. "It's me. I'm here."

"What are you doing here?" said a voice. "Who let you in here?"

"I'm her mother," I said.

"I know who you are."

"How is she?"

The doctor gave me a faint, exasperated smile.

"She was severely hypothermic. But her core temperature is rising. She's a fighter. She's not fully responsive yet but . . ."

Charlie's eyes half opened. "Mummy?" she whispered.

"I'm here," I said. "You're safe now."

Her eyelids started to close again. Her fingers relaxed in mine. Just as I thought she was asleep, she mumbled: "Happy birthday."

"It's been different, I'll give you that," I said. "Next year, I'd like to do something a bit quieter. Hey, you're wearing my bloody watch. So that's where it was. I needed it today."

A muffled sound came from her, then just regular breathing. She was asleep. I thought of when she was a baby. Sometimes I would creep up in the middle of the night, lean over her cot and listen for her breath. And even though I had often spent hours lulling her into sleep I would bend down and nudge her to wake her up, to make sure she was still alive. But this time I just stroked her hair as gently as I could. I needed to touch her to reassure myself that I wouldn't suddenly wake up and find myself still in some muddy corner of Sandling Island, running and running in an eternal quest to find her. So I stroked her matted hair and closed my eyes.

I had expected joy from this moment, euphoria— but what I felt instead was a peace such as I'd never experienced before. The nearest equivalent was that mysteriously beautiful moment after giving birth, when the struggle is over and there's nothing left that you have to do.

"I thought I'd find you here," a voice said, from behind me. I opened my eyes and smiled blearily up at her.

The stern nurse led me back along the corridor the way I had come, a firm grip on my upper arm. She told me as I shuffled along that I might be in shock and that people died of shock, and if I died she would be held responsible. I apologized humbly, like a toddler, but I couldn't stop grinning, though it hurt my face.

The hospital seemed to consist almost entirely of long corridors going off in different directions, and it was along one that I saw a small huddled group: DI Hammill, Beck . . . and someone else. Rory. They were awkwardly far away when they noticed me, too far for us to speak to each other. The two detectives looked embarrassed. Rory was evidently aghast at the sight of me and for the second time that day he started crying. He took a few steps forward, then ran towards me and gave me a hug, but stepped back when he felt me flinch.

"Sorry," he said. "Sorry. You look—but Charlie's going to be all right, isn't she? She's going to make it." Tears streamed down his face and into his mouth.

"Yes. She's pulling through," I said. "I thought I'd lost her, Rory, but she's safe."

"We," he said.

"Sorry?"

"We'd lost her. We. You and me. I'm still her father. Is she really all right?"

"She's fine," I said. I reached up with my free hand and brushed the tears off his face.

"I should have been there too," Rory said. "We should have done it together. And I would have been. If I hadn't been in custody. I hope you can see that I was telling the truth."

"You weren't . . ." I started to say, then stopped. It didn't matter. Nothing mattered. Charlie was safe. She had opened her eyes and smiled at me. I had stroked her hair and left her sleeping quietly beside a machine that pulsed steadily with the beat of her steady heart. Doctors and nurses watched over her.

"You should go and see her," I said. "They'll probably let you sit by her bed. It might be good to talk to her, even if she's asleep."

"I'm sorry," he said. "I didn't mean—"

"We never do," I said. "I'm sorry too. Sorry for everything. But she's alive, she's all right."

"Yes."

"Can you do something for me? Phone Jackson. He's at Bonnie's house. The number is—"

"I can get the number."

"I need to see him," I said. "He's had a terrible day. You've no idea how terrible."

"I'll call him."

"Now."

"Now," he said. "And I'll come and see you later. If you want."

I didn't reply. I didn't know if I wanted him to come and see me. All I wanted now was to hug Jackson and tell him I was proud of him, then turn my face to the wall and close my eyes. I waited for Rory to tell me I'd done well, but he only gave his characteristic helpless shrug and walked away. So now it was just me, the two detectives and, I could see from her nametag, Nurse Steph Bowles.

"This way," she said.

"Did you find Rick?" I asked.

Hammill and Beck looked at each other. Their expressions darkened.

"It took a while," said DI Hammill. "It was dark and muddy. They weren't able to revive him."

We had to move aside as a patient on a trolley was wheeled past us.

"I tried to save him," I said.

"Why?" said Beck.

"Does it seem stupid to you?" I said. "Maybe it is. I don't know why. Perhaps I wanted him to live so that he could think about what he had done."

"I think he's better off dead," said Beck.

"Do you?" I said, then started to shiver violently.

"We need to go," said Nurse Bowles, with a bossy solicitude that I was grateful for. "There'll be time enough for questions later. We need to get Ms. Landry into bed. She's in no fit state. Look at her."

"I don't mind," I said. "I'd prefer to get it over and done with. I need to." ·

"You're in no fit state," she repeated. I could feel myself swaying and her grip tightened. She waved at a porter walking past and barked for a wheelchair.

"I don't need a wheelchair," I said, but half-heartedly. All I really wanted was to lie in a bed, pull the sheet over my face, close my eyes and wait for the images to recede. But I needed to see Jackson first. Then I could let go, be swept out by the tide.

I was wheeled along the corridor by the porter,

Steph Bowles stalking ahead and the detectives following. I was shivering violently now and a flooding weariness was sweeping over me so that my eyelids felt leaden, my limbs heavy and boneless. We went into a small room at the start of an open ward, where I was lifted into a narrow bed and had more of the thin, pale-blue blankets piled on top of me. Hammill and Beck hovered awkwardly at the foot of the bed, waiting to be given permission to ask more questions.

"I'm going to leave you for a few minutes," said Steph Bowles. "I'll be back with the doctor. Be quick."

She left. Hammill furrowed his brow and Beck blinked at me and tried to smile.

"So Rick's dead," I said.

"That's right," said Hammill.

I stopped shivering but only because I suddenly felt even colder, as if the temperature in the whole hospital had dropped. The colours had drained away too.

"His wife's here," I said.

"What?"

"Karen. His wife. She was injured this morning. She's in a bed somewhere here. You'll have to go and tell her what's happened."

There was a long silence. Hammill started to speak but stopped before he had said anything intelligible. "No," he said at last. "Wait." He sounded dazed, as if he had received a blow to the head. "She's here? I don't understand."

"She had an accident," I said. "She had too much

to drink this morning. She fell over and broke her arm. Rick had to bring her here. They kept her in. She's still here."

"How do you know about it?"

"It happened in my house," I said. "That was the thing. He needed to get back to Charlie, if only to kill her. But suddenly he had to take Karen to hospital and stay with her. Then when he got back on to the island, I met him and gave him Jackson to look after."

"What?" said Beck.

"It's almost funny, isn't it?" I said. "He had one of my children and I gave him the other to look after." I thought for a moment. "But there's more. I can see now why he came to my house for the party. It makes sense."

"No," said Hammill, in a croaky, uncomprehending voice. "No. It doesn't."

"Yes," I said slowly. "He had Charlie, he was probably panicking, and he wondered what to do next. Then I phoned him, asking if he'd take a look at my car." I gave a little laugh. "Maybe if it hadn't been for the rattle in my car, Charlie would be dead now. It was a kind of alibi for him. It seemed that she went missing when Rick was with me. And then he must have remembered he was going to my house anyway, for the surprise birthday party that Charlie had organized. If he could do anything to make it look as if Charlie had run away, a serious police investigation would be delayed until he had killed her and disposed of the body."

As if a photograph had been put in front of my

eyes, I remembered walking up the stairs at the party and meeting Rick coming down. Coming down, as I now realized, with a few things he had seen in Charlie's room and grabbed to make it look as if she had left in a hurry.

"Yes," I murmured, more to myself than to the two detectives. "He stole those things from her room and, if he had been lucky, we might not have looked properly for a day or two and he could have—have done it and dealt with her and got rid of Olivia Mullen's body and never been caught."

DI Hammill shook his head. "But I don't understand how Olivia Mullen is connected with your daughter."

"No——" I began.

"The style of assault is different," he continued, interrupting me. "There is no link between the victim and Rick Blythe."

It was all so tiring. By now, Hammill and Beck were like two annoying wasps buzzing around keeping me from sleep. I just wanted to swat them.

"Stop this," I said to Hammill. My voice seemed to come from someone else, a stranger telling a story that had already started to seem unreal. "Just think about it. The death of Olivia Mullen is connected in every sort of way. Rick knew her. He taught her kayaking in the summer and they had a relationship, a fling that nobody must know about—he was a teacher, for God's sake, and she was only a teenager. He probably didn't mean to kill her—he throttled her in anger when she finished their affair. But then Charlie discovered what had happened. That was why he grabbed her. Charlie knew Liv, she knew about the relationship, she even met her on the day she died, and knew she was on her way to see Rick to break off their affair. When she saw her photo in the paper this morning, she must have realized what had happened. Then, when she was delivering the papers, she met Rick and probably she said something and he panicked and grabbed her. If you wait until tomorrow, Charlie will be able to tell you. We'll all know the truth."

"Right," said Steph Bowles, coming into the ward. "Dr. Marker is on her way to see you. She'll be here in a few minutes."

It was a cue for Hammill and Beck to leave. They made an awkward exit. Then Steph Bowles turned back to me. A watch hung from her starched breast pocket. I saw that it was past six o'clock.

"We would be taking off now," I said.

"What's that?"

"I was going to Florida today."

"Oh." She picked up a chart and looked at it, tutting. "Now then."

"And it's my birthday."

"Many happy returns," she said. "Pop this under your tongue."

I opened my mouth. The cold tip of the thermometer slid under my tongue and made me want to gag.

"Don't talk for a few minutes. Can I get you a cup of tea?"

"I'd like that," I said. It came out in a thick jumble.

"Just nod or shake your head. Milk?"

"Mmm."

"Sugar? Sugar's good for shock."

"Hate sugar in tea," I tried to say. "I'm very cold."

"Cold?"

"Mmm."

"Hold on. That's it. Now, let's see."

She removed the thermometer, frowned, looked at me as if I'd done something wrong, and wrote on the chart with a pencil that she had whipped out of her pocket.

"I'll get some more blankets in a minute. Tea and blankets. Do you want a biscuit with your tea?"

"I'm forty today. I had a birthday party," I continued, although I wasn't really talking to anyone in particular. My voice was fuzzy. I could hear how the syllables slipped and elided, but I needed to keep awake. I needed to see Jackson, my little boy who'd been wandering around all day like a lost soul. "Charlie gave me a party. It was a surprise party."

"Digestive biscuit?" Steph Bowles wasn't interested in my story: she wanted to know about my temperature and blood pressure and heartbeat. She wanted to put me back together again. I closed my eyes and the room swung round in my skull.

"It wasn't a success," I went on. "Surprise parties rarely are. They're good in theory, but—well, I wanted to pack and get ready and there were people I didn't know swarming all over the place and Karen fell down the stairs and Renata took to my bed and then I couldn't find Charlie. She wasn't anywhere." I squinted up at her face, which was going in and out of focus. "That's when it all started. No biscuit, thank you. I feel sick. I think I might be sick. Maybe you should fetch a bowl for me, just in case. Eamonn was at the party. Poor Eamonn, what'll become of him now?"

I opened my eyes and Steph Bowles was gone. I was talking to myself. It didn't matter.

"I wonder where Christian is," I said, through the waves of nausea. "He's been stuck in traffic all day. The M25 was closed in both directions. I've been running and running in circles, never stopping, and he's been sitting quite motionless. If I think about it, I still feel scared. Probably it will take time for that to go."

"Ms. Landry," said a voice. "I'm Dr. Marker. How are you feeling?"

She was slim, cool and blonde in her white coat, a stethoscope round her neck.

"Not at my very best," I said.

"Here." She sat beside me on the bed and held my wrist between her two fingers, feeling my pulse. She looked at my chart. She put her stethoscope to my chest, then my back. She ran her fingers down my leg, probing my knee and finding the pain there. She took my foot in the palm of her hand and rotated it to see where the ankle was injured. She pushed the hair back from my forehead and pressed her fingertips against the bruises on my temple and cheek while I tried not to cry out.

"I think you'll get away without stitches. This must hurt."

"A bit," I croaked.

"Do you feel sick?"

"A bit. Quite a lot, actually. I think I may be sick."

"The nurse is bringing a bowl. Cold?"

"To my bones. But it's getting a bit better."

"Dizzy?"

"Just tired, I think."

"How's your memory? What's your name?"

"I've done this. Nina Landry."

"Do you know what day it is?"

"It's Saturday, December the eighteenth, of course," I said. "Because it's my fortieth birthday. Never to be forgot." I smiled at her. Her face swam in and out of focus.

"Good. How many fingers am I holding up?"

"Three."

"Fine." She stood up. "You need warmth and rest, but I think that's all. You've been concussed so we need to keep an eye on that. One of my colleagues will be back later to check on you."

"Tea," said Steph Bowles, putting a large green mug on the table beside me. "And I've got a nightgown for you. Let me help you with it."

Dr. Marker left. With surprising gentleness, the nurse half raised me and, as if I was a tiny child, pulled the thin nightgown over my head, then tugged it down my sore, chilly body. It smelt of soap. She pulled the sheet and all the blankets back over me and withdrew. I lay back on my pillow and gulped at the tepid, milky tea. My hands shook so that I slopped it down my neck.

Then I heard Bonnie's voice. "Can he just go in?"

And another voice saying, "Mum?"

Jackson stood in the doorway, a small, bulky figure wrapped in a quilted red anorak so much too big for him that it came down almost to his knees and both his hands were hidden. He stared at me with beetle brows.

"Hello, my hero," I said. I sat up and held out my arms, but he didn't move.

"What on earth's happened to your face?"

"It's only a bruise. Come here and let me tell you how proud I am of you."

"It's all blue and lopsided." He wore an expression of faint embarrassment.

I grinned at him, my heart galloping with bruised tenderness. "Soon it'll be yellow and lopsided instead, then I'll look even weirder. Are you all right?"

"Bonnie gave me hot chocolate with marshmallows in it. Where's Charlie?"

"She's here," I said.

"Is she alive?"

"Yes."

"You promise?"

"I promise."

"Can I see her, then?"

"I think she's sleeping. Why don't you wait until tomorrow?"

"I want to see her." His voice quavered, then righted itself. "If you're telling me the truth and she's really all right."

I looked at his puffy face, the violet stains under his eyes, his ridiculously large padded jacket. "I don't think I can move right now, but as soon as a nurse comes, I'll get her to take you there."

"Bonnie can take me. She's waiting by the lift."

"All right, then. Can I have a hug before you go?"
He edged forward. "Where was she, anyway?"

"Charlie?"

"Yeah. Did she run away?"

"No."

"Are we going to Florida?"

"Not today."

"Can we go another time?"

"Yes."

"When?"

"I don't know."

There was a pause. He sat down by the bed and I put a hand into his sleeve, found his small, warm fingers. He didn't take them away, and I felt him soften gradually. After a few moments, he said, "Sludge will be going mad all by herself. She'll have chewed half the house down."

"I expect so."

"But you won't be angry with her?"

"No. I won't be angry."

"Will you have to stay in bed for ages?"

"Of course not. I'm just a bit tired."

"Bonnie said I'd have to look after you."

"Nonsense."

"That's good. It's Christmas in six days and a bit less than six hours. I'm starving."

"In a bit Dad can take you to the café and buy you something."

"Do they do chips?"

"Probably."

"Shall I go and see Charlie now?"

"Go on, then. Don't stay long, though. She needs rest, remember."

"Do you promise you'll still be here?"

"I'm not going anywhere."

He wriggled off the chair, gingerly planted a reluctant kiss on my bruised face, then turned to go.

Nurse Bowles returned, almost invisible behind the pile of extra blankets she was carrying. She spread them over my bed in layer after layer. I lay back with my eyes closed, heard her leave the room and return in less than a minute. I felt a rummaging in bed, as if she was reaching for me. Then there was something against my feet, something warm. The heat spread through my toes, my feet, my ankles and up my legs.

"A hot-water bottle," I said sleepily.

"Don't shout about it," Nurse Bowles said, "or everyone will want one."

I didn't reply, or even open my eyes. She went and I was alone. I knew that for the first time that day I wasn't needed and I let myself go, as if I were on a boat, releasing the painter and letting myself be carried out to sea.

H ello."
I didn't know if I had been asleep, if any time had passed. I opened my eyes. They hurt in the harsh light of the hospital room. A middle-aged man was standing by my bed, holding a clipboard. He looked tired, like a man at the end of his shift.

"Are you the doctor? I've just seen a doctor and she said I was all right."

"I'm Dr. Siegel. I'm sorry if I woke you. I need to check on you. You were hit on the head so I'm afraid you'll be woken regularly all night. Just to make sure you're not unconscious."

"I know I look terrible," I said.

He wrote something on the clipboard. "You wait until tomorrow," he said. "Then you'll look as if you've been in a fight and lost."

"I have been in a fight."

"Yes," he said. "That's what it says here. But you won, didn't you? And I've just seen your daughter."

"You have? How is she?"

"She's not too bad," he said. "But mainly, I'd say she's very lucky to have you. You can tell her that tomorrow."

"I don't think I will," I said. "She's had enough to put up with."

Dr. Siegel frowned. "I'm meant to check your comprehension and responses. How do they seem to you?"

"Not too bad," I said. "I don't know."

He grunted and wrote something more on the clipboard. "You live on Sandling Island."

"Yes."

"I've never been there. Isn't that funny? I work just a few miles away and I keep meaning to go, to walk along the coastal path and eat oysters and do the things you're meant to do there. Would you recommend it?"

"Not today," I said. "I'm not sure I'll be going back. I think I've fallen out of love with it."

"Don't make decisions now. Everything will

seem different in the morning. Let me see if I can find a pulse." He took my wrist in his left hand. "Happy birthday, by the way."

"What?"

"It says on the clipboard," he said. "Forty years young."

"Yes. It wasn't much of a celebration, though. I don't think this has been the best birthday of my life."

Dr. Siegel placed the clipboard on the bed and touched my hand gently. It felt very consoling. Then he stood up. "I'm not sure I'd agree with that," he said, "but, then, I don't know what the others were like. I'll see you tomorrow morning. Try to sleep. That is, until the nurse comes to wake you again in about twenty minutes."

He wrote something more on the clipboard, then caught my eye and, for a moment, I was sure he wanted to say something important. But he simply muttered, "You did well." Then he shambled his way out of the room, switching off the light as he left.

As my eyes grew accustomed to the dark I saw for the first time that there was a small window. From the bed, I couldn't see much out of it. A beam of light swept across the ceiling as a car drove past. I lay gazing out at the dark night sky. Was there a moon out there? Were there stars? Just a few miles away was the sea. The flooding tide was going down now, the waves ebbing, sucking up the pieces of driftwood, the broken shells and the litter. Out on that desolate waste of mud and shingle, underneath the subsiding cliffs, was the pillbox, the sea seeping out, only to return once more by dawn. The body had been dragged from the black waters, the blood had been washed away. The winter sun would hang on the horizon, and everything would look the same as it always had, peaceful, vast and undisturbed.

I turned on my side and pressed my face into the pillow. I took a long deep breath and, at last, I began to cry. I was here; Charlie was here; Jackson was here. And the morning would come to us all.

Read on for an excerpt from Nicci French's next book

UNTIL IT'S OVER

Available in hardcover from St. Martin's Minotaur

I had cycled around London for week after week, month after month, and I knew that one day I would have an accident. The only question was, which kind? One of the other messengers had been heading along Regent Street at speed when a taxi had swung out to make a U-turn without looking. Or, at least, without looking for a bike, because people don't look for bikes. Don had hit the side of the taxi full on and woken up in hospital unable to recall his own name.

There's a pub, the Horse and Jockey, where a whole bunch of us despatch riders meet up on Friday evenings and drink and gossip and share stories and laugh about tumbles. But every few months or so there'd be worse news. The most recent was about the man who was cycling down near the Elephant and Castle. He was alongside a lorry that turned left without indicating and cut the corner. That's when the gap between the lorry and the kerb shrinks from about three feet to about three inches. All you can do is get off the road. But in that case there was an iron railing in the way. The next time I cycled past I saw that people had taped bunches of flowers to it.

When these accidents happen, sometimes it's the cyclist's fault and sometimes it isn't. I've heard

stories of bus drivers deliberately ramming bikes.
I've seen plenty of cyclists who think that traffic
lights don't apply to them. But the person on the bike
always comes off second best. Which is why you
should wear a helmet and try to stay away from lor-
ries and always assume that the driver is a blind, stupid psychopath.

Even so, I knew that one day I would have an accident. There were so many different kinds, and I
thought the most likely was the one that was hardest
to avoid or plan against. So it proved. But I never
thought it would take place within thirty yards of
my own house. As I turned into Maitland Road, I
was about to swing my leg over the cross-bar. I was
forty-five seconds from a hot shower and in my
mind I was already off the bike and indoors, after
six hours in the saddle, when a car door opened into
the road in front of me, like the wing of a metal bird,
and I hit it.

There was no time for me to respond in any way,
to swerve or to shield myself. And yet the events
seemed to occur in slow motion. As my bike
slammed against the door I was able to see that I
was hitting it from the wrong direction: instead of
pushing the door shut, I was pushing it further open.
I felt it screech and bend but then stop as the mo-
mentum transferred itself from the door back to the
bike and especially to the most mobile part of the
bike, which was me. I remembered that my feet
were in the stirrups and if they remained fastened, I
would get tangled in the bike and might break both
my legs. But then, as if in answer, my feet detached

themselves, like two peas popped from a pod, and I flew over the door, leaving my bike behind.

It all happened so quickly that I couldn't protect myself as I fell or avoid any obstacle. At the same time it happened so slowly that I was able to think about it as it was taking place. I had many thoughts, but it wasn't clear whether they were happening one after another or all at the same time. I thought: I'm having an accident. This is what it's like to have an accident. I thought: I'm going to be hurt, probably quite badly. I thought: I'm going to have to make arrangements. It looks like I won't be at work tomorrow. I'll have to phone Campbell and let him know. Or someone will. And then I thought: How stupid. We're meeting for dinner tonight, one of those rare occasions when we all sit round the table together, and it seems like I won't be there. And I even had time to think: What will I look like, lying flung out on the road?

At which point I hit the ground. I had flipped over like an incompetent acrobat and landed on my back, hard, hitting the wind out of me, so that I made an "oof" sound. I rolled and felt bits of me bang and scrape along the road surface. When I heard my body hit the Tarmac, there was no pain at first. It was like a bang and a bright flash. But I knew that the pain was on its way and suddenly there it was, at the centre of everything, beating against me in wave after wave, light pulsing in my eyes in reds and purples and bright yellows, each pulse a different sort of hurt. I made an attempt to move. I was in the road. The road was a dangerous place. A lorry might

run over me. It didn't matter. I was incapable of
movement. All I could do was swear, over and over
again: "Fuck. Shit. Fuck. Shit."

Gradually the pain started to locate itself. It was
like rain that had fallen and was now settling into
puddles and rivulets. I felt dizzy but my helmet had
saved my head. My upper back was numb where I
had landed on it. What really hurt for the moment
were lots of other places—my elbows, the side of
one knee. One of my hands had been bent back and
was throbbing. With the other I touched my thigh
and felt sticky wetness and bits of gravel. A tiny
part of my brain still had time to think: How stupid.
If this had not happened, I would be in the house
and everything would be normal. Now I'm here and
I'm going to have to deal with it, and if only I didn't.

I lay back and the Tarmac was warm against me
and I could even smell it, oily and sharp. The sun
was low and yolky in the fading blue.

A shadow fell across me, a shape blocking the
sky. "Are you all right?" it said.

"No," I said. "Fuck."

"I'm so sorry," it said. "I opened the door. I didn't
see you. I should have looked. I'm so, so sorry. Are
you hurt? Shall I call an ambulance?"

Another wave of pain hit me. "Leave me alone," I
said.

"I'm so, so sorry."

I took a deep breath and the pain receded a little
and the person came into focus. I saw the vaguely familiar face of a middle-aged woman and I saw her sil-

ver car and I saw the open door, which had been bent outwards by the impact. I took another deep breath and made the effort to say something that wasn't just whimpering or swearing: "You should look."

"I'm so sorry."

I was going to tell her again to go away but suddenly felt nauseous and had to devote my energy to stopping myself vomiting in the street. I had to get home. It was only a few yards away. I felt like an animal that needed to crawl into its hole, preferably to die. With a groan, I rolled over and began to push myself up. It hurt terribly but through the fog I noticed that my limbs were functioning. Nothing was obviously shattered; no tendons had been torn.

"Astrid!"

I heard a familiar voice and, indeed, a familiar name. My own. Astrid. That was another good sign. I knew who I was. I looked up and saw a familiar face gazing down at me with concern. Then another swam into focus behind the first: two were staring at me with the same expression.

"What the hell happened?" one said.

Stupidly and inexplicably, I felt embarrassed.

"Davy," I said. "Dario. I just came off the bike. It's nothing. I just—"

"I opened my door," the woman said. "She rode into it. It was all my fault. Should I call an ambulance?"

"How's my bike?" I said.

"Don't worry about it," said Davy, bending down, his face creased with concern. "How are you doing?"

I sat up in the road. I flexed my jaw, felt my teeth with my tongue. I felt my tongue with my teeth.

"I think I'm all right," I said. "A bit shaken." I stood up, flinched.

"Astrid?"

"What about my bike?"

Dario walked round to the other side of the car door and stood the bike up. "It's a bit bent," he said. He tried to push it but the front wheel was jammed in the fork.

"It looks . . ." I was trying to say that it looked the way I felt but the sentence seemed too hard to construct. Instead I said I wanted to get into the house. The woman asked again about getting an ambulance but I shook my head and groaned because my neck felt sore.

"I'll pay for the bike," the woman said.

"Yes, you will."

"I live just here. I'll come and see you. Is there anything else I can do now?"

I tried to say something snappy, like "You've done enough already," but it was too much of an effort and, anyway, she looked upset and bothered and she wasn't defending herself like some people would have done. I looked round and she was trying to close the offending door. It took two goes to get it shut. Dario picked up my bike and Davy put an arm carefully round me and led me towards our house. Dario nodded at someone.

"Who's that?" I said.

"Nobody," he said. "How's your head?"

I rubbed my temple cautiously. "Feels a bit funny."

"We were sitting outside on the front step," said Dario, "having a smoke and enjoying the evening, weren't we, Davy?"

"Right," said Davy. "And there was a crash and there you were."

"Bloody stupid," I said.

"Can you make it? It's just a few more yards."

"It's OK," I said, though my legs were quaking and the door seemed to be receding rather than getting closer. Davy shouted for Miles, then Dario joined in even more loudly, and the sound echoed round my skull, making me flinch. Davy led me through the gate and Miles appeared from inside at the top of the steps. When he saw the state of me, his expression was almost comic. "What the hell happened?" he said.

"Car door," said Davy.

I was quickly surrounded by my housemates. Davy tried to hang the bike on the hooks on the wall in the hallway. Because it was damaged it didn't fit properly. He took it down again and started to fiddle with it, getting oil on the front of his lovely white shirt. "That's going to need some work," he said, with relish.

Pippa came down the stairs and said something rude to Davy about how it was me that needed checking, not the bike. She gave me a very light hug, hardly touching me. Mick looked at me impassively over the banisters from the floor above.

"Bring her through," said Miles. "Get her downstairs."

"I'm fine," I said.

They insisted and I was half helped, half dragged down the stairs into the large kitchen-dining area where we ate and talked and spent our time when we weren't in our own rooms. I was placed on the sofa near the double doors and Dario, Pippa and Miles sat staring at me, asking over and over how I was feeling. I was clear-headed now. The shock of the accident had settled into simple, ordinary pain. I knew it was going to hurt like hell the next morning but it would be all right. Dario took a cigarette from a pack in his pocket and lit it.

"We should cut her clothes off," he said. "The way they do in A and E departments."

"In your dreams," I said.

"Do you need to see a doctor?" Miles asked.

"I need a hot bath."

"About the hot part," said Dario. "There might be a problem with that."

There's something satisfying about the aftermath of an accident in which you haven't really been hurt. Especially when you look worse than you feel. I felt all right, but there was a lovely bruise flowering on my calf, a raw graze down my thigh, a gash on my hand, and my left cheek had an ugly scrape. My wrist was swollen. I stung and throbbed and ached, but in a masochistically pleasurable way. I kept pressing my cuts to make sure they were still bleeding. After a shallow, tepid bath, I lay on my bed in old jogging pants and a T-shirt, and assorted members of the household strayed in to ask me if I was all right and to hear yet again how it had happened. I began to feel almost proud of myself.

"It was all in slow motion," I repeated for the fourth time.

Davy and Dario, the two heroic rescuers, were looking down at me. Dario lit another cigarette, except it wasn't a cigarette, and a familiar illegal smell drifted across my room.

"You must have fallen in a really natural way," said Davy. "That's why you didn't get seriously injured. It's pretty impressive. It's the way they train paratroopers. But you did it naturally."

"It wasn't in my control," I said.

Dario took a huge drag on his spliff. "Or like a really, really drunk person," he said. "When really drunk people fall over, they don't get injured because their body's so relaxed."

"Let's have a look," said Mick, sitting on the edge of the bed.

I might have made a caustic remark if someone else had said that, but with Mick you don't really make caustic remarks. He's a man of few words. It's as if it takes a painful effort for him to speak, and when he does the rest of us generally fall silent. I wanted to ask why he was more qualified than anyone else to assess the damage, but I knew he would simply shrug.

"Does this hurt?" he asked, as I flinched. "Or this?" He pressed a hand against my ribs, then lifted each leg, one after the other, feeling along my calves over thick daubs of oil that no amount of scrubbing with warm soapy water had removed. "Nothing broken," he said, which I knew anyway.

Pippa appeared with a small bottle of blue liquid and a handful of cotton wool.

"Will it sting?" I asked.

"Not a bit," she said, and applied a liberal dousing of disinfectant to my cheek.

"Shit!" I yelled, squirming away from her. "Stop at once!"

"Be brave."

"Why?"

"Because, because," she said mysteriously, slapping another sodden wad of cotton wool on to my thigh.

"Have a drag on this," said Dario, offering me his spliff. "It's good for pain and nausea."

"I'll pass," I said.

"Are you all right for the meal?" said Pippa.

"I'm starving."

"Owen's bringing it on the way back from his studio."

He arrived with an Indian takeaway in brown-paper carrier-bags and put them on the table, then looked up and saw me at the head, in a large chair, propped up with pillows. He frowned. "You get into a fight?"

"With a car door."

"Those are some bruises," he said.

"I know."

"They'll be worse tomorrow."

"You should have seen her," said Davy, sitting beside me. He looked more shocked than I was. "She flew through the air."

"Like a human cannonball," said Dario, taking the chair on the other side.

"Does it hurt?"

"Not so much."

"Of course it fucking hurts," said Pippa. "Look at her."

"No. Don't look at me. My nose is twice its usual size. How much do we owe for this lot, Owen?"

"Eight quid each."

There was muttering as people fumbled in pockets and purses, counted out coins and demanded change. Dario pulled a roll of notes out of his pocket, peeled off a twenty and tossed it to Owen. "Keep the change," he said. "I probably owe you anyway."

"Did you win the lottery?" said Owen, with an expression of distrust.

Dario looked shifty. "Someone owed me," he said.

Everyone sat round the kitchen table and eased off the foil lids, pulled tabs on beer cans, passed round chipped plates and an odd assortment of cutlery. Pippa helped herself to Dario's spliff and took a deep drag.

"Are lawyers allowed to do that?" asked Miles.

"Not in the office," Pippa said, and looked round the group. "How often does this happen? It's us and just us."

"Now we are seven," said Dario, clinking his fork against his plate for silence, then immediately shovelled an enormous amount of rice into his mouth and chewed for several seconds while we all waited. "Like the Seven Dwarfs," he said at last.

"There are certain things we need to discuss," said Miles, rather formally. "To start with, can I say—"

"You're Doc," said Dario.

"What?"

"If we're like the Seven Dwarfs—"

"Which we're not."

"—you're definitely Doc," said Dario.

"Because I own this house? And who else is going to get the drains fixed and make sure the bills are paid?"

"The dwarfs represent the parts that make up the psyche," said Dario.

"Is this what I flew into a car door for?" I said. The beer was making me feel mellow and the pain had receded.

"You're Angry," said Dario to Mick.

Mick ignored him.

"Is there an Angry?" I asked. "I don't remember him."

"There's Grumpy," said Davy.

"Pippa's Randy, right?" said Dario, winking across the table at Davy.

This was a reference to the fact that Pippa was not in a proper relationship, but instead had a fair amount of extremely short ones.

"Oh, boys, boys," I said. "That's pathetic."

"I think we can agree that Dopey's taken," said Pippa.

"You can have Sleepy, then," said Dario. "No one can sleep like you."

This wasn't strictly fair. Pippa only sleeps at weekends, when she goes to bed in the small hours and gets up in the afternoon, looking puffy, dazed and replete. During the week she's a dutiful worker who rises at seven. Dario, on the other hand, sleeps whenever he likes.

"We're running out of the good ones," said Davy. "Owen can be Sneezy."

"Why?"

Davy looked at me. "Which leaves you and me fighting over Bashful and Happy," he said. "And you, Astrid Bell, are not bashful. Unless you want to be Snow White."

"I want to be the Wicked Queen. There's a real woman."

"You're spoiling the game," said Dario. "You're Happy."

Happy. And groggy. And relaxed. I sat back in my chair. I looked round the people at the table: a motley collection who were, just at the moment, the closest I had to family. There were only three of us left who had been here from the beginning, or perhaps the real beginning was before that, when we were at university together. Miles had bought the house when he was still a post-graduate student who wanted to change the world, paying a ridiculously small amount for this rambling, run-down place at the rougher end of Hackney. Then, he had had no beard and his hair was long, often tied back in a ponytail. Now he had a closely trimmed dark blond beard and no hair at all. If I ran my hand over his head I could feel all the bumps of his velvety skull. Pippa was the other long-termer. In fact, she and I had met in my first term at university and we'd shared a house in our final year, so by the time we moved in with Miles I already knew her domestic habits well. She was tall and willowy, and had a delicate kind of beauty that could mislead people.

So we were the original trio and we'd survived, even though for a year of that time Miles and I had been sort of a couple and for another six awful months had been sort of not a couple and then definitely not a couple. Now Miles had a proper new girlfriend, Leah, and that felt good, like a fence between us. "Good fences make good neighbours," someone had said.

Around us, there had been various others, and the current seven was bound to change sooner or later. Mick was older than the rest of us, and carried his years as if they were a burden that weighed on his broad shoulders. He was stocky and short. He stood with his legs apart as if on the deck of a ship in stormy weather. His eyes were pale blue in a face creased by the sun and wind. He had spent years travelling restlessly round the world. I didn't know if he'd been searching for something, or even if he had found it. He never talked about it. Now he worked, doing odd jobs, and had drifted to a temporary halt in Maitland Road. When he was at home, he spent much of his time in his small room at the top of the house, though I never knew what he did up there and I'd rarely visited him. None of the doors have locks on them, but some are more firmly closed than others. Sometimes I went downstairs in the middle of the night because I couldn't sleep, and he was there, sitting quite still at the kitchen table with the steam from a mug of tea curling round his face.

We were never quite sure how Dario had come to be living here. His previous girlfriend (who I suspected was the only real girlfriend he had ever had) had rented a room for a year so he had often stayed over. Then we blinked and she was gone and somehow he was still there, digging himself into the smallest room, which was on the second floor, then gradually colonizing the empty room next door.

Although he had no job and couldn't pay the rent, no one had the heart or the necessary steel to throw him out—perhaps because he didn't look much like a Dario. He had untidy ginger hair and thick freckles; his teeth were slightly crooked and when he smiled he seemed like a goofy little boy. In the end, Miles came to an agreement with him: that he should renovate the house, top to bottom, in return for living there. I don't think it was such a good deal for Miles. As far as I could tell, Dario spent most of his time smoking weed, reading astrology columns, watching daytime TV, playing games on other people's computers and doodling on walls with stiff-bristled paintbrushes that he wasn't scrupulous enough about cleaning or replacing.

Davy was the most recent member of the household, being here just a couple of months, along with Owen. He was a carpenter and builder. A real one, not like Dario. Despite the disadvantage of not being Polish, he had plenty of work. Enough of it was outside so that he was lightly tanned. He had light-coloured hair, which fell thickly over his shoulders, and grey eyes. He was good-looking, but he didn't seem to know he was, which I found charming. He had the anxious manner of a new boy in the house, but also a nice smile that crinkled the corners of his eyes, and when he arrived I had let myself think, Perhaps? and then decided probably not. Sex in the house felt like a taboo, and my experience with Miles was an awful warning.

And then there was Owen Sullivan, sitting across from me right now. With his pale skin, his straight, shoulder-length dark hair, and his wide-set, almost-black eyes, he had a faintly Oriental air, though as far as I knew all his ancestors had been Welsh. He was a photographer. He hawked his portfolio round magazines and got the occasional commission. But what he really wanted was to do his own stuff. He had once said he hated magazine work. I had giggled and said then it was lucky he got so little of it. He hadn't replied but he had given me such a sharp look that I had realized you couldn't safely tease him where his work was concerned. He used to watch people as if he was sizing them up for a photograph, checking the light, framing them. I sometimes wondered if he really saw, really listened to what they had to say.

"Seven ages of man," said Dario, dreamily. "Seven seas, seven continents . . ."

"That's not right."

"Listen," said Miles. "I hate to break into this, but it's very rare that we're all together like this. Just the seven of us. Don't you dare start again, Dario."

"You're right, it *is* rare," said Davy. "Why don't we have a group photo to mark it?"

"We even have an official photographer."

"I don't do snaps," said Owen, with finality.

"Let's not forget he's an artist," I said sarcastically.

Davy just smiled. "I'll take it," he said.

"My camera's in the drawer over there," said Miles, wearily.

Davy stood up and pulled it open. "It's not here. You must have moved it."

"Someone's nabbed it, more like, and forgotten to put it back."

"I've got one upstairs," said Davy.

"Let's just forget it," Mick was starting to say, but Davy was out of the room and bounding up the stairs two at a time.

A silence settled over us. Outside, a car horn blared several times and then we heard footsteps running down the road. A door slammed upstairs.

"Who else thinks this lamb tastes like dogfood?" said Dario.

"What does dogfood taste like?"

"Like this."

Dogfood or not, there was the sound of chewing and plates being scraped. There was little conversation. Everybody seemed distracted. Then Davy returned, breathless and slightly flushed, but triumphantly brandishing his camera. "It wasn't where I thought. Now, all squash together. No, you don't have to move, Astrid. Everyone can stand round you. Owen, you're out of the picture like that. I still can't see you."

"Good."

"Dario, your face is hidden by Pippa's shoulder. Mick, you look a bit weird with that smile. Scary, actually. OK, ten seconds. Are you ready?"

"What about you?" said Pippa.

"Just wait."

Davy pressed a button and ran round to join us. His foot hit the table leg so he stumbled and half fell on to the tightly massed, scowling, smiling group as the light flashed. That was how the camera caught us, a blur of flailing arms and legs, and me in the centre, mouth open in surprise in my grazed and swollen face, like the victim of a drunken attack.

"Look at us!" screamed Pippa in delight: she came out the best of us all, of course—dainty and gorgeous in the scrum.

"My eyes are shut," groaned Dario. "Why does that always happen?"

"Right," said Miles, once we'd sat down again. He pushed away his plate of congealing orange curry. "I want to say something."

"Yes?"

"This isn't easy, but I'm giving you plenty of warning."

"It's about the state of the bathroom, I know it."

"Leah and I have decided to live together."

Pippa gave a little whoop.

I frowned. "So why the solemn face?" I asked.

"She's moving in here."

"We can cope," said Dario. "Can she, though? That's the real question."

"I mean," said Miles, "it will be just Leah and me."

For a moment, nobody spoke: we stared at him while his sentence hung in the air.

"Oh," said Mick at last.

"Fuck," said Pippa.

"You're chucking us out?"

"Not like that," said Miles. "Not at once."

"How long?" I asked. My face was starting to throb.

"A few months. Three. That's all right, isn't it? It'll give you time to settle in somewhere else."

"I was just settling in here," said Davy, ruefully. "Oh, well."

"You couldn't all stay here for ever," said Miles.

"Why not?" Dario looked stricken. His freckles stood out in blotches.

"Because things change," said Miles. "Time passes."

"Are you all right, Astrid?" Davy asked. "You've gone a bit pale."

"I need to go to bed," I said. "Or at least lie down for a bit. I feel odd."

Pippa and Davy levered me to my feet, hands under my elbows, making tutting noises.

"I'm sorry," said Miles, wretchedly. "Maybe it was the wrong time."

"There's never a right time for things like this," said Pippa. "Come on, Astrid, come into mine for a while. It's one less flight of stairs to manage. I can rub Deep Heat into you, if you want.'